Odd Is Left

a novel
by
Michael Frederick

Books by author:

White Shoulders

Places

Ledges

Blue River

The Paper Man

Different

Missouri Madness

Zed

Shy Ann

Drop 50 & Magnify

Summer of '02

Autumn Letters

Stuck

Indie Writer

King of Slugs

Golly Springs

Already Bad/Volume 1

Already Bad/Volume 2

Dedicated to my brother, Johnny

October, 2017/1st printing/2000 copies
Copyright 2017
all rights reserved

Cover design by Paul Coy
www.paulcoy.com

A Fresh Start

" The better I tell this story…the better my life will be." That's what 42-year-old Johnny Tower wrote in his journal a month ago on December 1st, 2019, the first day of his self-imposed retirement, the day he began living his life full-time…*odd is left.*

Only 3 hours remained of 2019 as "JT" finished scoop-sliding 3 inches of fresh snow off his massive lime-green, heart-shaped patio, a faded North Woodbury, South Dakota landmark in this area known by locals as *"Superland."* Superland is a place just inside the middle of nowhere, where South Dakota meets Nebraska and Iowa halfway across the Big Sioux and Missouri Rivers; and (historically) not far from the only fatality of the Lewis and Clark Expedition. JT wrote about his visit to Sgt. Floyd's Grave in a 7th grade English assignment that was posted on the Tower fridge door for 2 years, the beginning of JT's writing habit.

Rather than trying to describe JT, most people agree that he's just an average-looking guy…except for one distinction: JT's dominant right eye is dark blue, and his left eye is brown, a chocolate-brown. It's called *complete heterochromia* when one iris color is different from the other. John Eldon Tower is the 3rd consecutive generation of Tower men to have this oddity of *identical* different-colored eyes. That's rare. *"Ten million-to-one,"* bartender Charlie Tower would inform his loyal regulars who truly liked Charlie and *loved* his wife Ruthie ever since the day she was born...literally. Anyone who could win the heart of *Baby Ruthie*...had to be a great guy.

Charlie, JT's dad, could be odd at times. Like one hot August day when Ruthie was getting her (red) *hair done*, bartender Charlie asked one of his newer customers to *watch the bar for a minute* so he could run next door to his double-wide to change into a pair of fresh boxers waiting for him in the freezer.

John Eldon Tower is a closet writer, having consistently made daily entries in his journal ever since he was in the 7th grade. In over thirty years he's missed a few dozen days of writing if that. Every year of JT's writing is organized and stored in boxes in the family cabin in Yankton, South Dakota, about 60 miles northwest of North Woodbury. After logging thousands of days about his past life in journal entries JT has a story worth telling. That's what this story is about: making sense of a dead past, finding truths that resolve it, then reaching your potential. Otherwise for JT –it's a life unlived, all because of some big *family secret* that he believes has been holding him back from experiencing substantive intimate relationships with women. No. JT *knows* it's holding him back.

There it was: that same glaring floodlight mounted on the roof of his 1977, 70-foot, 3-bedroom double-wide. The light was put there by his dad, Charlie, to shine on this green heart-shaped basketball court that made his son a remarkable overnight success story. Then...came humiliating failure for JT in this upper Midwest tri-state area, a failure that wouldn't stop Ruthie and Charlie Tower's *plan* for their only child's security. JT is a small-town Gen X success story that Millennials supported too, because in every subconscious mind of these younger generations -they know their Baby Boomer grandparents are coming...and staying longer and longer, costing all working-class members of the X *and* M Generations more than they care to imagine. It's too frightening to think about...and if one of us can make it —we all make it.

Souvenir hunters over the last 25 years (mostly drunks stumbling out the back door of Tower Tavern) would stagger over to the green heart and break off a crumbled chunk of green concrete around its edges. In the winter of '95, not long after JT's stardom was at its brightest, a couple of "*drunk bastards*" with Nebraska plates backed up a flatbed truck to the fold of the heart and felled the pine in-ground basketball goal, backboard-and-all with a chainsaw —then drove off into the darkness. Even today, it still makes JT laugh when he thinks about it: that night the *sound of a chainsaw* woke him, then the *falling thud* onto the truck's bed...and that *drunken cackling laughter* from two idiots who drove off into the ink-black night of Superland with a trophy JT would never miss.

Now: JT walked over to the fold of his cement heart, removed his gloves and took a long look at the remains of his sawed-off basketball foundation post, now half-buried in wind-swept snow, exposing a mere stump of weathered wood sunk three feet into the earth. He spiked his shovel into the crispy-old snow piled around

3

the edges of the green heart and turned to look at the faded white arc of the 3-point line, now nearly invisible after 27 years of weather as increasing New Year's Eve bar noise reverberated from the back door of Tower Tavern, exactly fifty steps from the Tower trailer.

His parents had bought the bar in '76, a year before John Eldon Tower was born. JT's parents sold the bar and the Tower Tavern name for a fortune to Marty Gunderson's parents in '95, right after JT graduated from North Woodbury High. Marty was a junior at North Woodbury and idolized JT. *Old Man Gunderson* owned a massive mobile home park in Woodbury, Iowa; he bought the popular bar for their son to manage when he graduated, an investment that would keep young Marty and their only child around Superland.

After selling the bar, Charlie and Ruthie Tower moved to Julian, California, to retire in a warmer climate, leaving their only child, JT, the trailer and the family cabin in Yankton. They also left him *a great gig,* as Charlie would tell everybody.

Charlie and Ruthie created their own *gold mine* because they knew how to keep their business *as busy as possible*, especially after video slot machines were legalized in the fall of '89. From the very first day gambling was legalized, all 10 Tower video lottery machines were busy day and night, speeding up retirement for JT's hard-working parents. Charlie and Ruthie Tower managed to keep the bar's maximum capacity of 200 entertained for six nights a week with a vintage '56 Wurlitzer 2000 jukebox filled with 45 records that played a song for a quarter, 3 songs for fifty cents. It was Charlie's idea to stock his jukebox music selection with songs picked by *regulars.*

The bar had a good pool table, known to be *level* by local pool players; and an 8'X8' dance floor sprinkled lightly with sawdust in front of *Charlie's Jukebox,* as Ruthie called it. Tower Tavern was also known to be clean, not to mention *Baby Ruthie's* delicious food specialty items that came 'round the weekly calendar with anticipated regularity. Yes, Tower Tavern was one respected business and landmark, well-run by the beloved couple Ruthie and Charlie Tower. They knew that Marty Gunderson would keep it that way.

This entire month of December of 2019 has been JT's time to move out of the trailer, the only home he's ever known. He sold the family trailer and lot just before Thanksgiving to a young couple who liked its location under a majestic oak tree that was older than the town. Tomorrow he was to be out, on the first day of 2020, and begin a fresh start.

JT put the shovel inside the back door of his blue and brown '95 Dodge cargo van that held the last load of his stuff he'd move into the cabin in Yankton, including his queen-size bed. He thought about leaving now, but then he'd miss his annual New Year's Eve *appearance* in his parents' old bar, where he'd have a seat on his dad's reserved barstool at the end of the bar, order a Coke and bring in the new year with old friends that revered him as a local celebrity, a star that remained bright in their eyes for 25 years. And: this was the night Marty never failed to play that highlight video on all 7 screens of JT's first basketball game his senior year in-sync with Charlie's old jukebox to R.E.M.'s "Losing My

Religion." Recently, Marty told JT he'd done *some editing* to the video Ruthie and Charlie professionally made, and he was anxious for JT to see it tonight. It was always embarrassing for JT to get that much attention from a bunch of drunks when he was allergic to alcohol...like his parents.

"No, they'd be expecting me," he told his mind to drop the idea *to leave now,* deciding to write a bit in his journal before catching a *power nap.*

It's been a month since JT reached his goal that he'd set for himself at the turn of the century: *"To retire from chasing money."* Since graduating high school in '95 he's managed to remain single with no attachments. JT's aversion to intimacy with women is no secret to his family and friends...as well as the few women he's had brief relationships with...since Iris Jean Prescott.

Partly because of Iris -he's stayed here, hoping she'd return some day. JT went to every one of his high school reunions hoping he'd see her there. Not once did she show. Then last week, with one week before moving out of his trailer, a slice of irony hit this romantic sap at the speed of sound. Mary Parrot, a friend and the organizer of North Woodbury High reunions called JT and told him that Iris was on the list of attendees for their 25-year reunion June 18, 2020. June 18th has always been the biggest day of every year for the Towers. And: reunion organizer and Class of '95 gossip Mary Parrot told JT that the reunion was going to be held in Tower Tavern, the family bar that sports nut Marty Gunderson now owned and managed with an obvious loving respect for the bar's history. One thing about Marty: even though he was not even close to being

6

the fun-loving Charlie and Ruthie, he was at least smart enough to keep the name of the most popular neighborhood bar in Superland (aside from the fact that Ruthie had it stated in the sale of Tower Tavern that the name would remain the same). More about that later.

Now: JT got behind the wheel of his van and took a discreet hit of his weed he buys legally in Colorado. He named his vice "Creative." It was a winter habit to get stoned before he wrote in his journal. *"It changes my thought patterns,"* he told his now 99-year-old Grampa Tower several years back when the retired Minnesota farmer asked his only grandchild why he smoked *"that stuff."*

The Tower trailer was dark and nearly empty, the utilities off and out of his name since earlier this evening. The trailer's thermostat read 62 degrees and would drop quite a bit more since it was going down to 22 tonight. Right away he peeled off his clothes to his birthday suit, stepped up and onto his inversion table, the only heavy item left to haul to the van. In the middle of the living room he hung upside down at about a 60-degree angle, perfect for releasing the effects of gravity and shoveling. It only required about a half a minute, since right away the cracking and popping meant he was back in alignment. But now he slipped a black sleep mask over his forehead and reached back to turn on his infrared light therapy lamp before covering his eyes with the protective mask. He'd hang upside down while bathing in the red light that JT says keeps his mood positive during these dreary months of winter; and he claims it keeps his body free of aches and pains after an automatic-timed 15 minutes a day.

Back on his feet after the infrared light went off, he was warmed by the light treatment; he put on his jeans and sweater and socks before going over to his narrow futon to lie on his belly before turning on a lamp standing on the cool linoleum beside his leather-bound journal. A well-placed pillow under his chest, then he wrote:

"I'm off to another odd is left after I stop in the bar. A new decade is here in a few hours. Ever since I retired I feel like I'm in this invisible cell, this closed room with no door or window. This last month has shown me I'm locked up on the inside by these memory cells that keep circulating in my blood, the same blood that feeds my brain first...before my heart. Isn't that where my mind lives, in the same muddied blue blood of these memory cells we inherit from past generations, just as my dad and I inherited Grama Tower's eyes. Tomorrow I visit my Grampa Tower; then I head north to Elmdale, to the farm in Minnesota where Grampa T raised my father alone. Something awful happened to my dad there, and they won't ever talk about it. Whatever happened to my dad, I believe more than ever that a big part of why I have never been able to forgive Iris and have an intimate long-term relationship with any woman, is related to this big 'mystery thing' that happened to my dad not long after he graduated from high school. My mother enlightened me about this paternal Tower trait I inherited from my dad and Grampa: one mate for life. My mom said that 4% of mammals practice monogamy, and in that way Tower men are like wolves, beavers, and otters. My dad said he tried to break that pattern in the service many times, yet once he met my mother: '...that was it,' he said. Over the years in the bar I've seen my

8

dad around many attractive women and I just know that he's never strayed or cheated on my mother. And their lives together have flourished. I think every man wants that. I know I do. So, I'm in that 4%; and I do believe that roughly the same percentage of men today live in a monogamous relationship. I had my first love. Her name was Iris Jean Prescott. And because of Iris I leave the only home I've ever known for the unknown...to break this pattern. Odd is left."

JT turned off the light, moved onto his back, adjusted his pillow, and could see the silver glow of the floodlight behind the curtains. The light would deter any thieves from messing with his van while he rested and reflected, until he would walk over to the bar in a few hours just before the new year. He checked the time on his cell phone and saw that he still had about three hours before he made his reluctant/anticipated appearance in Tower Tavern.

JT was proud of himself for not living in his past *for most* of the last few years. And yet: he'd *planned* this time, these very moments before the new year. Another trait besides writing that he'd inherited from his mother: *planning.* Ruthie Tower planned important things over a long stretch of baby steps and a sense of purpose that gave her son his strong will. Strong enough to reflect on how he was going to bring his past back to this moment, in these few remaining hours before 2020. He *needed* this time before leaving the only home he's known, to truly reflect on *why* he had to know all about this *family secret* that happened to his father when his father was a young man. JT could close his eyes now and go back ten thousand days to anywhere, and his mind chose to show him that awful time during late

August at the front of his sophomore year during late-summer football practice when Indian Summer pollen was thick and the game became *too mean* for JT.

Bull in the Ring

J T didn't want to go out for football his sophomore year, a most dangerous time for young American athletes with fragile egos. Internal peer pressure made him. He was 140 pounds of over-developed fear. Now JT would practice with the big boys, the juniors and seniors who were 17, 18, and even 19-year-old *men* who were bigger, faster, shaved every day, and welcomed any chance to steamroll and punish some pimple-faced cipher who dared to tackle or block them.

#14 was string bean JT, who'd be *lucky* to make the traveling varsity team as a 3rd string quarterback this year. Some of his peers would make the team as one of those crazy special teams' players who wasn't afraid to sacrifice his body by throwing himself in front of a 200-pound senior running back who relished punishing underclassmen on a punt or kickoff return. Football practice for these North Woodbury High Warriors was nothing less than a hazing for sophomores like Johnny Tower. This rite of passage for the younger players would be tested from late August until the last game of the season.

JT's biggest concern: Coach Blodough. Dowd Blodough was a 27-year-old walking ego who flirted with high school girls. He'd been promoted to coach the varsity running backs and quarterbacks. Handsome Coach Blodough never let JT play with the starters in practice, even though JT had a better arm than the starter. Refusing to play #14 became a habit since Blodough did the same thing to JT in gym class. That's when JT started hating *Blodough*. Like some unconscious parent who favors one child over another – Coach Blodough did not like John Tower at all.

The young coach's aversion to JT was made obvious in *Mr. Blodough's* science class at the beginning of JT's sophomore year. It was an early afternoon class for JT and stifling-hot after the disgusting boiled wiener winks and sauerkraut wolfed-down in the lunchroom. He sat at the back of the science room close to a hot radiator, nodding off now and then, feeling bloated with gas. Blodough would lean against or sit on his long science table at the front of the room, his dry-cleaned slacks and shirt with tie an impressive look for the prettiest girls he'd have sitting in the front row, an obvious seating arrangement for a man who liked flirting with teenage girls. Although JT thought his science teacher/coach was ugly with his deep pock mark scars from acne, certain girls thought he was handsome *"in a rough way."*

During one of his *science naps* JT was jolted awake when Blodough removed JT's notebook from under his elbow and read aloud the three words JT had doodled all over the paper: *"science kills mystery."* The class giggled, then Blodough walked up to his big table, leaned against it with his bulge facing the front row and

12

asked: "*Mr. Tower...stand up and explain how science kills mystery.*"

Later that night in his bedroom after football practice JT wrote in his journal:

"*I'm exhausted from bull in the ring. It started in Coach B's science class when that jerk had me stand and tell them all that 'the mystery of life is constantly being destroyed by science...and that's why science bores me.' I paid for that comment at the end of football practice when Coach B blew his whistle and barked 'Bull in the ring! Tower, get in there!' Bull in the ring is this chalked circle that I had to stay in while each player charged at me one at a time and I had to fend them off. I was tired to begin with from my ragweed allergy and by the time the trampling stampede was over...I was face-first in the dirt and barely able to get up. He punished me for what I said about science. So, I quit football. I threw my sweaty uniform, jock and all, into the barrel of dirty towels. I hate that fucker. Walking home tonight I realized that my dad was right about staying clear of football and basketball until my senior year. He said my body would be more developed and less likely to get injured. When I got home I told my parents what happened and my dad said he has a 2-year plan for me that would make Blodough eat his whistle my senior year. My dad even knew that Blodough was from Watertown and that the football season opening game my senior year would be at Watertown. My parents named this 2-year plan the 'Johnny 3 Plan.' My dad showed me their plan, and he told me that If I can get serious and make this plan work...Blodough won't like it one bit...and that's good enough for me.*"

Johnny 3

That late-summer of '92 - the day JT quit football - 43-year-old Charlie Tower had been planning for this day, knowing with certainty that his son would quit the team before the season even started. He was right, because he knew his son better than anyone. That early evening when JT walked home from his last practice, Charlie was standing near his butt can at Tower Tavern's back door enjoying his hourly smoke break, a habit he's had since the service. Charlie knew something was wrong with his kid.

"What happened?" the popular bartender called out to his haggard boy.

"I quit!"

"Really?" Charlie stepped toward his son, prepared and hoping for this moment.

"Yeah. I hate that bastard, Blodough."

"I got this *plan* for you. A two-year plan I call Johnny Three. It'll make Blodough eat his whistle. I'll bring it over and show you! "

14

Charlie watched his whipped kid step gingerly into their mobile home before he tossed his Marlboro *Red* in the Folgers butt can, most anxious to tell Ruthie what just happened.

Charlie and Ruthie Tower were making a fortune with their 10 "slot machines" combined with "Ruthie's Loose-meat," a delicious lean beef recipe involving brown sugar and a homemade low-calorie sourdough hamburger bun. Shrewd Ruthie, a 102-pound, 5'2" redhead, drew up a contract with a local bakery to supply her with her own packaged/microwaveable loose-meat sandwich, using her recipes. Tower Tavern was selling over 300 of Ruthie's Loose-meats a day at three dollars a sandwich; about half the Tower sandwich business was carry-out.

Charlie brought his tired son an ice-cold bottle of Mexican Coke from the bar's cooler, along with his "Johnny 3 Plan" marked on the front of a file folder. Charlie sat on JT's queen-sized bed listening to his whipped kid.

"He put me in bull in the ring, Dad!" JT's voice faltered with emotion.

"That's stupid! You don't put a QB in the ring! But I came up with this plan…"

As Charlie opened the file folder to reveal a legal-sized yellow paper with drawings on it: "Don't you mean you and *Mom* came up with a plan?"

"Hey, your mother might have the *long-term* idea, but this is the vehicle to *get it there.*"

"Johnny Three…is that my name now?"

15

"Shut up and look at this. I've spent hundreds of hours working on this. Wait... Not here. I want you to come out to the kitchen table and look at this under the light."

***

Later that night when Charlie was back at work, JT wrote in his journal:

"Dad was right. My mom had a money-making idea with a new sandwich called 'Johnny 3'; it's her loose-meat recipe scooped onto her yummy sourdough bagel instead of a hamburger bun. The meat would go through the bagel hole just like Johnny 3 made 3-point shots, and it would sell for 3 bucks a sandwich (at first). My mom had all the figures down to the penny and believed we'd sell over a thousand Johnny 3's a day, even if we had to get a couple distributors. Then my dad flipped over the page and showed me his drawing of a green, heart-shaped patio with a regulation-size basketball goal standing at the top of the heart. There was a 3-point line shooting arc exactly 19' 9" from the rim; except the target was not a regular basketball hoop: it was a florescent golf ball welded onto this spring-loaded arm that would drop down and trigger this counter device that would count the number of hits. The golf ball would be placed exactly 10 feet off the patio and in the exact center of where a regular hoop would be. His theory: shoot at a target so small over 2 years and the real target will be easier to hit. My dad told me this was a classic 'odd is left' and that if I promised to shoot 200 shots a day until my senior year basketball season –he'd buy me a new van the day I graduated. I agreed and went to sleep knowing my dad

16

was going to have a friend stake the patio and pour the concrete asap."

***

Within a few days the massive green heart-shaped patio was dry and the white 3-point arc painted and dried shortly thereafter. Charlie's buddy, a licensed electrician, installed a floodlight atop the Tower home, the identical lighting used in every high school gym. Now: the stage was set and ready to light up Johnny 3's 3-point shots. Before his boy's first shot at the yellow fluorescent golf ball, Charlie stood atop a step ladder while finishing testing the counter connected to the spring-loaded arm attached to the golf ball. After watching a few of JT's missed shots from atop the ladder, Charlie talked seriously to his son:

"I think you should shoot a *higher* arc, hit the *top* of that golf ball with *lots of backspin* so you're not shagging your rebounds all over hell. I want you to believe that your *persistence*…will make this plan a success. That's *why* it's a *green heart*…to promote prosperity and to *put your heart* into *every* shot. And I want you to begin shooting your first hundred shots at the *same time* every night around seven, the exact time of your games. Then, you'll take a halftime break for twenty minutes before shooting your hundred second-half shots. In time, you'll be able to control your shot to the point that you can get your shot to backspin back to you any place around the three-point line that you want. At halftime, I'll come out and count your shots made and later when you're finished with your second hundred. This only counts your shots *made*, so you *must* keep track of a hundred shots for each half. Okay?"

17

JT nodded yes and took his higher *rainbow shot* from the patio corner, chasing the rebound and then another rainbow from behind the 3-pont line from the other corner, missing the golf ball entirely. After his dad chased down the ball:

"Quicker release. Shoot from your core," the bartender/coach pointed to his son's belly. Just then: Johnny 3 hit the golf ball, his first 3 on his makeshift target. Charlie went back up the step ladder to check if the *hit* was clicked off to '1' on the counter. It was.

"We'll count that as your first shot," Charlie said, then rebounded all misses as JT began his first half of 100 shots. Soon, Charlie walked back toward the bar, telling JT to call him when he finished his first 100 shots, adding:

"Remember, this is a *two-year* plan!"

Charlie had lit a cigarette on his walk back to his butt can; while standing near the bar's back door he watched his son taking 3-point shots and rebounding each one. Charlie was into his head about Ruthie's ingenious part of the Johnny 3 Plan, to turn this into a way they could retire when JT graduated from high school in '95 instead of after at least four years of college. Their friend and one of Ruthie's oldest customers, Jake Martin, wanted Chuck and Ruthie to buy his cabin in Julian, California, before he died of lung cancer and his daughter sold the place. Martin put so much work into upgrades; he really wanted his friends to enjoy the home he had built. Just then: Charlie heard the *sound* made by the spring-loaded counter when JT's basketball hit the golf ball. *"Maybe we can fly out to California this winter,"* Charlie thought, then butted and canned his smoke before going back to the bar, anxious to tell Ruthie that JT was "shooting threes from the heart"; and, that the Johnny 3 Plan was off to a good start.

Mother's Garden

J T sat up on his futon in the dark trailer and checked his cell phone time at 9:20; not even 3 hours remained of 2019. He didn't want to go over to the bar now. *"Too early,"* he thought, and decided to go for a walk in the decade's last night of winter. But then: he changed his mind and decided to drive up to the cabin *now* and pick Grampa Tower up for breakfast tomorrow...*early.* So, while sliding and side-stepping his folded inversion table out of the trailer and into his van along with the futon, the red light, and a few items, he thought of how many years Grampa Tower had gotten up alone like this in the dark for thirty thousand Minnesota mornings. And how it must've changed him when his only child ran off to the Air Force that early spring of '69. Like his father's move *into* the service, JT felt he had to make this move *back* to Elmdale...to his father's dead past.

It's an hour-long drive to the cabin. That's where he'd bring in 2020, in the family cabin his parents bought when Grampa Tower moved to Yankton Manor 12 years ago.

On every monthly weekend drive to Yankton, JT never failed to think of Elmdale, that rural speck of earth

20

where *nowhere meets just outside the middle of nowhere.* It was his dad's incredible research when his dad was in the service that intrigued JT. Charlie found out from insurance actuary stats that Elmdale was right in the heart of a "longevity belt," a 60-sqare mile area in South Dakota/Minnesota where its residents live to be the oldest Americans. *"And by far,"* Charlie would brag to anyone in the bar who asked him about where he was raised.

JT was also moving to Elmdale in the dead of winter to find out why those people live to be so old. Uncovering his dad's secret past was his new *oil* resolution motivated by a mailing list Mary Parrot showed him, a list of attendees from rsvp reunion letters that the reunion organizer received back confirming Iris Prescott would join her *Class of '95* graduates. Iris, who JT hadn't seen in 25 years, was going to attend their 25-year high school reunion…on the most sacred day of any year for three generations of Tower men: June 18th. This was proof to JT that irony still exists in the universe.

He took the exit from I-29 North and soon cruised west through Vermillion, home of the University of South Dakota, the only school that offered Johnny 3 a basketball "tryout" without a scholarship. *Creative* often gave him humorous insights: like how strange it is that his mom's Johnny 3 Sandwich has sold consistently-well for three great distributors in three different states for over 25 years, *while I break scoring records that still stand today…and this is the only place that would look at me.*

At the Hy-Vee in Vermillion he parked and went inside to get a fountain Coke as fireworks were going off around the college town, even though ninety minutes remained until 2020. This was another celebration for JT: no more retirement goals to chase. *"I'm there,"* he'd reminded himself the entire month of December. Now he was free to think about his past life with "Wild Iris," the troubled neighbor girl who stood with him on Mother's Garden on the farm his senior year, and believed he'd be the Johnny 3 legend his family had been working toward.

He started his van and headed west on Highway 50; he had 27 miles to think about her and the impression she made on him the first time he saw Iris that mid-September night his sophomore year. That was when he was into his early weeks of his nightly 2oo-shot Johnny 3s on his green heart-shaped patio. He thought of that summer and how his parents had gotten their usual summer tans on the patio while playing gin every Sunday afternoon, their only day off.

It was easy to recall that night, because he'd written about it in his journal and read it later at the cabin in Yankton to Grampa Tower during one of his monthly weekend visits.

Johnny Blue Eye

"*They arrived like gypsies in the late-summer night of early September, parking a 31' silver Airstream travel trailer in the space next to ours on the other side of the shared septic tank and oak tree, its leaves rustling above my bedroom window. My parents decided to rent that space for $150 a month plus utilities to this single mom from Omaha who was raising her 16-year-old daughter alone. My mom is a softie for people in need. Earlier today this woman from Omaha named Libby came into the bar right after getting a job at the casino across the road from our place. She asked my mom if she knew of a place to park her Airstream. My mom said Libby looks like a brunette Dinah Shore with this perky personality and beautiful teeth. That night of their arrival I could see a tall slim man in cowboy boots hooking up their waste hose into the septic tank while Libby held a flashlight. He must've known what he was doing because soon I saw lights on in the Airstream and heard water running. The guy unhitched his truck from the trailer and then I could hear three people talking. The daughter was smoking a cigarette and complaining about how awkward it was going to be starting a new school when the new school year began a week ago. She*

*was a bit taller than her mother and tomboy-thin with
brown curly hair. My mom said her name was Iris."*

***

The next morning, Libby and her cowboy/trucker
friend were arguing on Tower Tavern barstools while
Iris had a smoke outside the bar's back door. She was
facing the Tower trailer's front window where Charlie
and Ruthie kept their office for the bar. JT watched her
from that window, her brown bangs seemed to be hiding
her eyes as she smoked like an old pro, blowing smoke
rings now and then.

Meanwhile, Charlie and Ruthie couldn't help
overhearing the angry cowboy's words to Libby: "That
sneaky bitch rips me off *every time* I come off the road!"

"Glen, keep it down and *watch* your language," Libby
warned her friend after Glen downed his bloody Mary, a
warning Ruthie and Charlie had seen hundreds of times
when couples were fighting.

"I'm *not keepin' it down* when I KNOW Iris is rippin'
me off! Am I s'posed to sleep with *my frigin' pants on*
so I DON'T GET RIPPED OFF?"

"You ain't sleepin' in my bed no more...pants or no
pants," Libby was done with this guy.

Charlie had heard enough and told the cowboy, "No
domestic bullshit in here. Take it outside."

Glen saw Charlie's dominant blue eye and then saw that
the bartender had a brown left eye; Glen nodded
respectfully and left out the bar's back door just when
Iris was coming in. "F... you," the trucker muttered,

24

causing Iris to follow Glen outside right when JT was coming out of his trailer. She called out, "Hey Glen!" and *fingered* him when he turned to look back. JT watched the angry man's truck peel out of the dirt lot, then waited for the dust to settle until he started sneezing from his allergies. When he was done with his allergy attack and the dust had cleared...his new neighbor had gone back into the bar.

Libby Prescott, the new Tower tenant, went to pay for the tab Glen was supposed to pick up, but Ruthie stopped her: "It's on the house, sweetie. Welcome to North Woodbury."

"He's not comin' back," Iris stated with certainty to her mother while both new tenants were enjoying Ruthie's Loose-meat.

"*Amen,*" her mother smiled.

"I took his carton of smokes he bought at the casino last night."

Libby could only laugh at her crazy daughter and then compliment Ruthie on her sandwich. That's when the girls got a closer look at their landlords' son, "Johnny," when he reached into the cooler behind the bar in front of them to get a bottle of Mexican Coke that he opened right away with a bottle opener.

"That's Mexican Coke," Iris smiled while holding out her glass of ice: "Can I get a little? I love Mexican Coke."

As JT poured Coke into her glass he quick-glanced at her dull jade-colored eyes; he could see that she noticed *his* eyes, and she surprised him:

"My name's Iris and your name must be...*Johnny Blue Eye*," she smiled.

JT looked at his mother and gave her that *look* for calling him "Johnny." His mother called him Johnny; he didn't mind it, but he didn't like being called Johnny Blue Eye; and since this girl seemed so confident and forceful...he didn't tell her how he felt about it. She surprised him again:

"We used to have a cat named Johnny Blue Eye. He had one blue eye and one yellow eye. I've never seen a person with different-colored eyes."

"I have. My dad. It's genetic," JT said while walking away from his new neighbors, causing Iris to try and see Charlie's eyes at the other end of the bar.

***

Now: cruising into the outer city limits of Yankton, JT figured he could be unloaded before the new year and have the van loaded with what he was taking to Elmdale. He wanted to leave for Elmdale right after his breakfast visit with Grampa Tower. Now, the old man would be asleep since nine, often telling his grandson that he stopped staying up for the new year after Charlie ran off to join the Air Force in '69.

He parked his van close to the Tower cabin, an isolated 2-bedroom, 1 bath, 900-square-foot log cabin tucked into dense woods not far from the Missouri River. He wanted to get to his stored writing and look up things he'd written about Iris. For JT, this cabin had a *writing energy* unlike anywhere in Superland. He could sit on Grampa Tower's favorite leather recliner in

26

this space where technology was not allowed: cell phones were usually off, no TV sets, and computers were forbidden. Ever since he retired the first of December, JT has phased out TV and got rid of his ancient Gateway monitor, having planned this "*slower life*" for many years at this point. And tonight, he would think about seeing Iris at the reunion in June and the perspective he had about seeing her again after 25 years.

After getting a roaring fire going in the fireplace, he checked his watch at 11:52 from his grandfather's recliner under the same reading lamp his grandfather used for as long as JT could remember. He turned off his cell phone, not wanting Marty to call him from the bar after missing his annual New Year's Eve appearance and Johnny 3 highlight video. This time: JT would not sit on his dad's reserved barstool that Marty would place behind the bar near the back door where Charlie used to read his paper and sipped Ruthie's great coffee that regulars would buy every morning on their way to work. Libby loved Ruthie's coffee. About noon every day except Sunday Libby would get out of bed to grab a cup of Ruthie's coffee to start her day. Libby Prescott loved to talk. Ruthie was a great listener.

This was the time JT planned to read about Iris and her crazy life, as the *sound* of exploding fireworks beyond the woods told him that a new decade was here. He started looking through a stack of his journals he'd removed from his storage closet. Soon he found the journal he was looking for: those first days of having new neighbors.

Sore Loser

"*My* *dad was telling Libby about the 'ripeness' from the septic tank they shared and how it goes away in colder weather. Mom and Dad were happy because the slots were full earlier than usual. My new neighbor, Iris, asked if I played pool. I wanted to beat her for calling me Johnny Blue Eye. Skinny Iris wore these stringy, jean cut-offs, a dark-red halter top and flip flops with specks of pink polish on her toenails. She chalked her que and said she wanted to play last pocket, scratch-you lose, ball in hand...for a pack of smokes. I told her I don't smoke. She went over to the cigarette machine and we agreed to play for four bucks. I thought Iris was sexy in a wild and dirty way. She didn't like small-talk but she said she was a sophomore like me and bragged that she dated older guys. After I racked she broke and the que ball sailed off the table and Arnie Kutcher barked fifty cents in the jukebox from his barstool. I covered her penalty and she wanted to pick the song. Hot Chocolate played "You Sexy Thing" three times. Iris danced with her mother while I ran the table before the music stopped. She got mad because she thought I hustled her. My dad verified that I'm not a hustler as Iris got four bucks in quarters*

28

from her mom, paid me, and left out the back door. My mom said I could let the girl shoot at least once."

JT closed his journal to recall that day, his words in his journal giving him a clear picture: He recalled taking a seat on the barstool across from his dad, who was reading the paper. JT had just run the table on Iris.

"She thinks I hustled her, Dad."

"It sure looked like it," Charlie kept his eyes on his paper.

"*She's the one* that wanted to play for a pack of smokes."

The bartender *whispered* from behind his open newspaper while Ruthie and Libby chatted: "I want to be discreet for our new neighbor, *tenant,* and *customer,"* Charlie said to his son's dominant blue eye. "Would it hurt you to let the girl at least shoot a few times, for Christ's sake?"

"She called me Johnny Blue Eye."

Charlie shook his head in jaded disappointment and told his son that most things can be ironed out if you do it right away.

"What should I do?"

"I want *you* to figure that out."

Charlie went back to his paper and JT thought about what he could do. *"Odd is left,"* JT said to himself, three words that his father and Grampa Tower have always lived by whenever creative action was called for.

29

JT went over to Libby and asked her what brand of cigarettes Iris smokes.

"Marlboro Reds," Libby said, then watched Johnny Blue Eye get a pack of reds from the cigarette machine with the quarters Libby had given her daughter to pay him. He came back to Libby and handed the pack to her, saying, "You can tell her *you* bought 'em...'cause *you did,*" JT smiled.

***

Even now in Grampa Tower's favorite chair he could almost *hear* Libby's laugh that day in the bar, a good sign that he'd turned things around with his new neighbor Iris. He went to bed in his cozy Yankton cabin, anxious to begin the first day of 2020 living his life in "oil" full-time.

30

Sleepy-poor and So Alive

JT got up early to pick up Grampa Tower at Yankton Manor. It had warmed to 37 with sunshine. At ninety-nine years young, retired farmer Eldon Charles Tower's butterscotch-colored hickory walking stick was under hand as he stood outside the front entrance to the retirement home, known to be one of the nicest assisted-living facilities for seniors in the area.

"When are you leaving for Elmdale? the old man asked John while walking to the van.

"After this visit."

"Tomorrow?"

"Yeah...tomorrow," John decided right then while helping the retired Minnesota farmer up and onto his van's front passenger seat where the interior always smelled like weed.

They went straight to the Hy-Vee and had breakfast sitting at a front window table, where Eldon could watch people coming and going. Grampa Tower was the only person that John shared his writing with. It was Eldon who promoted *"daily writings about one's life makes life real and even more of a mystery. And there's nothing more beautiful than a mystery."*

The old farmer was impressed with the way his recently-retired grandson had marketed Ruthie's Johnny 3 Sandwich the old-fashioned way, by going door-to-door to businesses, handing out business cards for all three distributors...for over 24 years. The card showed all 3 locations and when brought in was redeemed for a *buy one, get one.* This doubled the contracted dime per sandwich JT received, because he was also paid a dime for every free sandwich, another shrewd part of the distributor's contract that Ruthie had written into the agreement: that JT would get a dime for *every Ruthie Tower Bagel* delivered by Ruthie's supplier, adding up to 12 million Johnny 3 Sandwiches sold in Superland since JT graduated in '95.

"How much do you have saved for your retirement?" Eldon asked his grandson about every other visit.

"About eight hundred thousand."

"And you did this with the buy one, get one?"

"At first I was getting only a couple hundred dollars a month from each distributor. Then I created the two-for-one card and gave out cards to every business. It started to grow from there."

"You were smart to stay single and save money. Now you can go anywhere you want...and you *go to Elmdale?*"

"Grampa...I *could go anywhere* like you say, to a thousand places, but I'd be taking whatever happened to my dad with me. And this reunion is coming up on your birthday..."

"I knew this was about that girl Iris," Eldon smiled.

"Yeah, that's part of it." JT leaned across the booth to say: "I don't want to live alone like you did after Grama died. I saw my parents' life together...and I want that. I've lived alone long enough, putting everything into this early retirement, and... Don't get me wrong, Grampa, I don't *want you* to tell me what happened to my dad. I respect the fact that you promised my dad not to talk about it. What's hard to believe is that my mom knows about it and she won't tell me. And she tells me *everything.*"

"Did you tell your mother or Charlie about Iris?"

"No."

That's when Eldon leaned in a bit closer and said: "I think everyone has something in their past that they would never tell anyone about. Have *you* ever told anybody about why you broke up with Iris?"

"Just you."

Eldon reached into his plaid shirt pocket and handed John a safe deposit box key.

"What's this?"

"It's for your research. Take it to the bank in Ortonville."

That was all that was said about the key. John put it on his key ring and went off to get a few things in the store while Eldon waited, looking out the window, watching the people coming and going; he felt good about giving John the key, the same safe deposit box key that his banker gave him that spring in '69 in the bank. It was one of the few times he'd seen or spoken to Betsy Mueller, the music teacher who lived in *The Pink House* across the lake in South Dakota. Charlie had left to join the Air Force. Eldon hadn't lived alone on his farm since before he met Ellie; and then he raised Charlie there by himself. And soon: his grandson would know what happened.

"Water under the bridge," Eldon told his quiet mind and got up from the booth with the aid of his cane, wanting to be ready when he saw John coming toward him with a snub-nose grocery cart holding their groceries.

***

Arriving at the Tower cabin, John's passenger asked him, "What was it that you called Iris in your journal, sleepy-something…?"

"Sleepy-poor and so alive."

"That's it. How'd you come up with that?"

"Iris and her mother Libby had these droopy eyelids. Even though they were poor, they were *so alive*. And there was this song titled "So Alive" that customers would play on my dad's jukebox. It always reminded me of Iris and her mother. From my room, I could see them dancing to their music… Libby would sing on *Karaoke Night* where she worked. She'd sing these sad

Billie Holiday songs. Both Libby and Iris were disappointed by men all their lives. Iris told me that when she was sad and really needed a good cry she'd always play this Anne Murray song, "I Just Fall in Love Again." She said that song made it easy for her to let go of all the poison built up inside her. And whenever I'd hear her play that song, sure enough the next time I saw her she'd look...*so alive.*"

They talked while John escorted Grampa Tower into the cabin, where Eldon soon found his favorite chair and JT got a fire going after putting away the groceries. Leaning against the wall on the mantel above the fireplace was the memorized framed quote of his grandfather's that used to hang on the wall in the farmhouse bathroom: "*What we do not grasp...is forever lost. When all is lost...odd is left.*"

He turned away from the framed quote of his grandfather's, wanting to say more about Iris.

"Iris and her mom lived day-to-day in that sardine can. If Libby was a few days late with her rent it was because tips were slow at the casino. My mom would tell her to just add it onto next month's rent."

From his chair, Eldon told John, "Iris was the one who got this thing started about Charlie and Karen. It was when she came to your football game in Watertown with Charlie...and then to the farm."

John agreed, telling Grampa T that last night he found and read a chapter in his journal about that, adding, "That was my senior year, the opening game, and the only game I wanted to play-in that year."

"Wasn't your coach from Watertown?"

"Yeah. I want to get something to show you."

The old man knew that his grandson had been planning on living his life in oil full-time, as he and Charlie had done. They talked about it every weekend they spent here. The longer he waits, the harder it is to act, Eldon knew. For even though youth has the energy to go there –it's the older ones who need it the most. So, Eldon Tower was happy for John. *"Better late than never,"* he mused, since he and Charlie were forced to live in oil when they were in their roaring 20's, when tragedy came to them in Elmdale, in the God-blaming, fist-pounding fury and form of freak accidents, where guilt could have destroyed them both...if not for the oil Ellie Tower gave Eldon, her beloved and devoted husband for only 2 short years.

***

JT and Grandpa T stayed up talking until the old man's usual bedtime at 9. After reading a few passages from his journal John wanted to expound on his aversion to technology to a very old man who never owned a computer, cell phone, or debit card. Yet Johnny 3 had used those very tools to save a fortune and retire early, explaining his business to his grandfather while John sat on the floor with his back against the leather sofa, another piece of familiar furniture they'd brought from the farm.

"It wasn't easy for me to promote the Johnny Three Sandwich. I started out just giving out my two-for-one business cards all day, to as many people as I could find without much conversation. Because I *didn't like* everybody I met. So, I became this *false-positive* guy…because I was not authentic with those people. If I was happy I didn't feel or show it like I could've. If something upset me or angered me –I tried to conceal it to avoid conflict and possibly lose a potential Johnny Three customer."

Eldon's positive nod encouraged John to continue:

"I really wanted to be like my parents were with their customers: *Real*. If my mom or dad were upset with each other, they'd feel it and show it to each other…without a public display of anger. After watching them all my life you'd think it might be easier for me to show positive feelings to people like my parents did. It's something I inherited, this lack of emotional candor…with *myself*. And yet I see this all too often in my friends I went to school with. It's as if technology and science have diminished the mystery in us all by giving us faster data. I've read that over ninety per cent of our brains are unused, unconscious, and that only relaxation can reach that part of the brain. Doesn't that mean we have to slow down?"

Now it was Grampa Tower's turn to talk. So, John shut up…and waited until it came out of the retired farmer, a man who talked slow and steady, like everyone JT ever met in Elmdale during his visits over the years.

"That's where we are," Eldon said while staring into the fire, his pale-blue and cloudy eyes twinkling a bit. "We're gorillas with hammers, sitting on our territory, fearing any intruder and willing to go to war with the world every ten years when the anger separates too far from sadness… And the race to war is the *lazy* human

37

nature of things. God forbid we should mask our sadness with more technology."

Then JT said: "And we get further and further away from ever being a united country, let alone a united world. That's what I did, Grampa, I slowed down and really talked and listened to people as if *every word* really mattered. I gave out a third of my cards, and yet the commission checks every month really grew from then on."

"Slowing things down is a big part of living in odd is left, or oil, as you call it in your journal. When you go there to research why those people around Elmdale live to be so old...don't forget to tell 'em I sent you," Eldon laughed his big/silent way.

Past his bedtime, Eldon had his own opinion about why Elmdale is in this *longevity belt:*

"If you live on the prairie, just outside the middle of nowhere for most of your life, the mind has to find that balance between anger and sadness. And loneliness lives with sadness...I know."

"Uh huh," John knew that to be true for himself.

"And *if* you get connections to these people living in and around Elmdale...they will help you find that balance. Your grandmother told me about that balance and she helped me know it. It's all about owning your sadness and anger, then watching it vanish in awareness. Those two stressors are killers over time. You connect with the people there and they'll help you."

He watched the old farmer flex and fist his right hand, a signal in wintertime that his *"bones are ready for bed."*

38

John escorted Eldon and his cane to his old bed, the same one he had at the farm for 10 years before Charlie and John moved it here when the old farmer retired and moved into the Yankton Manor.

In wintertime, JT liked sleeping on the sofa instead of the other bedroom when Grampa Tower was here. The other room was much colder and he wanted to be near the fire since it had to burn all night. He'd have to get up once or twice during the night to throw a log on the fire.

It wasn't long before he could hear his grandpa's *snoring*, a familiar sound to John as he was covered with his favorite blanket and his bamboo pillow comfortably holding his head. He wondered if this *balance between anger and sadness* was the key to longevity for Grampa Tower or anybody else. Now: he closed his eyes to see clearly how he would write that chapter in his life, when he was still in his Johnny 3 training of 200 shots a night on the green heart and yet preparing to lead his football Warriors north to those massive Buffalo awaiting on their turf in Watertown, Coach Blodough's hometown. It was that *one* football game he wanted to start his senior year. Then he would *quit*…win or lose. That was Johnny 3's Plan.

Sounds of the Flurry

Iris was 18 at the front of her senior year. She heard JT's basketball bouncing off the green heart, causing her to look at the clock on top of the Airstream fridge. She'd made it to her senior year somehow without studying for anything. She's heard her persistent neighbor over the last two years, shooting his daily quota, aiming for that golf ball, beginning every night at 7 p.m. Over time, the sound of the flurry of 200 shots increased to a furious pace of maximum shooting speed, since now JT was hitting his target frequently and getting the ball to return to him quick…then a fast release…real fast. Speed and accuracy. That's what Johnny 3 was all about on his green heart, shooting from his core, his center, and always imagining the game was on the line. To Johnny 3, *every* shot he took could be the game-winning shot.

Last time she counted that slicing metallic spring-loaded "BOING" sound, Johnny 3 was making about 80% of his shots from behind the 3-point line. Wind could mess with his shooting and lower his average to 70%. Iris knew he was good at adjusting to wind and hitting that fluorescent target by this time in September,

40

when daylight diminished every day and JT prayed for
an early frost to end his allergy suffering.

A couple times a week she'd go out and rebound for
him, getting fewer rebounds she noticed as time went by.
And she was fun for JT, by trash-talking and trying to
block his shot, shouting: "*Johnny Blue Eye shoots! And
nails another three! He misses! Johnny Three choked!*"

Then: the first half of his shooting regimen was over.
The silence after the flurry had its own familiar sounds:
the ball would stop hitting the concrete; she'd hear the
front door of the Tower trailer open then slam shut while
Johnny 3 rested, sitting on the end of his bed as if it was
the bench in the locker room at halftime. Then: that
sound of the ball bouncing on concrete and 100 more
shots until she'd see Charlie coming out the back door of
the bar carrying his 5-foot step-ladder, pausing to light a
red, just as Johnny 3's last shot *BOINGD* another spring-
loaded hit. Charlie would get the count then reset it to
zero with a penlight from his apron pocket.

"*One hundred and sixty shots made,*" Charlie would let
Johnny 3 know while logging in the numbers and
percentages in his *J3 calendar notebook* he kept in his
apron with rolls of quarters. This was the best time of
the day for JT, when he'd just finished his regimen of
200 shots. He'd pace around the 3-point arc, not quite
able to palm the ball when he'd leave the heart to snort
allergy snot from each nostril while watching his father
on that step-ladder, his burning cigarette pooched in his
mouth as he got the total number of hits for the 2nd half.

And this was the time for Iris to come out of her
trailer and bum a smoke from Charlie, the affable
bartender who reminded his regulars of a best friend they

41

wished they had. In-character, landlord Charlie would offer his neighbor a red and light it for her, then he'd head back to the bar with his ladder as JT was removing his black high-tops on the front door steps. That's when Charlie surprised Iris by asking her if she wanted to go to JT's *"first* and *last* game*"* in Watertown Friday, explaining how Ruthie couldn't go because she had to cover for somebody at the bar and that he didn't drive at night because of his *"night blindness."*

"Can't stand those headlights. I get these awful David Jansen headaches every time I drive at night."

"I'd love to go!" Iris declared with such joy on her face that it made Charlie feel good that he asked her to go. *"It was like seeing a young girl going to Disneyland for the first time,"* he told Ruthie later.

"I've got to pick up my dad first," Charlie explained, "...then head to Watertown. We can get a bite to eat on the way and after the game. We'll go right after school."

"Great!" Iris excitedly skipped away.

"Tell your mom you'll be home late," Charlie said.

*"*I will!" she waved at Charlie as he neared the bar's back door. Iris had to ask JT why this was his *"last game,* because isn't this the first football game of the season*?"*

"Yeah. It is." Then he explained, removing his socks, looking haggard from this brutal season of ragweed pollen.

"See...I hate Coach Blodough. He's from Watertown. I promised my dad I'd quit after that game. I'm starting at

42

quarterback and I'm quitting whether we win or lose. Either way, it's because I hate that jerk."

"I think he's handsome," Iris remarked.

"Yeah, right," JT scoffed and went inside his trailer, *slamming* the door behind him.

Iris stood outside the Tower front door finishing her smoke, then the floodlight went off. She wished she'd bummed a couple more smokes from Charlie to tie her over until her mother came home with tips at 2 a.m. when her night shift at the casino was over. That's when Iris would buy her smokes at the 24-hour liquor store across the road, where the clerk has never carded her since she moved here.

This wasn't the first time she'd opened the Tower front door without knocking and slipping into Charlie and Ruthie's front office just to the left of the door. Quickly she removed a pack of reds from Charlie's desk drawer in a carton she'd hit before. Thirty seconds later she was ready to exit the trailer when she stopped, having second thoughts. She looked down and saw JT's basketball shoes and could hear *faint music* coming from behind his closed sliding bedroom door. She walked quietly to his door, wanting to tell him she took a pack of his dad's smokes and would replace them tomorrow. But: she backed away, deciding she'd rather get away with stealing a pack than bothering JT right now, who looked tired after his Johnny 3 shots.

Outside, she lit a red from Charlie's pack and paid attention to the rustling leaves above their trailers; they were dark leaves now, brittle and curled and rattled loud from gusts of warm Indian Summer air. Last week she

43

was rebounding for him and he cupped his ear with his hand before taking a shot, telling her after pointing to the leaves, *"Hear that? That's the sound of a crowd wanting another three."* And then he'd shoot fast; to her it seemed that he wasn't even looking at the target, and yet he launched the ball so high, way above the arc of the light, and soon from darkness this orange ball smacked down that florescent ball that dipped with the arm of the counter while the ball bounced back to him. He didn't move. It was so compelling to her to see him do something she could never come close to doing. And now: this was Iris Jean Prescott's happy time: a fresh pack of free reds, a lighter, a short walk, then alone-time in her sanctuary under the train trestle behind the casino where her mother worked as a waitress/bartender and consistently made really-good tips.

Even in Omaha little Iris had her private place where she could *get lost* when she and her mother lived with Granny Prescott. Now, she crossed *Casino Road* across from Tower Tavern and walked through the casino parking lot to the dirt trail that led to an escape from her mother, or from an unwanted visitor, who was usually an older boy out of high school with a car, smokes, weed, and maybe a fake I.D. to buy beer at the liquor store not fifty yards from her mother's work.

Under the iron trestle she'd chain-smoked another red from Charlie's pack by using the fire from the first one she butted-out on the concrete slab she sat on. She marveled at how Charlie and Ruthie had put up that huge orange and black banner across the front of Tower Tavern, advertising the *JOHNNY 3 SANDWICH/$3.00*; *and, "using the school colors was smart,"* she thought, admiring her landlords' business plan.

44

Alone with the orange glow of a stolen burning red, she reflected on Ruthie's idea to put one *precisely measured* scoop of her delicious loose-meat recipe onto a bagel, the hole representing Johnny 3's basketball hoop; and early sales were terrific, *"sellin' like gangbusters,"* Charlie told Libby this morning. And Iris thought of the pressure JT must be under with all the work he and his parents put into the Johnny 3 Plan. *"He has to be good,"* she thought.

***

All of Tower Tavern's regulars knew about JT's dedicated shooting at a golf ball from 3-point land. They'd step out the back door with Charlie to have a smoke and he'd go over the Johnny 3 Plan with such confidence on his face; even Charlie's dimmer brown eye would twinkle with aliveness whenever he'd talk about his son's progress on the green heart. "Coach Charlie" would proudly point out the progress his future star was making when the metal arm of the counter would spring down and back again while his customers watched in awe each time the ball returned to its master after a 3-pointer fell out of the darkness.

"He makes a higher percentage of shots every week," Charlie bragged. "And he walks around the three-point line at school without taking a shot. He says the rim looks bigger and bigger to him."

The Blowout

Those first weeks of varsity football practice were pure hell for 6', 155-pound quarterback John Tower. Ragweed pollen count was so high that his over-the-counter medication did little to help his runny nose, itchy eyes and violent sneeze attacks. By the end of every practice, JT was so weak he felt like quitting before the first game in Watertown. But he didn't. He was hanging in there, because of Coach Blodough; this was Dowd Blodough's first season at the helm of any varsity football program. It was obvious to anyone that "Coach B" wanted to improve on the Warriors' 4 wins and 4 losses last season when he was an assistant coach.

At first, Blodough alternated quarterbacks, splitting evenly the plays in practice with JT and junior Jake Webb, forcing them to compete for the starting QB position. Webb was not close to being the passer JT was; and both were not option runners. However, the junior was proficient at handing off and faking a bootleg. What Coach B liked about Webb was that the junior knew the playbook far better than Tower, and he knew every running back and receiver's responsibility on every play. It was uncanny how Webb could see a play

46

once and memorize it. Blodough wanted his QB to have a powerful arm like Tower that would help his running game –so he gave JT the starting nod for the season opener with a disclaimer he told both of his signal callers: *"I'll jerk ya if ya don't produce."* To JT, that was a direct threat that put more pressure on him, not to mention that Blodough was one of those hothead idiots that yelled and screamed at his players, creating this constant state of fear that intimidated everyone who played for him...except Johnny 3.

Thursday, the day before the game in Watertown (where Blodough graduated from high school), the science teacher/coach messed with JT's head by giving his #14 jersey to Webb. Rather than stew over Blodough's intentional slight, JT picked jersey #3, wanting to start early as his parents had with the Johnny 3 Sandwich promotion weeks before his fame manifested over the coming basketball season. JT was conscious of the fact that either way, his first and *last* football game was building his foundation for his mother's brilliant business plan.

The night before the game, he wrapped ice cubes in a wash cloth and covered his eyes while lying on his bed in his dark bedroom. He was going over the plays in his head, confident he knew them well. His pollen-weary body fell asleep.

***

Game day on Friday afternoon, #3 sneezed and stumbled onto the bus on weak legs after snagging his football cleats on a step, dropping his orange helmet that rolled over to the bus driver. There: on the front seat above the open front door was Blodough, looking down

47

at his starting QB with obvious disdain. JT caught a glimpse of those beady black eyes and thin lips pursed together in anger. The head coach was already regretting his decision to start Tower as JT wanted to get as far away as possible from this man that nobody really wanted to play for.

Fear was Blodough's game, and JT learned to hate this self-conscious fear that he felt every single time he was around that man. From his seat at the back of the bus he watched the Warriors filling up the bus with their black and orange uniforms. He closed his itchy eyes and recalled his dad's sage words last night about Blodough:

Charlie had come into his son's room with an iced wash cloth right after Johnny 3 finished shooting his last 100 shots on the green heart. Because of the game tomorrow night, he'll miss his 200 Johnny 3s for the first time since last Thanksgiving's ice storm. JT was complaining about Blodough giving Webb his jersey, while pressing the cold wash cloth covering his eyes. Charlie had to say:

"He's doing you a favor. You wear number three and like it. And remember that nobody can intimidate you without your permission. You take on his fear and anxiety," Charlie stated with certainty. "I do it all the time in the bar to connect with a customer. Some guy'll come in sober and all tense about something. I can feel it. But I don't take it on like you do with Blodough."

***

Bouncing north on I-29, behind closed itchy-red eyes, #3 was wishing he felt better for this game since Grampa Tower would be there. He opened his swollen red eyes

48

and could see the back of his team: a busload of 40
Warriors and a chief who was an asshole. He knew his
teammates resented him for starting after quitting his
sophomore season and skipping his junior year. He
wondered if his oversized offensive linemen would
protect him today, give him the time he needs to pass.

***

Charlie drove the Tower Buick to Elmdale in three
hours. Considering he was observing Ruthie's *no
smoking in the car rule* by stopping every 40 minutes to
have a smoke break with Iris at some obscure exit on I-
29...both Charlie and his passenger agreed that they
made "good-time." The fun bartender brought iced
Mexican Cokes in his cooler and gave his passenger a
pack of reds from his glovebox. Apparently, Charlie
was ready to talk to somebody about his first love, Karen
Mueller; that is, somebody besides Ruthie, his best
friend. On their first Coke and smoke break at an exit
ramp near Beresford, Iris had asked him how old he was
when he moved off the farm. Iris was in *mystery heaven*
when Charlie talked about his life with Karen from the
summer of '67 until winter of '69. Never had she
listened with such rapt attention, finding them reaching
Eldon Tower's farm before she knew it.

***

They picked up Grampa Tower at the farm and left
right away for Watertown. The old man was waiting on
his porch when they pulled up to his little 2-bedroom
farmhouse that Charlie could see was getting more and
more rundown in recent years. Everything looked more
weather-beaten: the house, the barn, the sheds were
leaning from storms long gone. What made the drive to

49

Watertown longer for Iris was that her driver told her just before Grampa Tower got in the car and when she was moving to the back seat…to *never tell anyone* about what he'd told her about Karen Mueller….*"and that includes my dad and JT."*

The drive to the game was a real drag for Iris, since out of respect for Grampa Tower –no smoke breaks. They arrived late, two minutes into the game and within a minute after taking their seats on the third row of the visitors' bleachers the Buffalos were beating the Warriors 14 to zip. #3 was getting sacked and pounded by these big Watertown farm boys who looked like full-grown men, some well over 250 pounds. Iris didn't like seeing her neighbor getting trampled, so she took a couple smoke breaks under the bleachers at the back where she could hear Charlie barking out at the Warriors: "Block for your quarterback, for Christ's sake! Zero pass protection out there, Blodough!" She saw Charlie wince whenever JT was sacked trying to pass and heard him expressing his anxious concern toward his dad's good ear: "If he gets injured…Johnny Three is over."

At halftime, the Buffaloes were trouncing the Warriors 28 to 0. While the teams were inside their locker rooms she could hear Charlie explaining the details of the Johnny 3 Plan, everything from the 200 shots on the green heart to the sandwich sales they were counting on. The old farmer nodded positively, a satisfied smile on his face that belied his pale-blue eyes clouded with cataracts.

It was hard for Iris to continue sitting there on those visiting team bleachers listening to Charlie go on and on about Ruthie's loose-meat recipe inside a bagel she created just for *John's* upcoming basketball season. She wanted to talk to Grampa Tower about his wife and his life after losing her to hailstones when he delivered Charlie right there in the garden on his farm. It was going to be difficult for Iris Jean Prescott to keep this secret, but she respected Charlie and his past life with Karen Mueller.

***

When the Warriors returned to the field for the 2nd half to face that massive herd of Buffalo, the field lights were turned on and Charlie covered his sensitive eyes with sunglasses. That's when Charlie told his father about the *perfect cabin* in Julian, California, that he and Ruthie were buying soon from an old customer who's dying from lung cancer. Charlie went on:

"Dad, if our Johnny Three Plan works, we can buy the cabin for two hundred thousand. It's a steal, Dad. I'd say it's worth *twice* that after the work he's put into it. He's only got one kid, a daughter, and she wants him to sell it to us."

"Do you think John will go to college?" Iris heard Eldon ask Charlie.

"Whether he does or not, Ruthie says she can get three exclusive locations to market her Johnny Three Sandwich on year-to-year contracts so that John gets a cut on every sandwich sold."

"I see. So, you're counting on Johnny Three making the sandwich take off?"

"That's the plan, Dad. If he gets a basketball scholarship, his sandwich cut can support him while he's in school and we can sell the bar quick and get out of Dodge *before* we're too old to make a move."

Then: Charlie saw #14, Webb, warming up on the Warrior sideline while JT sat on the bench with his helmet off, snorting snot onto the Watertown grass from each nostril.

"Blodough's putting Webb in for the second half!" Charlie pointed to the back of his benched son, pretending to be outraged.

That's when Iris went over to JT to talk to him. #3 put on his helmet when she called out to him just when Watertown kicked off to the visiting team to begin the 2nd half. JT had a plan, and he talked discreetly to his neighbor:

"I'm out of here."

Just then, on the first play from scrimmage Webb completed a long touchdown pass.

"See that?" JT remarked to Iris during the din of celebration from the visitor's side of the field. "They block for Webb," #3 complained to Iris. Then JT pointed to the distant scoreboard and told Iris to get the car and pick him up there, "behind the scoreboard."

Iris was caught off-guard yet was thrilled by this dangerous exit plan of JT's.

"You're quitting *right now*?" she had to ask…discreetly.

"I'll be there in ten minutes," he said while scouting his route from the locker room to the scoreboard. "Have my dad and grandpa head over now."

Soon, JT turned around to see Iris telling his dad *his plan*; then Charlie gave his son a big smile and thumbs-up from his bleacher seat before handing Iris his car keys. JT watched her hurry off toward the car in the parking lot behind the school not far from the locker room; then he saw his dad and Grampa Tower with cane in-hand slowly making their way toward the distant scoreboard. #3 went over to #10, the 3rd string QB, and told him:

"Hey Steve, do me a favor… After the headcount on the bus, tell Blodough I rode home with my dad."

"Monday, it's bull in the ring," Steve warned his friend.

"Not this time. I quit."

***

By the time Iris reached the Tower Buick she'd made up her mind to take a few quick hits from the roach in her cigarette pack. She put the keys in the ignition and rolled down the Buick's electric windows to rid the smell of this very sweet grass that always made her laugh. Meanwhile her mind raced with this part she was playing in this *great escape* the whole school would be talking about Monday. She laughed at her thoughts about Monday, about this *Johnny Blue Eye who quit during the game.* For the first time, Iris found herself attracted to this Johnny 3 character.

Meanwhile, #3 had made it into the locker room unnoticed; he'd removed his uniform and left it with his pads on the floor in front of the coaching staff door. Wearing his cleats, gym trunks and T-shirt -he hustled toward the scoreboard, whereupon he told Iris he would drive.

"Take off your spikes!" Charlie barked from the back seat with Grampa Tower.

Iris was on the front passenger seat; JT was exhausted when he got behind the wheel after tossing his spikes in the trunk. Before the dome light went off she could see perspiration glistening on his face and neck. Nobody said a word the first few minutes until they were out of Watertown and on their way back to Elmdale. Charlie was thankful his son wasn't injured. Then Charlie reminded #3 about Johnny 3, saying to his son into the Buick's rear-view mirror:

"Don't forget that the first basketball game of the season is *at home* against *Watertown.*"

Iris saw Johnny Blue Eye nod positively, giving his dad a thumbs-up without taking his eyes off the county road that was dark with no traffic coming from either direction. Like his dad, JT was confident that he had set the stage for the biggest game of his life, when a quitter gets a chance to show everyone in the Warrior gym that Blodough was wrong...about Johnny 3.

Sticks and Stoned

That 40-minute drive from Watertown to Elmdale at night was automatic for JT, despite having his head filled with self-talk noise about quitting the team halfway through the Buffalo stampede and leaving his soiled uniform for Blodough to find. As if Coach B wouldn't be pissed enough after getting blown out in his hometown.

74-year-old Eldon Tower was the only quiet mind riding in the Tower Buick. He was happy for his grandson for making an *odd is left* move. The old farmer was aware that if John could make a name for himself on the basketball court, a free ride to college and spending money from Johnny 3 Sandwich sales were possible.

Before leaving South Dakota, crossing Big Stone Lake to Ortonville, Minnesota, Charlie directed their driver to Ted's Chicken Bar, where they stopped for the best fried chicken in the area. Charlie went to school with Ted here in Ortonville. Like Charlie, Ted was a popular host and bartender; unlike Charlie, Ted didn't drink. JT recognized Ted from stopping here to eat about every time he visited the farm with his dad.

While three old friends chatted at a booth, Iris wanted to play pool, so JT racked. She laughed when before removing the rack he turned his blue eye to her: "Last pocket for a pack of sticks?"

"Scratch, you lose," she added. "But you don't smoke."

"That's right. So…you can't lose."

She laughed and broke the table with that same competitive spirit he'd seen the first day he met her in Tower Tavern. One of JT's journal entries:

"I could feel her intense desire to win. It was as if Iris would rather die than lose at anything. Even when a coin toss came out against her, she'd take it as a personal affront, as if the gods of luck were against her. There'd be this flash of anger at some invisible entity who wanted her to lose. That was Iris. She wanted everything, and would sacrifice any relationship to win. Even if it meant going against her mother's rules –Wild Iris had to win, be in control. Boys and weed, alcohol and cigarettes, those were the four most important things to her. Most people never understood why those things were so important to her. I did."

***

During their Ted's Chicken feast Eldon told his grandson he could use this experience to fuel his motivation for basketball season.

JT nodded in agreement.

"Now you'll have more time to practice your shots," Grampa Tower smiled.

Iris said to Eldon with sincere animation: "He's so good at shooting and hitting that golf ball and getting the basketball to return to him without moving from his spot. A hundred shots without stopping. It's amazing."

Charlie had to clarify to Iris and his dad that Johnny 3 has been taking *200 shots* a day for 2 years.

***

A few miles north of Ortonville on the Minnesota side of Big Stone Lake, JT parked the Buick close to his grandpa's little farmhouse now lit by a lone front porch light. Indian Summer nights like this were always cooler here, a few hundred feet from the lake, a secluded place where Dakota winds blew across Elmdale year 'round.

Iris thought it *a lonely place*, especially at night, with no sign of neighbors or any traffic on Moe Road in front of the Tower farmhouse. When Eldon got out of the car Iris asked him if he has neighbors. The farmer pointed to a stand of tall scrub pine, an emerald-green row of darkness, the boundary lines for the Tower and Moe property lines. Iris watched the old farmer move toward his front door; the way he walked reminded her of Charlie and JT, how they had this sense of urgency and purpose when they moved.

She wanted to finish her roach and have a smoke, telling the guys she'd be in after she had *a stick*.

JT followed her, and caught up to her when she stopped to have him lead the way to a tool shed out of view from the farmhouse.

"You got any weed?" he asked her.

"Johnny Three wants to get high?"

"Why not? Basketball doesn't start for a couple months. Now's a perfect time to experiment."

She liked his choice of words: "Experiment," she repeated. "Your first time?"

"Yeah," he admitted as she followed his steps in darkness until they stood behind Eldon's tool shed. The farmhouse was out of view from here, and a safe place for JT to lament, "I wish my grandpa hadn't seen me play."

"He's into your Johnny Three Plan, the whole sandwich thing."

Just then: he had a pollen attack, sneezing then snorting snot as she used a hairclip to hold the roach. Then, she held the roach close to his lips and lit it with her lighter as he inhaled and coughed, causing her to laugh so loud that he hushed her with his finger to his lips, whereupon she had to ask, "Out here? We're in the middle of nowhere, JT."

She took a hit from her clip before lighting it again, until he got a better hit this time. He could see her candy-apple-red nail polish chipped in places when she flicked her lighter on. Nothing else about Iris seemed feminine to JT —except for that nail polish. And yet, her sexual maturity scared him. A girl like Iris could ruin his chances at waiting for *"the right girl,"* that myth that mothers buy into and try to sell their sons, as Ruthie had tried with her son.

They stood close together, huddled with their backs to the cooling wind; that's when he asked her, "How come you always look at my blue eye and not the brown one?"

She thought about it when she saw that he was serious; and she could also see he was really stressed out now from his allergies and the game.

"I didn't realize I did."

She lit her lighter in front of his face and purposely looked at his dimmer brown eye, holding her gaze on it...until she looked over at his pollen-red blue eye and told him in her brusque way, "I don't know. I guess it looks brighter."

He nodded as if he understood.

"It's so *weird* that you and your dad and grandma have the same blue and brown eyes."

Before awkwardness took over —she asked him what he saw in her eyes. He took the lighter and flicked it on, going back and forth from each jade-green eye while cupping the flame he said:

"I don't know how to describe it..."

"You're a writer. What do you see?"

"Each eye is different. Your right eye is more alive and brighter; but your left eye is...sad or something...like it's been hurt."

She broke away from him, not wanting to be analyzed; she headed up the hill in the direction of the tractor path, talking as she walked:

"What's over the hill?" she pointed ahead of her.

"The lake."

She stared ahead at the ascending corn, a dark cluster of rows that ran north and south with the lake. He could see she was headed for the tractor lane that was nothing more than a worn path for tractors and combines; he started sneezing again. He watched her walk to the lane between the corn until he told her his allergies were too bad now and he was going inside.

***

"Where's Iris?" Charlie asked JT when she didn't come into the front room with him.

"She wanted to see the lake."

Charlie's voice seemed agitated when he asked, "Why didn't you *go with her*?"

"My allergies…"

It seemed strange to JT to see his dad scramble for his grandpa's flashlight in a kitchen drawer and then exit the house with it as if Iris was in danger. JT got some ice cubes from the fridge and wrapped them into a washcloth in the bathroom, pressing the cold cloth over his swollen and itchy eyes while seated on the toilet bowl lid. His eyes closed behind the cold compress as he thought back to that terrible game when he was pounded into the Watertown turf. He remembered lying on his back with a couple sweaty 300-pound Buffalo on him, snotty sweat strands dripped onto his face as these farm boys with beard stubble and smoker's breath pushed themselves up by using #3's facemask, purposely twisting the visiting QB's face as if it were a rubber pretzel. That instant: Miguel Champa came over him, and for a moment he could see in *super slow-motion* one of the 200 shots he wouldn't be taking on his green heart tonight. And then: on Grampa T's toilet and without opening his swollen eyes he could also see the framed inscription his dad gave Grampa Tower for a birthday gift when *John* was a little boy. It was there, framed and nailed to the wall across from the toilet. He mumbled the memorized words out loud, feeling more intensely this pot stupor now that made him feel sore and tired from the recent beating he took.

"What we do not grasp...is forever lost. When all is lost –odd is left."

"-Eldon Tower" was printed below the quote that all three generations of Tower men certainly have used in their lives. Johnny 3 has been living this Tower way of life on a green heart-shaped patio that his parents believed would benefit their son's financial security. If so: Charlie and Ruthie could retire early to live their lives in the California sun, far away from the cold past of things forever lost.

Eldon was reposed in his favorite chair, a worn brown leather recliner that faced a black and white TV with rabbit ears and one local channel. John sat across from the old man on a dark hickory rocking chair Joe Moe gave Eldon right after Charlie was born on the farm. John placed the cold cloth over his eyes and sat back, rocking slowly...and...feeling paranoid about something... Was it this old front room of the farmhouse that was making him feel weird now? This *paranoia*, he had to blame on the weed he smoked with

61

Iris. His mouth was so dry and he had thoughts of being with Iris now...if only he felt better.

***

Meanwhile, Charlie struggled up the worn tractor path, his father's flashlight in-hand raking the ground before him and further up the hill to see if Iris was coming back from the lake. Now: emotions were churning inside Charlie's gut, since he purposely hadn't looked at the lake and the view to Karen's house in South Dakota from atop *Tower Hill* at night...in over 50 years.

Charlie's Brain Freeze

R uthie waited for the right moment to wake her husband. The same retired bartender who put his boxers in the freezer in summer, wanted his wife to wake him whenever he was in the throes of a *Brain Freeze*, a name Ruthie gave to describe her husband's unforgiven past life when he was young and in love for the first time. Images and scenes came to Charlie in these *quick dreams* about his past life with Karen Mueller. Ruthie's been tracking Charlie's dreams seriously since before they were married. In her journal, after dating Charlie for a couple months and already talking about marriage:

"Charlie told me about a dream he had after waking up in my trailer. He said he was eighteen and parked outside the Dairy Queen in Ortonville waiting for his girlfriend Karen to get off work. Karen always brought him a cherry slush and he'd get this 'brain freeze' headache. This one time, he had this headache from his cherry slush and Karen played this David Bowie song that Charlie didn't like. That was Charlie's brain freeze

from his past. He's got this uncanny thing about songs related to events in his life that just interests me to no end. I love this guy."

***

Now was the right moment. Ruthie turned on her bedside lamp in their Julian cabin. Brain Freezes were more frequent now that Charlie knows JT is moving to Elmdale soon. They sat up high on their pillows to talk. Ruthie listened:

"It was the time Iris came to the farm after JT's football game in Watertown. I went outside with Dad's flashlight looking for Iris… I was climbing that Tower Hill again…"

"And your legs were giving out."

"Right. I could feel them aching in my dream."

"Did you reach the top this time?"

"I didn't have to. I called out for Iris after I'd fallen. She came up from the other side of the hill and tried to help me up. But I didn't want to get up. I was pissed at her for even going near that lake at night after telling her about Karen."

"What did Iris say?

"She said she was sorry and didn't mean to upset me."

"Aw…that Iris Jean was a sweetie."

"This time I remembered that Iris and I had a smoke right there on Dad's tractor path. I was exhausted from trying to make it up to the top of that frigin' hill. I asked

64

Iris if she said anything to JT about Karen. She said she didn't. Then I told her I don't know *why* I told her about Karen and that I wished I hadn't told her. She asked me why I didn't want JT to know. I got real upset with her and told her how I didn't want to lay that on my son…and that I felt responsible. So, Iris promised she wouldn't say anything about Karen to anybody."

"Then what happened?"

"We went inside the house and JT was on the floor looking through my senior yearbook. Right then, JT asked me who Karen Mueller was. I told him she was an old girlfriend after JT read out loud what Karen wrote in my yearbook.

It was Ruthie's turn, to recite from memory the words Karen wrote in Charlie's yearbook: "Sweet Charlie, promise me you'll always be my friend…no matter what!!! Love you forever, Karen."

"Was that *it*?" Ruthie laughed in her husband's flushed flabby face.

"Yeah."

She turned off her light and asked her husband if he'd consider flying back home to spend time with JT in Elmdale, adding, "Maybe it's time to tell JT what happened to Karen."

"He might get too cold or bored and leave before I'd even get there."

"He's going to find out what happened."

"I know that," Charlie said.

"Jerry or Ronna could tell him."

"No. Dad asked them not to. And they won't."

Charlie turned away from Ruthie to sleep on his side; then, close to sleep, he said to his wife, "Promise me you'll always be my friend."

"No matter what," Ruthie patted Charlie's leg and turned away from him to recall that time in her life when she first met Charlie Tower. This memory always made Baby Ruthie go to sleep with a smile on her face:

The Poor by the River

R uthie was the first prolific writer in the Tower
family, keeping extensive journals long before
she married Charlie. Charlie and Ruthie were
married 3 months after they met, and right
before they bought the bar they named Tower Tavern.
They used all their savings and secured Charlie's G.I.
loan at a low interest rate that business-savvy Ruthie
managed to handle with ease. A powerhouse couple was
formed.

Ruthie started keeping a journal ever since her long-
term residency in Good Shepherd Home, an orphanage
in Woodbury. She really believed she was *damaged
goods*, and that's why nobody adopted her. When she
was a freshman in Woodbury Central Jr/Sr High School,
her first boyfriend dumped her for a prettier girl with
bigger tits. She'd write about things she'd imagine
doing and then actually do to them: like walking the
halls in school with a new boyfriend –just to get even
with the *"pencil-neck loser"* that dumped her.

***

*"The first time I saw Charlie Tower, he walked into the
bar looking and smelling like he just crawled out of the
river. He'd recently been discharged from the Air
Force. It's funny how he thought I owned the joint
because he saw the 'Ruthie's Taverns' banner and he
thought it said 'Tavern.' He was a little drunk when he
came in and sat on a barstool at the end of the bar
drinking Coke while wearing these blue-lensed
Polaroids. And he loved my sandwiches. He ate 4 of
them, wolfed them down like he hadn't eaten in days. I
told him all about me...and he sobered up from that
crazy story, I'm sure. At first, I thought he was one of
the low-life drunks that come and go. 'The poor by the
river are the first to drown.' That's what he said after
he told me this incredible story how he ended up in N.
Woodbury. Then: he became this funny guy who bet me
a 'quick shower in my trailer' that I couldn't guess his
eye color. He won. We stayed up all night just talking
about our lives. I fell in love with Charlie Tower's story
in my little trailer. His story is a perfect psych match for
a girl raised in an orphanage. I kissed him goodbye
outside his truck parked by the river near the bridge
where Karen's body was found the spring of '69. I kept
waving goodbye to him long after he was out of view. I
lit a cigarette and walked down to the riverbank. I
remember hearing about a woman's body found there
back then. I tried to recall where I was at that time, and
all I know is I was here...waiting for Charlie Tower to
find me. Already I think about spending the rest of my
life with this man. So, I must live this 'odd is left' stuff
he talked about, with him, and love Karen Mueller with
him, for if not for losing her the way he did...I'd never
feel this happy today. This morning in the light of things
while sitting at my table for one, I sat on his lap sharing*

a cup of coffee. He's the funniest man alive that I know. I could see into his blue eye, the one that glowed with such confidence...until I saw how it watched me move my gaze to his brown eye; it was like this quick blue flash of a guilty boy who had lived through the worst kind of thing I could imagine. He said he would see me tomorrow after he finds a place to live. I really hate waiting...now that I've met someone I don't want to stop thinking about...for as long as I live. God help me. Who am I? 'Baby Ruthie' is my nickname, and that's what he called me before he drove off. I've never felt so alone in my life."

Yankton Visit

The second day of 2020 was freezing-cold outside the Tower cabin in these rural Yankton woods south of town where homes were few and far between. This was JT's favorite place to write, and he was considering making this his permanent home after his time in Elmdale, however long that would be. His parents bought this place twelve years ago when Grampa Tower moved off the farm and into the assisted-living apartments of Yankton Manor.

Although the cabin was more crowded now with John's things that he'd been moving in over the last several monthly visits here, Eldon liked the feel of his furnishings from the farm mixed with John's stuff. It felt more *"lived-in,"* he told John during early morning coffee.

Later that morning, Eldon made his way with his cane to the cabin front window and looked out at the van parked 20 feet away. He could see John behind the wheel while he warmed the van's engine and listened to his music he liked to blare at times. When Eldon asked his grandson *again* about *"that stuff he smokes."*

"I buy it legally in Colorado."

"Charlie used to smoke it in his room with his girlfriend. She got him started. It grew wild on the farm. Ditch weed, Charlie called it."

"How did you know he was smoking weed?"

"I could smell it."

After an awkward pause, John asked if *Karen* was his dad's girlfriend. The old man nodded yes, and for some reason, again the *family secret* was off limits, and her name was Karen Mueller. That's all Ruthie ever told her son whenever JT brought up Karen's name. So, John backed off.

"Did you say anything to my dad when you knew he was smoking pot in his bedroom?"

"No," the old man scoffed. "I was a live-and-let-live kind of dad. He was a good kid. He helped me on the farm more than he wanted to," Eldon chuckled.

John didn't want to tell his grandfather that the first time he smoked that stuff was on the farm with Iris. Instead:

"Remember that time you first told me about odd is left?"

"I don't remember what I told you yesterday," Eldon grinned.

"I guess it was my dad who told me. It was right after he talked to you on the phone. That's when you reminded him about *odd is left*, and it gave him the idea for the golf ball target for Johnny Three."

"Yes, very good and very odd," Grampa Tower laughed his silent way.

"How did you ever come up with this odd is left thing?"

The old farmer reached into his overall pockets with both hands and found his lip balm that he smeared on his lips before telling John:

"It was your grandmother who used to tell me that. It was something she always said about the *hard choices* and what to do about them."

John understood; and after lunch together, and snowed-in by 6 inches of fresh snowfall by late afternoon, it was better to spend another night here when the roads were cleared.

***

It was always tough on John saying goodbye to Grampa Tower after their meal together at a downtown Yankton café they both liked. There was always this tinge of sadness whenever he escorted the old man into his cozy apartment at the end of his assisted living wing and they hugged goodbye.

***

From his front-room window, Eldon watched JT's van drive away...on his way to Elmdale. It reminded him of a memory he'd lose and then he'd find again at times like this:

72

Charlie's Home

Early spring of '72, Charlie Tower was honorably discharged from the Air Force after serving his 3-year hitch. Eldon was dressed in his worn gray-blue overalls when he picked his son up at the Watertown bus station in Charlie's old Ford pickup. Charlie wore jeans and T-shirt with a pair of sandals, his full sea bag riding on the truck's flatbed as Charlie drove them home to the farm.

"You've filled out, gained some weight," his dad mentioned from the truck's passenger seat.

"I weighed one-sixty when I went in and I'm one-ninety now."

"Ten pounds a year. Uncle Sam must've fed you good," Eldon smiled. After a mile of awkward silence: "I drove your truck now and then, changed the oil every six months."

"Thanks Dad."

***

During lunch in Ortonville, Eldon found out his son picked up 2 habits in the service: beer and cigarettes. Eldon asked his son what his plans are.

"I've been thinking quite a bit about what I want to do. I'm moving to North Woodbury."

The quiet farmer nodded positively, understanding *why* his son would move there. They chatted, enjoying their visit, catching up on the last three years since Charlie left home. Charlie did most of the talking. Eldon wanted to hear about the places his son had seen, since Charlie was the only Tower to serve in the armed forces. Hawaii, Japan, Guam, and Thailand –all fascinating to the farmer who'd never traveled anywhere outside the Upper Midwest. Only once did he visit Minneapolis, to get a tractor part. *"Too many cars and one-way streets. Hicks like me are lucky to come back alive,"* Eldon would joke.

Charlie was aware that he owed his sanity to the Air Force; and he was *not* going to be another generation of Tower men to stay home to farm the land. Nothing was said about Charlie's past with Karen. Eldon talked about Joe and Jerry Moe and how the farm was doing.

***

Later that evening on the farm, seated on *their chairs* in the small front room of the Tower farmhouse, Charlie informed his dad that he wanted to *"take off"* after breakfast at Moe's tomorrow. That's when Charlie got into his sea bag and showed his dad these detailed aerial maps that he rolled open on the kitchen table. Eldon followed his son's finger pointing out this amazing route:

74

"It's the only *possible* course Karen's body could've taken to end up at North Woodbury, Dad. I plugged this course into a computer and the odds were over a *million-to-one* that she'd end up way down there. That's why I'm going to live there...to start a business and live in the place Karen found for me."

Eldon caught a glimpse of that pain he could see in his son's brown eye; he stayed positive about his son's plan, saying with a nod and a smile, "Odd is left."

Those were the words Charlie needed to hear, to validate his choice he had made after 3 years of thinking it over. Charlie Tower was thrilled to have his father's support.

"You need any money?" Eldon asked.

"I got plenty of money, Dad. I saved eighteen thousand in three years. And I'm going to start a business in North Woodbury with it."

Eldon was impressed with his son's plan.

***

Now: Eldon and his butterscotch-colored cane moved away from his apartment window in Yankton Manor. The old man was confident that Charlie's past life with Karen would come to light in Elmdale for John. *"I hope I live to see it,"* Eldon thought.

A Star is Made

J T was ready for a writing session when he parked his van at the familiar rest area at the I-29 Vermillion exit where he peed before having a hit of his stash. He would write on his futon on the cold cargo bed that held the journals that he wanted for his research to complete this book he planned to write after he retired. Well here he was, in rural America, headed for a place just outside the middle of nowhere, a place that devastated his father when he was a young man just out of high school in the late 1960s.

From Yankton to this spot was 30 miles; he'd spent most of that drive thinking about how he would write about that time in his life when the basketball hoop seemed as big as a swimming pool after over 700 nights of aiming for that golf ball. He caught his mind trying to make him feel guilty for not showing up to bring in the new year at the bar, and so, he dived into his story. Writing as Miguel Champa:

"Early-on in practice, head varsity basketball coach George Bergdorf saw this Tower kid as an obvious 3-point threat from anywhere behind the line. It was uncanny how several times during a scrimmage Coach Bergdorf would be ready to blow his whistle whenever

Tower took a 3-point shot instead of passing it off to an open teammate breaking for the basket. But the whistle never came –because Johnny 3 never missed.

Meanwhile, the Johnny 3 Sandwich, the bagel with Ruthie's popular loose-meat recipe, was growing in sales in all 3 Superland locations. Coach Bergdorf loved Ruthie's Johnny 3 Sandwich and had no problem assigning Tower a #3 Warrior jersey after Charlie delivered a free lunch to the head coach a week before the opening game at home with Watertown. Coach Blodough, a Watertown High graduate, was now the sophomore boys' basketball coach. Coach Bergdorf received plenty of negative feedback from Blodough, calling Tower a showboat, a glory hound out for himself. 'He's a quitter,' Blodough scowled. 'He quit my team during the game. Starting a kid like that sends the wrong message to the rest of the team,' Blodough complained."

Miguel stopped writing and thought about how Coach Bergdorf would often get complaints from other faculty and parents about starting *the quitter*. The head coach always ended up saying the same thing: *"He shoots threes like nobody's business. Until he starts missing – he's starting."*

***

That first basketball game of the season was tomorrow with those same Buffalo that trampled Johnny 3 into the turf, embarrassing him in front of his dad and Grampa Tower. He knew that the Buffalo basketball starters would be part of the same vicious herd that humiliated him in Watertown. This was number 3's only chance to get even.

Lying on his bed after a light practice, he felt pretty good; and yet, he was denying the stress he felt for tomorrow's big game. The pollen was long-gone after an October freeze. Through his closed window he could *hear* the familiar sounds of Iris and one of her "boyfriends" hanging out in the Airstream. More and more guys seemed to be stopping by the Prescott sardine can. They were older guys who had dropped out; or they were the non-athletes who smoked and partied with other non-jocks. They smoked with Iris just off school grounds; and he'd seen plenty of guys dropping her off in front of the school at the end of lunch period. Miguel wrote in his journal the night before the big game:

"I keep hearing jocks at school calling her 'Wild Iris.' Seems like she only likes those older tough guys who boss her around. I always believed Iris liked older guys because she didn't have a father figure around at all. This morning she wished me good luck and said she was going to the game. Jocks are afraid of Wild Iris, betting she'll be knocked up before she graduates. Libby told my mom that she had one rule for her daughter: 'no smoking, drinking, or sex in the home.'

At night when Libby was at work I'd hear this loud engine arrive and park outside the Airstream; then her music would stop, the trailer door would slam shut and I'd hear her drive off with her friend. Iris would return home just before her mother got off work at 2. One night I saw Libby come home early and Iris hadn't returned home yet. I never heard two people yell so much at each other."

JT was having trouble falling to sleep after writing and hearing one of Iris's boyfriends leave the Airstream and drive away. But then he could hear Anne Murray's voice singing "I Just Fall in Love Again." He cranked open his bedroom window to let in the song. He remembered this was the song she said always helped her have a good cry when she needed one. As he listened to the love song, it got to him, under the covers, curled into a ball of tension, he started sobbing and convulsing –trusting her words that he too was releasing toxic poisons he had to let go of when the world got to be too much. Then: the song was over; he could only hear the flapping of winter's cold breath blowing against his curtain...until...he fell...fast sleep...from this natural anodyne sent at the speed of sound from a caring neighbor and friend called Wild Iris.

***

At game time around 7 p.m. - the exact time of day JT had been shooting at a golf ball in every kind of South Dakota weather - the North Woodbury High gym and stage were packed to the rafters with Warriors wanting revenge. Even the visiting Watertown fans were anxious to see this Johnny 3 *buzz* that was going on all around them, not to mention a professional camera crew hired by the Towers set up on one wing of the bleacher-packed stage near the school band. Charlie and Ruthie sat on the bleachers at half court and halfway up, all staged by Ruthie, who saved a space for Iris, now getting stoned in the school parking lot with a couple of friends.

When the black and orange Warriors came out of the locker room to warm up, every eye watched this #3 *Tower kid* taking 3-point shots with a designated rebounder (Marty Gunderson) feeding the ball back to

Johnny 3 as he moved quickly around the 3-point line from corner to corner…unable to miss if he wanted to, swishing each high-arching shot that even the same big and tall Buffalo football jocks on the team had to watch with their loyal fans who'd traveled so far from the north to see them rout these same Warriors they'd trampled on their turf just a few months back. Then: JT saw Blodough; he was leaning against the wall under the scoreboard with hands behind him after just chasing a couple guys out of the boys' bathroom he caught hot-boxing a red that Iris had given them.

The game began with the Buffalo ahead 6 to zip…until Iris entered the gym and stopped to watch that familiar rainbow shot she'd seen thousands of times; it razor-zipped the net upside down so the ref had to stop the game to get the net back down as the crowd *roared* with the score cut in half 6 to 3. Iris squeezed in-between her neighbors on the bleachers and sat there awestruck as Johnny 3 made 5 more 3's in a row with a 21 to 19 lead at the end of the first quarter.

In the 2nd quarter the visiting head coach put a taller Buffalo on Johnny 3, but it made no difference, because it freed up the middle for easy lay-ups where Tower could get easy assists. On offense, #3 ran back and forth, prowling behind that 3-point arc where screens were set by Warriors running the bigger Buffalo to exhaustion while 3 after 3 rained down from the rafters until something odd happened: *"Johnny 3 missed one,"* the crowd quieted, which caused a *cheer* from the Buffalo faithful, who were sadly witnessing another kind of first-half in North Woodbury by Johnny 3, the same QB they had trampled out of the game. 7 more 3's in a row zipped through the cotton twine in the 2nd quarter, giving #3 39 total points *at the half.*

On their way into the locker room at halftime, Blodough applauded the varsity squad while he stood on the same spot under the scoreboard that had the home team ahead 47 to 30. Johnny 3 had scored 39 of the 47 with one missed shot, and Blodough was as phony as could be about Tower's success. It was obvious.

Coach Bergdorf - who looked like he could stroke-out any minute - was on fire at halftime in the locker room drawing up frenetic double screens on a chalkboard to get Johnny 3 open, telling his Warriors, "until he misses...we go with Johnny three."

On the way to the court for the 2nd half, the team manager, Marty Gunderson, told JT he was 4 points shy of breaking the all-time Superland scoring record of 42 points in one game. The warm-up chanting was "Joh-nee-three!" a 3-syllable chant that Ruthie, Charlie, and Iris started and ended with a thousand feet stomping the bleachers with *Joh-nee-three* as if this was a state championship game. *Then*: from Charlie's POV, the bleachers across the court revealed a rare *brain freeze* to Charlie Tower:

***

It was that summer school dance in Milbank in '67. Across the gym floor on the bleachers he saw 17-year-old Karen Mueller talking to a girlfriend, Elizabeth Snow Bear; they were giggling, having fun. Then:

***

A Johnny 3 *swish sizzled the net* and the *roar* of the crowd brought Charlie out of his reverie.

***

A new star named Johnny 3 sent 200 wounded Buffalo fans back home after humiliating state records were broken against them by the same Warrior they all but destroyed last September. Coach Bergdorf let his star keep shooting until a total of 25 3's burned through the cotton net, a 75-point total that was professionally recorded. This was *the game* played every New Year's Eve at Tower Tavern; and, on all the screens in all three Johnny 3 Sandwich locations that night after the game…thanks to Ruthie. And Ruthie would need help keeping up with the demand for her 3-dollar Johnny 3 Sandwich that thousands of customers from across Superland were scrambling to buy after her son's record-breaking performance. The Johnny 3 Plan was off to a great start.

***

Charlie slid the Saturday morning paper under his son's bedroom door, then knocked before barking, "Time to get up! Check out the paper and come over to the bar! Okay?"

"Okay," JT said while getting out of bed after his record-breaking first game of the season.

He looked at his headline performance and knew right away that he'd peaked; he was destined to slide down the hill as a one-hit wonder from now on, for a weakness in his game was revealed to him near the final buzzer when he was intentionally fouled. Free throws. He couldn't adjust to the shorter distance, because his shot was set from behind the 3-point line, around 20 feet out. He thought it was funny when he missed all 3 free throws. And then, another weakness: when he was in bed late last night he heard a loud muffler outside and he cranked open his window and saw Iris looking all sexy in her winter-tight jeans getting into Ben Marshall's old Pontiac, a baby-blue Firebird without a muffler. JT resented this wild neighbor girl and her promiscuity. Iris was rumored to have done Marshall in his car at the sand dunes last summer. Nevertheless, he couldn't imagine his life without that sardine can of histrionics, where every emotion under the sun was played out to the max. Yes, this virgin star named Johnny 3 knew he was at his brightest now…and diminishing soon. By the time he finally got to bed last night he was exhausted from his mother's post-game publicity schedule, including a lecture from his mother warning him not to party with the wrong girls, to *"save yourself for the right girl."*

Last night before sleep came for restive Johnny 3, he was certain he hated Iris –because he wanted to be with her, to be one of her "boys." He wanted every wild and crazy part of her. It was a sentimental feeling, a paternal desire to rescue her, to save her from a life of ruin he's seen acted out a thousand times in the bar.

"Now, maybe she'll come to me," he'd whispered last night and fell off to sleep with the *roar* of the crowd still there in his head, this intoxicating sound that made him *flinch awake* as if one of his teammates had passed the ball to him. And yet: this was the same crowd that said he was "odd" for shooting at golf balls every night; the same that said he was *a quitter*. Then, his best *Cool Hand Luke* smile had to come to his face when he caught a glimpse of Blodough watching him with contempt all over that despicably-clenched iron jaw of his when the frenzied Warrior fans stormed the court after witnessing a local sports history moment for the record books.

Last night, at bedtime, Charlie and Ruthie went to sleep cuddling like snuggle bunnies on their king-size bed. This was the start they'd planned for their son...and their long-awaited dream to retire in the California sun. They had a buyer in-mind who was rich enough to pay them what they wanted for their bar: Harold Gunderson. His son Marty is the team manager for the Warriors varsity basketball team. Things were really lining up for their Johnny 3 Plan.

Birthdays, Hailstones, and Home

J T's 3-hour winter drive north to Elmdale was purposely sidetracked by *oil*, (as abbreviated in his journal). In downtown Sioux Falls, he took a long brisk walk along the Big Sioux River in subzero weather. He found a cozy coffeehouse where he wrote: *"I want to arrive in Elmdale in the morning, have breakfast at Moe's. I'll get a motel in Watertown or Milbank and leave early tomorrow. My river walk was packed with oil: I smoked a bowl in my van and during my walk I stopped to talk with 2 Native men sitting on their haunches under a pedestrian bridge; they were rolling and smoking cigarettes and offered me one after pointing out a coffeehouse. I told them I don't smoke...cigarettes. They laughed and wished me a 'good journey' after telling them I was going home to where my father and grandfather are from."*

***

85

Next morning, JT's winter approach into Elmdale from the south on Moe Road was like driving into a Norman Rockwell painting. Every little thing he noticed had its weather-beaten rustic charm as in a thousand such obscure American towns and villages not found on maps. Elmdale was a destination for only *its* residents. Moe General Store was still the only business. Moe Road was a mile-long stretch of plowed gravel that ran the length of Elmdale with Joe Moe's store and cafe in the middle at the bottom of the road where a speed limit of 15 m.p.h. was posted and never enforced.

On his left, he could see the frozen blue-gray ice atop Big Stone Lake winding south along the western boundary of his grandfather's land that was now leased by Jerry Moe, Joe's son and working manager of the general store. It was Ruthie who made a deal with Jerry Moe, that his company would pay Eldon's annual Yankton Manor costs for leasing the Tower land out to local farmers. It was a sweet deal for everybody. Eldon especially liked it: since it was like his life in Elmdale was taking care of his golden years in Yankton without touching his life savings and social security.

He stopped his van on this familiar road of rural desolation to look at his grandpa's farmhouse, now abandoned. Then, on the east side of Moe Road up ahead he could see the plowed entrance to the one-room church Eldon Tower and Joe Moe built soon after moving here from Winner, South Dakota, when they were young men. They wanted to escape the strict elders for a *softer* house of worship, Eldon told Ruthie when she first met Eldon here after their honeymoon in Custer.

JT remembered stopping at the church cemetery
every time he and his dad came to visit Grampa Tower.
They'd walk over here to Grama Tower's grave behind
the church, where JT parked his van now. He took a
quick hit of Creative before brushing off *Ellie Tower*'s
flat headstone with the date of death "June 18, 1950"
exposed. He never failed to imagine her death whenever
he stood at her grave, even now as icy-cold winds blew
stinging shards of snow off the granite banks of the
frozen lake that always seemed more like a river to JT
whenever he visited. He dipped his chin into his coat
and saw a blank headstone beside Ellen Tower's grave
after clearing it of snow. Something he figured his
grandfather had done before moving to Yankton.

For the first time in his life, JT was alone here; this
was another shot of oil for him on these early days of
living in oil full-time. Thanks to Creative he could stand
here in the blast of winter and imagine that summer day
in June some twenty thousand days and nights back; and,
after seeing Grampa Tower outlive his bride by 70 years,
JT could see how Grama T's short life was impacting
her grandson's life now, *"in this odd way,"* he thought.
And now: he could see clearly that her death was the
beginning of oil for 3 generations of Tower men, men
who had lost their first love.

Back inside his warm van he found an old journal
entry he wrote after talking to his father about Grama
Tower's death:

*"Eldon Tower turned 30 on June 18, 1950; his bride
Ellie of two years was 27 and pregnant some 8-plus
months with my dad, Charlie, when she was killed by
hailstones while fetching vegetables for her husband's*

87

birthday dinner. Instantly, with no time to grieve the death of his wife, Eldon delivered his son right there in the garden. 'Odd is left made me act,' Eldon said."

***

It was the future Ellie Tower who first told young Eldon about *odd is left*, the very first time they met in Moe's General Store at the lunch counter. Grampa Tower would talk about those early days of courting *Ellie*, and John would write them down in his journal:

"Eldon talked to Ellie for the first time when she was having breakfast in Moe's and talking with Joe Moe at the counter. Eldon came in and sat a few stools away from her. She was talking to Joe about how when she gets bored she does this 'odd is left' thing, that she'll do something out of character and it changes everything. For example, she said: 'This morning I got up and walked here from Ortonville because I heard there was a rather good breakfast to be had here. So, here I am,' she laughed with Joe. And then I saw my Grampa Tower's face light up when he recalled his first oil; and all because he knew he would have one chance with this girl...or she's lost forever, gone like the wind-swept lovers of yesterday, he said. Then, Eldon said he moved onto a stool closer and told the pretty girl from Ortonville how he got up to do chores as usual and now he's here, talking to this attractive woman. That's when Eldon moved right up to the stool next to her, looked right into her mismatched-colored eyes, one blue and one brown, and told her how he wanted to do something odd and walk her back home today after they had breakfast. It was the best time of his life, he told me."

***

JT coasted his van down Moe Road until on his left he saw the grand 3-story *Moe House* Joe built in the mid-1950s with Eldon; it was atop a hill overlooking the store with 25' stands of scrub pines obstructing the view from any direction all around the house. He could see red and green holiday lights blinking behind some of the front windows of the stately Moe House.

Then, he reached the old store, still as rustic as any milking barn, and clean, with its retired Fire-Chief gas pump now a faded-red sandwich sign: "Good Food/Good Coffee/No Gas." He parked in back near the back door where 70-year-old Jerry Moe was scooping sawdust onto his oak floor. Jerry recognized JT right away and was happy to see Charlie's boy and Eldon's grandson.

"I heard you were comin' to do some writin'," Jerry smiled.

"I hope to, Jerry."

Over a great breakfast made by Ronna, Jerry's wife, JT discovered that Joe Moe's old summer cottage behind the house was ready (at no charge), and that 102-year-old Joe Moe would be glad to see Eldon's grandson at dinner this evening in Moe House.

"Did my dad call you?" JT had to ask Jerry.

"Ruthie called," Jerry smiled.

***

He parked his van near the cottage door at the top of the steep driveway behind Moe House. He remembered when he'd spent the night here with his dad on one of

89

Charlie's many visits here to convince his dad to sell the farm and retire.

Jerry was a great host, helping JT carry in from the van his inversion table that JT set up on the back porch of the cottage. Jerry told JT to help himself to anything in the Moe House kitchen, and *the back door is always open.* Upon leaving his guest with a key to the cottage, Jerry said to be sure and call his parents to let them know he was settled.

"I will, soon."

Whether it was the preserved furnishings that reminded him of Joe Moe, the Elmdale founder and corporate owner; or, the real love that Jerry showed him when he arrived in his store –the cottage felt like home to JT, and "*a good place to write,"* he hoped while unpacking.

***

Dinner went well in the Moe dining room, a familiar place that had a good-feeling vibe for JT. "John" was seated at one end of the oak dining table directly across from the 102-year-old patriarch of Elmdale, Joe Moe. *The General* had a slender patch of silver hair above his pointed ears, and the egg-shaped head of an old goose who appeared to slump forward from his long sagging neck. Jerry and Ronna flanked both sides of the old man's end of the table, adroit at handling or interpreting anything since Joe moved into his spacious attic apartment when he was 90.

Earlier, before dinner, Ronna escorted her father-in-law from his 2-story motorized chairlift that raised and lowered him safely to and from his attic apartment, the warmest room in the house in winter and directly above Jerry and Ronna's huge master bedroom. Joe was awe-struck by how much John resembled a young Eldon, Joe's best friend. Several times during dinner, Joe had to pause to stare at the face across the table as if the old man was into a flashback that John's uncanny resemblance to Eldon had triggered. Jerry and Ronna were amused by it all, this obvious light that came over this retired grocer of Elmdale staring at Eldon's only grandchild.

After dinner, Ronna poured Joe a cup of decaf tea she would raise to his chapped lips ever so carefully; that's when Joe whispered to Ronna, inquiring about his old buddy, Eldon Tower.

"He wants to know how your grandfather is," she translated to John.

"He's fine. Living well in Yankton," John nodded at the old man.

When Ronna tried to repeat to Joe what John had said, Joe snapped at her, "I heard what he said."

Later, John watched Jerry walk alongside Joe and his ascending chairlift chair that would climb to the 2nd floor, then it would turn to climb the narrow stairway that stopped before Joe's attic apartment door, whereupon Jerry or Ronna would help Joe into his living space. Ronna explained to John how Joe liked to sit and look out at the land for *hours-on-end* during the day. JT could tell that there would be no answers coming from Joe about his dad's life here; the same was true for Jerry and Ronna, as again, when Jerry returned downstairs after getting Joe situated, Jerry asked his guest if he'd called his parents yet. Again: "I will, soon."

Just Outside the
Middle of Nowhere

After a great breakfast at the store, and after a good night's sleep in the cozy Moe cottage - JT was ready for the bank when they opened at 9. On his slow drive to town he couldn't help thinking how his dad was right whenever he'd described Elmdale; it was always, *"just outside the middle of nowhere."*

He parked near the bank, where he saw the temp was a -5. On the frozen main street, the wind was biting at a 20-below wind chill on his exposed face below his purple beanie from Bud Grant's Viking days. *"Odd is left,"* he told his mind when crossing the street, taking in the gray-stark minimalist order of things all around him. He could see that mining granite was an old business here, underfoot and on the buildings, and its color matched overhead in the gray overcast of a sustained cold front that was bound to have all 3 bars in town busy all day. It was his dad who taught him to appreciate weather like this. That's when the bar was busiest, his dad would say every winter.

***

Inside Eldon Tower's safe deposit box was a house key and a deed to that house and lot in rural Big Stone City in South Dakota. The deed was transferred to John Eldon Tower in '95. On the drive to the house JT realized when he turned off and onto this unmarked gravel road –he'd seen it a hundred times. It was bought by his grandfather in 1970, who paid the taxes on the abandoned house ever since. Karen's mother, Betsy Mueller, was the seller, JT confirmed in the bank when one of the tellers knew that Mrs. Mueller was a music teacher in Milbank and that she did have a daughter named Karen that lived with her.

The Pink House was the lakefront house directly across the lake from Grampa Tower's land. It was weathered to a moldy watermelon-pinkish color with no trees on the lot. He parked facing the lake close to the house. After a hit of Creative he realized he's owned this house ever since he graduated. He could see the tops of the trees on the Moe/Tower property line from here. No neighbors in sight. And Elmdale might've been the closest neighbors in winter when you can walk across the frozen lake.

He walked down to the weathered barn-wood dock and stepped onto it, relieved when it held his weight. The dock *creaked* from ice and built-up snow so much that he stepped off it and looked at this ugly house on the prairie with no trees for summer shade on the entire lot. It looked like a crooked barn on stilts from lakeside. Half of the lower first floor facing the lake was empty space for parking, supported by six rotting beams of timber. He walked around to the front door of the house,

94

where the "front door key" fit. Before turning the key, he looked around and could see no sign of neighbors on this side of the house, and mumbled, "…just outside the middle of nowhere."

Women Lived Here

That was JT's first thought: *"Women lived here."* And he could see this *had to have been* an oasis in its day from the bleak winters here. The people who lived here were alive with music, he knew upon seeing the curling and faded lavender wallpaper with inch-high black musical notes in scale. This was the home of the music teacher, Betsy Mueller.

He followed the fog of his breath upstairs to 3 small bedrooms, each one had a high ceiling and reminded him of a bird cage. In the bedroom facing the lake he knew this had to be Karen's room. At the east window, across the lake, he could now see more of the trees and the roof of Grampa Tower's old barn. Just then: his cell phone *rang*. "Dad" was calling him. He did not want to talk to his dad now. *"Odd is left,"* he thought…and so:

"Hi Dad!" he moved to the south window and saw his van.

"You in Elmdale?" Charlie asked his son.

"Yeah, I'm here," he answered, knowing his dad had probably talked to Jerry.

"I *can't believe* you'd go there *now*," Charlie's voice wanting an explanation.

He knew his mother was listening to him on his dad's speaker phone, and Charlie was speaking for Ruthie too when he declared, "There's nothing for you there."

"That's right," his mother injected as JT made his way downstairs.

"I found out I own a house here," JT said.

Awkward silence from California.

"That pink house across the lake from Elmdale. Dad, why would Grampa buy this house in 1970 and transfer the deed to me?"

More awkward silence, until:

"I don't know. I had *no idea* he bought it," Charlie was angry now.

"Dad, you would *never* talk to me about Karen or this place."

"It's *my past*! Why bother *you with it*? Just *sell* the place...or list it with some real estate agent there... It's the *dead past*, JT."

In California, Charlie's head was spinning with the fact his father bought Mrs. Mueller's house and kept it from him all these years.

***

"And why *not* sell it? Why leave it to Johnny?" Ruthie asked her husband at their Julian kitchen table after JT said he'd call back after he charged his phone.

"Dad wants him to know," Charlie said, absently.

"Then why wouldn't Dad *just tell him, for Christ's sake?*" Ruthie wondered out loud.

"Because I *asked him not to*!" Charlie snapped.

When Charlie Met Karen

Since Charlie was frugal - combined with his fear of professional help with his issues about Karen Mueller - Ruthie was the only person Charlie would talk to about his *first love* whenever he had one of those *brain freeze* dreams about Karen. Ruthie had a clear image of the first time Charlie and Karen met:

***

It was July of '67, the summer before Charlie's senior year at Ortonville High. From atop Tower Hill on the tire-rutted lane of his dad's cornfield, 17-year-old Charlie Tower could hear *music* coming from the Mueller dock across the lake in front of The Pink House. He could see Mrs. Mueller's daughter in her black one-piece bathing suit, her auburn-blonde hair short and attractive to him.

He'd seen the music teacher last winter with her daughter in Moe's store after they'd walked across the lake to buy cocoa for hot chocolate. If winds blew from the east he could *hear* piano lessons going on day and night during summer break. He knew that the music teacher's daughter went to school in Milbank, where her mother taught music, and was pretty sure she was also going to be a senior this fall.

When a young man takes a risk, he's being young. When Charlie Tower stripped down to his cut-off jeans and sunglasses before making his way down to the lake –he was being the son of Eldon Tower after saying out loud to himself: "...odd is left."

She *heard* his distant splash and groan coming from across the cold lake, a lake that was 26 miles long and looked like a river without a current. The sound of his approaching swim thrilled her, for she had seen him many times standing on the hill across the lake, and recently this summer before the corn was tall. Karen Mueller turned down her transistor radio so she could hear him if he said something to her. Right when he seemed to be right there at the dock...she could *hear* his heavy breathing, and he said nothing...for the longest time...until she sat up and had to look over the edge of the dock, where she saw him floating on his back, his hand holding the dock while wearing these blue-tinted sunglasses.

"Hello there!" she called down to this farm boy she'd also seen from afar in the old general store.

"You're the music teacher's daughter. I saw her flyer for piano lessons in Moe's," he pointed east.

He stood up in the shallow water and asked her how he can get a piano lesson.

"Just call the number on the flyer and my mom will schedule you."

"I've seen you from the hill," he pointed. "I could hear your radio."

She stopped herself from telling him she's seen him on the hill, instead:

"You live there, right?"

"Yeah. That's my dad's land," he pointed again.

"We don't have a phone," he said, referring to the piano lesson.

"Really?" she almost laughed. "Are you going to the school *Summer Dance* this Saturday in Milbank?" she smiled.

"Maybe. Do they give dance lessons there?" he smiled, and she laughed. "I'm Charlie."

"I'm Karen."

***

Charlie told Ruthie that he swam back across the lake with a boner after meeting Karen for the first time. Ruthie thought that was funny and *"raw teenage hormones at play."* To these career bartenders who'd seen and heard everything tending bar over the years…they could only be real to each other.

First Lesson

That summer of '67, music teacher Betsy Mueller was *so busy* with her "students"; she was now making enough extra money from piano lessons at home to make double mortgage payments on The Pink House. The organized teacher was booked solid every day tutoring 8 students a day, 7 days a week for a ten-dollar hour-long session.

Charlie admired Karen and her mother living alone in that old 2-story house that Mrs. Mueller had painted pink two summers back when she moved from busy Minneapolis to this rural house on the prairie. Karen was nearly expelled from the school in St. Paul where her mother taught music. Freshman Karen was caught smoking marijuana in the girls' bathroom soon after her parents were legally divorced after a long separation. Betsy decided to move her daughter to a *"slower life"* after securing her South Dakota teacher's certification and her new position at Milbank K-12. With her teaching job and credit rating, Betsy was approved for a mortgage loan at the Ortonville Bank. Charlie and Eldon admired the teacher for having their bank pay for

a new hot water heater and a new coat of pink paint with
white trim to close the deal.

***

The night of Charlie's first piano lesson was to be his
only one, since the *only* reason he took a lesson was to
see Karen again. Last night, Charlie drove his truck to
the Milbank *"Summer Dance"* that Mrs. Mueller
organized. Right when he walked into the gym he saw
Karen dancing on the gym floor with a girl. Karen
spotted Charlie right away, waved at him, and when the
song "Come See About Me" was over, she ran over to
him, telling him about his piano lesson she scheduled for
him tomorrow at her house with her mother, who was
playing the records and overseeing this school function
from the stage.

He didn't like to dance, he told her; then she told him
she had some *"awesome weed,"* and to *"meet me
outside."* He got behind the wheel of his truck and
watched for her to come outside to the school parking
lot. Earlier tonight at home after getting dressed for the
dance and putting on English Leather cologne he'd
bought at the Ortonville Drug just for tonight, he pressed
his dad about getting a phone, telling his dad they were
"living in The Stone Age without a telephone."

Then, later at the dance in his truck, she kissed him
after they smoked her weed. He'd seen her paying
attention to his eyes. Charlie liked her for not saying
anything about his eyes. Because of her weed: he ended
up missing turns on his familiar ride home.

***

103

The next evening at 6:30 Charlie splashed English Leather onto his palm and rubbed it over his face and neck; he was into his head about seeing Karen again. He'd only gotten to 2nd base with two local girls the summer after his sophomore year. But Karen was no local girl, he knew; and to see her again after kissing her last night meant more kissing and more blue balls…unless Karen would be his *first time*.

Eldon thought his son was dressed up *"pretty snazzy for a piano lesson,"* before heading out the front door and on his 6-mile drive to the Mueller place that was just across the lake from the farm.

"How much is your lesson?" Eldon asked his boy.

"Ten bucks."

The farmer reached into his overalls pocket and pulled out some cash, handing Charlie a ten-dollar bill.

"I got money," Charlie said.

His dad just smiled and went back to his reading chair, so Charlie pocketed the ten.

***

Charlie was the only one who could tell Ruthie about his 6-mile drive to Karen's house to his first piano lesson, and how *"excited"* he was.

"You were nervous about seeing Karen again?" Ruthie had asked Charlie.

"No. I was nervous about meeting Mrs. Mueller with a *woody* that wouldn't go away all through my piano lesson."

"What happened?" Ruthie laughed her big loud laugh.

"Karen saw me drive up and she came outside from her back door, and *right away* started kissing me under the carport. Then she had me follow her to the dock where she lit this big joint and our hands ended up all over each other until the next thing I knew I was sitting with Mrs. Mueller on her piano bench with *more than cotton mouth.*"

Ruthie knew the next chapter in the Charlie/Karen story was sex in Charlie's truck behind the Ortonville bowling alley. What Ruthie *didn't know*: was that her son's first time…was closer to home.

Shame

That first Sunday morning in May of '95, Iris and JT had a month to go before they graduated. To Iris, it was one of those cool spring days when everything was coming alive, including her skin on her bare legs and arms when she burst out of her Airstream with a fistful of quarters in her silver silk pajamas and barefoot. She was out of smokes and knew JT was cleaning the bar, like he did every Sunday morning. She also knew that her mother was getting ready to go to brunch with Ruthie and Charlie; and, this was Charlie and Ruthie's morning to rest after selling record numbers of Johnny 3 Sandwiches.

As Iris tip-toed her way to the bar's back door on the spring-cold earth, watching for broken glass, she saw the remains of the Johnny 3 basketball target that was brutally chain-sawed down last winter and hauled away as a souvenir after Johnny 3's fame on the basketball court vanished as fast it appeared. Opposing teams figured out that Johnny 3 couldn't make a free throw. Teams started sending in scrubs to intentionally foul #3, who missed enough free throws to ride the bench for the rest of the season. It was embarrassing for all to watch this dying star boiled down to a *Superland* sports joke and a 3-dollar sandwich.

Although JT was depressed and humiliated for being this joke that couldn't make a free-throw, incredibly –the Johnny 3 Sandwich kept growing in popularity at all 3 distributor locations. That's what Ruthie wanted, a family-made product that would help support her son long after she and Charlie retired to their cabin in Julian.

Despite JT's self-imposed low profile, Iris *pounded* on the bar's locked back door; she could hear "Stairway to Heaven" playing loud on the jukebox. After no answer: she walked around to the bar's front door where she knelt and pushed open the vertical mail drop slot. She could see him standing in the open doorway of the men's restroom taking a hit from his pipe. She yelled at him, startling him, causing him to conceal his pipe and smoke he'd been aiming at the ceiling vent.

He walked over to the front door palming his pipe; he was glad to see it was his neighbor who saw him smoking. He knelt to the mail slot:

"What are you doing here?" he fake-smiled like a depressed kid who was happy to be stoned.

"Can I buy some smokes?" Iris smiled her sexy way he'd seen many times when she was with one of her boyfriends.

He let her in. She went right over to the cigarette machine and dropped in 16 quarters.

"You finished cleaning?"

"Yeah," he started putting the barstools back down on the floor.

She asked him when he started smoking weed.

"*With you...on the farm*...remember?"

She laughed at his cynical remark then followed him over to the restroom doorway where he unwrapped his stash of green weed in foil to show her.

"Where'd you get it?" she was curious.

"I can't say," he smiled.

"It looks like Eddie Lee's weed."

She took the foil of buds and smelled it.

"That's Lee's weed. I can't smoke that ditch weed. It gives me a headache."

JT put the foil in his pocket as Iris went to the jukebox and played her favorite song she had Ruthie order, "Shame," sung by Evelyn King. She started to dance as he'd seen her dance to this song several times with her mother in the Airstream. Before the song was over she hopped onto the pool table, lying back under the light with her eyes closed until the song was over. JT turned off the light above the pool table and talked to her.

"I really blew it, didn't I?" he said.

"How so?"

"Johnny Three...when they started fouling me."

"Johnny Blue Eye, are you feeling *sorry* for yourself?" she made her pouting face that embarrassed him.

She sat up, her legs dangling over the end of the pool table; she was waiting for an answer. He changed the subject:

"My parents sold the bar."

"Really?"

"They're retiring to California right after I graduate."

"So, what's the problem?"

"They gave me the trailer and their Johnny Three Sandwich contracts."

"Yeah, and again...the problem is...?"

"Ever since I was benched for not making free throws I lost my chance for a scholarship. I don't *want* to go to college now and burden my parents with that expense. So...if I *live here*, market the Johnny Three Sandwich, I'll always be *that guy* that couldn't make a free throw. A big frigin' *joke!*"

Iris hopped down from the green felt table, getting in JT's face with: "Johnny Blue Eye, do you *know* how *lucky* you are? You are a *star* around here, and the Johnny Three Sandwich was a *brilliant* product timed *perfectly* by your parents. All done for *you* so that *you* can make a living off that product when they retired. Only *you* can go out there and sell your sandwich like *nobody else could*...and have some *frigin' fun* with your missed free throws. Your attitude about it...is up to you. And lots of folks would love your opportunity. And a free place to live? Give me a break, JT."

Iris went out the back door to have a smoke; she knew she'd hit the mark by telling her neighbor to change his attitude. Iris had other problems; she was worried about not graduating, since she was short a credit or two, and it was time for desperate measures, she believed. When JT came out the back door then locked it, she'd decided to treat him like any other boy she could manipulate.

He was glad she was still finishing her smoke, standing near the butt can she and Charlie used many a time.

"You're right about that attitude thing," he sounded grateful.

Just then: they saw Charlie and Ruthie exit their trailer when Libby came out of her Airstream, all going to brunch in the Tower Buick.

"I heard Ruthie call my mom this morning. It must've been about sellin' the bar."

"You could still live here if you want," he said while watching the trio get into the car.

"No. My mom wants to move back to Omaha when I graduate. I'm tired of this place."

"Last time I talked to you, you said you weren't sure you'd have enough credits to graduate."

"If I don't fail any classes I'm okay," she said as they waved goodbye to the faces smiling at them in the moving Buick.

"Want to hang out at my place? Get some breakfast?" he asked with a shrug that told her he was not confident about fooling around with any girl…even with this obvious perfect timing staring him in the face.

110

"Sure," she smiled, and they went inside his trailer.

***

Two weeks until final grades at North Woodbury High and Iris Jean Prescott let the whole school know she was the girl Johnny 3 was scoring with now. They'd walk the halls together holding hands, talking discreetly dirty about their *"ten times"* in eleven days. Their first time was in his trailer on his bed after he made her breakfast. Now, she talked about something crazy as they approached the dreaded science classroom, her first class of the morning with Mr. Blodough. And there he was, standing there in his tight slacks with every hair in place, in front of his room watching Tower and Wild Iris, a clashing couple if he'd ever seen one. They stopped at her locker and she shocked JT.

"I told Blodough I'd do him on his science table the day I get my diploma."

"What?"

"If I fail his class I don't graduate. I hate his boring class. He could flunk me just because he doesn't *like you* and he *knows* we're dating."

"I thought we were a couple?"

She face-laughed loud, slammed her locker and headed for science class leaving JT beside himself.

He couldn't believe what he heard. Her words and face-laugh were like a *siren* going off between his ears that wouldn't stop. Even though he'd grown up with that kind of bar talk his whole life...it now was clear to JT that Iris was using Johnny 3 to make sure she graduated.

111

And that was the last time they walked the halls together as a couple. The fling was over; and yet, he didn't want to believe that she'd be with Blodough, that it was only *bar talk*, words forgotten when morning came.

***

On the day of their graduation, he could hear Iris getting ready in the Airstream, playing "Shame" loud on her CD player as if to remind him what she told him at her locker. He could see her black and orange gown with cap and tassel move to the dance of her seductive body across the trailer window. She knew he was watching her, like she knew he would watch her later…and be devastated. "Strike first," was Iris Jean Prescott's way of surviving another man leaving her. And Miguel Champa knew that about her, writing, *"I could hear her arrive home from her dates with these older guys. Quick as I could from a dead sleep I'd get up and go to my window and sit on the end of my bed and watch my sad neighbor being alone in that crowded sardine can. Then: she'd play a barrage of Dusty Springfield songs on her stereo: "Son of a Preacher Man"; then, the tears came hard, especially in the summer during allergy season when she played "You Don't Have to Say You Love Me"-pure torture for a romantic sap like me. And then the song, "I Just Don't Know What to Do with Myself." Before that maudlin song was finished…so was Johnny Blue Eye…balled up under the covers sobbing like a scared boy; yet all the while knowing this was an emotional cleansing for me, something that Iris had helped me with when I was humiliated at the free-throw line. She told me to let go of that shit, and don't stop until you do, to give it my full*

112

attention like I did in my Johnny 3 training days. She was right. I miss her."

***

Libby sat with Ruthie and Charlie on the same bleachers where Johnny 3 had packed the house to standing-room-only. It still bothered Charlie that he didn't have his son shoot even 10 free throws after each half during those 2 years on the green heart; then he wouldn't have witnessed the awful shame and humiliation Johnny 3 endured on the court, then benched for the entire 2nd half of the season. And yet: he respected his boy for not quitting the team as many might have done in the same situation.

Libby *cried out her joy* above the crowded gym when her daughter's name was called to receive her diploma from the school principal at center stage. JT watched *"Iris Jean Prescott"* receive her diploma then wave to her mother in the bleachers, exiting the stage and out of the gym, into the hallway like a strong woman on a mission.

When JT's name was to be announced, Ruthie and Charlie and Libby started the 3-syllable chant "Joh-Nee-Three! Joh-Nee-Three!" that quickly spread to hundreds on folding chairs and on the bleachers, all joining in and cheering *"John Eldon Tower"* when he walked across the stage, by far the loudest reception for any Class of '95 graduate.

JT found himself in the school hallway in a daze after hot-boxing a joint with a classmate in the bathroom. Now: he was unable to move his legs toward Blodough's science room door upon reaching her locker, the same

113

spot where *Wild Iris* told him about what she will do right after she gets her diploma. He opened her locker and saw her cap and gown hanging there, her diploma on the top shelf. And: he could smell the fragrance of Champa she must've put on. Other graduates were going in and out of the bathrooms at the other end of the hall, changing their clothes and howling their joy to be done with this place forever.

"Did she leave already?" he hoped, then stepped toward the closed door of Mr. Blodough's classroom, his mind in these first minutes of being free was showing him the time Blodough made him stand and tell the class *science kills mystery.* And now: a few feet from the narrow vertical window, he could hear the familiar sounds of Wild Iris having sex. He cupped his face to the narrow glass and could see the dark profile of Blodough, who appeared to have the grimacing wizened face of a fetus while he took Iris on his science table. He walked away dry-heaving.

Closing-in-on the school's front entrance he realized how close he came to ruining his life over a girl who would do something like that. Then: when pushing open one of the front doors he felt nauseous again and *almost* dry-heaved once...*then again* upon seeing his happy retired parents and Libby standing next to his graduation gift: a new custom-painted blue-brown cargo van he could use to deliver Johnny 3 Sandwiches to his distributors. He handed his mother his diploma, then he gave her his cap and gown after removing them. When Charlie handed his son the keys to his van, Libby asked JT where Iris was.

"She'll be out soon."

114

Just then: out stepped Iris, her cap and gown draped over one arm, she handed her diploma to her mother while JT was getting behind the wheel of his new van. When Libby asked Iris if she wanted to get a bite to eat with them, Iris opened the van's passenger door and got on the front passenger seat before JT had a chance to say anything.

"We made plans," Iris waved goodbye to her happy mother.

***

When JT started heading for home in his new van:

"Where are we going?' Iris asked her driver.

"*We?*" he was pissed. "Don't you *need a shower*…after Blodough?"

"You saw us?" she laughed.

"I thought you were kidding about *doing Blodough on his table.*"

"I graduated. That's all I care about," she started to light a cigarette.

"No smoking in here," he said.

She put her smoke back inside her pack, then told her driver, "If I didn't graduate, my mom would've freaked."

"So, *that* makes it *okay*? I get it. You *had* to graduate. And Blodough, who you know I *hate*, just had sex with a girl I really liked."

And when she laughed again:

115

"Seriously, Iris, don't you feel *any shame* for what you did?"

"Relax Johnny Blue Eye. It was just sex. Nobody got hurt...'cept your *big ego.*"

He parked his new van near the green heart and she hopped out, leaving the door ajar while she lit a red. Then before closing the door, the last words she said to him:

"It'll pass."

And that was it. Science *had killed* the mystery of Iris Jean Prescott for Johnny Blue Eye.

***

"It'll pass," JT thought while he stood at the Moe cottage front room window watching heavy snow fall after recalling one of the worst chapters of his story. He hadn't thought of that awful Blodough scene in many years, at least to that degree. Perhaps it's because of The Pink House combined with hearing his parents on the phone, the way they keep holding on to whatever happened to Karen Mueller.

***

JT finished shoveling a path from his cottage door to the Moe House back door before joining Jerry, Ronna, and old Joe for dinner. It was time for some answers...if he could *get any* from these people who knew his family better than anyone else around here.

During dinner, John talked about his tour of The Pink House across the lake when his parents called him, telling his hosts that he just found out that he own's Mrs. Mueller's house, The Pink House across the lake.

A big *answer* came when Jerry was escorting his father to his room. As Ronna poured John another cup of her great coffee at her dining room table she told John, "Betsy Mueller lives in Ortonville…at Prairie Home. It's that nursing home on top of the hill on Ortonville Road."

It took him a while to ask Ronna, "How long has she lived there?"

"A few years. She must be in her nineties I would imagine. I don't know how much she could tell you now."

Prairie Home Companion

Next late morning, JT waited at a table in the empty Prairie Home dining room for Nurse Dee at the front desk to return, to let him know whether resident Betsy Mueller would see a visitor now. JT told the friendly nurse to let Betsy know he was John Tower, Charlie Tower's son; *"and to be sure and tell her my name."*

He got up from the round dining room table to walk over to a bulletin board collaged with pics of residents under the rainbow colored-and-shaped letters that spelled *Prairie Home Companions.* He realized that these were his grandfather's people, like Joe Moe, people who lived to be the oldest Americans. Then: he heard quick footsteps at the entrance to the dining room. Nurse Dee told him, "Mrs. Mueller will be in to see you shortly, Mr. Tower."

"Thanks."

He went back to his round table nearest the open entrance to the dining room. To JT, this place was as nice as Yankton Manor, and it appeared that the music teacher must've done well for herself to live here.

Soon: he heard the approaching front wheels of Betsy Mueller's walker nearing the dining room. She came into view wearing her beige jogging outfit that appeared new. Her hair in a gray bun and covered quickly with a red and green scarf adorned with snowflakes. She kept her gaze on the floor, careful of each step until she stopped in the entryway of the dining room and looked at her visitor standing at the first table. Dee came over and helped the old lady get herself seated, whereupon John introduced himself.

"I'm John Tower, Charlie Tower's son. I'm glad to see you, Mrs. Mueller."

She nodded politely and asked if Charlie was here with him.

"No, he's in California. He retired and moved there with my mom."

"Retired? What kind of work did Charlie do?"

"He owned a bar in North Woodbury with my mother."

"Oh, he did well," she seemed pleased with that news.

"I was surprised when I heard you lived here," John said. "When did you move here?"

"When?" she turned her *good ear* to him, her pale blue eyes clouded with age, yet she was alert and cheerful.

"Yes... Have you lived here *long?*" John repeated.

119

She didn't answer, and smiled at him, noticing he had his father's eyes; she pointed at his blue eye and winked at him before giggling.

"He smiled, pointing to each eye, "Yes, just like my dad."

Then, as if an afterthought she said: "North Woodbury…that's where Karen was found."

"Found?" he wasn't sure what that meant.

"Didn't Charlie tell you?"

He nodded *no* through "My dad never talked about Karen." Then added, "That's why I came to see you. To find out what happened…if you want to tell me…"

"A mother isn't supposed to outlive her children," Betsy said, her slumped shoulders moving slightly in resignation.

John's understanding nod made her keep talking for quite some time, until residents started coming into the dining room for lunch. Soon, Nurse Dee brought Betsy her lunch tray; that's when John asked Betsy if he could come by tomorrow, same time, "to visit some more."

"Yes, I'd like that, John."

He patted her cold frail manicured hands goodbye and left Prairie Home in a daze.

***

Once outside the retirement home, walking to his van into the wind of 2-below atop Ortonville Road, he stopped, to face north in the direction of Elmdale from

120

here. From this vantage point he could see distant stands of trees familiar to him. He couldn't see The Pink House, since the Elmdale trees blocked any view of South Dakota's west side of the lake. His Tower eyes moved south following the frozen gray-blue lake slicing through the vast winter whiteness that covered Ortonville and dozens of farms splayed out in every direction.

As soon as he reached his van he wanted to call his dad and tell him he talked to Betsy Mueller, and that she was so loving and forgiving about losing Karen; and, that she had hoped Charlie had healed from his loss. Before driving anywhere, he had to open his journal and write down what Mrs. Mueller told him:

"I just visited with Mrs. Mueller, Karen's mother, and I'm beside myself with this secret my family has been keeping from me. Karen had an argument one night with her mother over marrying my dad. Mrs. Mueller said that after Charlie got a telephone at Grampa Tower's she overheard Karen talking to Charlie about eloping, running off to Canada to avoid the draft. The next morning, Betsy went in to Karen's room and her bed hadn't been slept in. She called Charlie and he hadn't seen her. Apparently, Karen had fallen into the lake on her way to see my dad. Her body wasn't found until nearly 3 months later in N. Woodbury."

***

JT didn't have to call his dad. While warming the van up, he'd turned on his cell phone and had a message from Charlie, one of his dad's direct and serious tones, telling him to *"Pick your mother and me up at the*

121

airport in Sioux Falls tomorrow at 5:25...in the
evening...and don't be late."

This was incredible news. His first thought was that
Jerry or Ronna must've told his dad that he was visiting
Betsy Mueller. Whatever, this was a *real chance* for a
big healing for his dad and Karen's mother, he believed.
Then: he thought about tomorrow, his next visit with
Betsy; he'd have to go inside now and let the sweet old
lady know he couldn't visit her tomorrow since his
parents were flying in from California tomorrow.
Halfway to the front entrance of Prairie Home he
decided not to bother Betsy now while she was having
lunch, so he waited for Nurse Dee at the front desk to
have her deliver the message to Betsy after her lunch.

Life Without Her

Charlie and Ruthie grabbed their matching suitcases from the luggage belt in the Sioux Falls airport, the Tower's favorite airport over Woodbury and Omaha.

"Keep it light with Johnny," Ruthie reminded her husband as they rolled their luggage out of the airport, where JT was waiting in a parked SUV he rented in Watertown.

After JT hugged his mother, he put her suitcase in the back of the rental with his father close behind and grumbling about being here "in the middle of frigin' winter"; and, "I'm starvin' here. What is this...the Donner Party?"

"Your father won't eat airplane food," Ruthie reminded their son.

"I know, I know. You got sick once and spare me the details, Dad."

Then Charlie took over from the back seat:

"Let's get something to eat...with good coffee!"

***

From behind a Sioux Falls coffeehouse window the Towers could see that a winter storm had blown in from the north as forecasted. They were finishing their sandwiches and enjoying good coffee when – in good humor – Charlie looked at his wife, who was happy to be reunited with her son, and said:

"What are we doing here *in January* for Christ's sake?"

"I'll tell you *why*," the feisty retired bartender shot back at her husband. "*You* were having sleepless nights ever since your son called you about The Pink House. *And*...after talking to Ronna, when she told me Betsy lived in Ortonville and that she'd told JT, that's when I booked our flight for you to have a meeting with Betsy Mueller...before you both go to your graves without truth and forgiveness. *That's why* we're here, buster."

Then, Ruthie winked at her son, saying with confidence, "This'll be the best trip ever."

***

Ruthie knew that Charlie was also anxious about seeing Grampa Tower. The plan was to first drive to the Yankton cabin to prepare it for a 2-day visit. Ruthie found out on her new phone that Yankton got 12 inches of snow, so JT knew he had some shoveling to do after this estimated 3-hour drive in a blizzard that normally took half that long. Following a semi at 30 mph, JT could see his father was into his head about this coming visit with Karen's mother.

"I know if you didn't go along...Dad wouldn't!" their driver said to his mother.

JT could see in his rear-view mirror that his dad agreed. Then Ruthie spoke from the front passenger seat to her driver and loud enough so Charlie could hear:

"You're right! He's like most men! He'd rather *pretend* that nothing was there! Many a time I tried to get your father to find Mrs. Mueller and get some closure…but it was always put on the back burner! Some day! Right, honey?" she wanted her husband to respond.

Charlie really felt he was ready to meet with his dead girlfriend's mother, if only because of this pain in his chest he'd told Ruthie about right after Ronna called Ruthie to let her know that last year she found out Betsy Mueller was living in Prairie Home, and that John was on his way over there to visit her. That was all Ruthie needed to hear. Ruthie booked their flight, and itinerary calls were made to Grampa T and JT within forty minutes.

Later, during their slow drive to Yankton, JT wanted to know from his dad when he first heard about odd is left. Charlie said that it was something his dad used to tell him when *options seemed unclear.*

That's when Ruthie said to Johnny, "Just before we bought the bar, your dad said we should do something out of our comfort zone. 'Odd is left,' he said. So, we did! We bought the place!"

***

Charlie and Ruthie went to bed early, sleeping in the cooler bedroom of their family cabin so that Grampa Tower got the warmer bedroom. JT was finishing cleaning up after Ruthie made Eldon's favorite meal:

meatloaf with mashed potatoes and gravy with cucumbers and *lots* of pepper. It was the brown sugar that made her tomato sauce topping *"good,"* Eldon complimented his daughter-in-law.

Eldon sat in his favorite chair from the farm, reposed all the way back in his brown leather recliner and staring into the roaring fire before him…and not absently, as some of his Yankton Manor neighbors. He was debating inwardly whether to go with his family to Elmdale, knowing it *could be* the last time he'd see his best friend, Joe Moe. For that is the key to longevity, he knew, that desire to stay healthy, if only for the friends and family you want to see again; for that precious chance to return to your people, to a place where you are always welcome and loved.

The old man couldn't be sure Charlie and Ruthie would let him go along in wintertime. Nevertheless, he wanted to be there *after* Charlie had his long-overdue meeting with Betsy.

JT was stretched out on the cabin floor, his back to the fire and facing Grampa Tower.

"You found out some things," Eldon smiled at his grandson.

"Grampa, why did you buy Betsy Mueller's house?"

"She came to the farm when Charlie was in the service. I could see she was hurting bad. I made some coffee and we sat at the kitchen table…"

Meanwhile, unbeknownst to JT and Eldon, Charlie and Ruthie stood in JT's bedroom doorway in their pajamas, listening:

126

"She told me she wanted to move back to St. Paul to teach at her old school, but she couldn't leave unless she sold her house. She cried about Karen and said how life without her was unbearable in that house. '*Too many good memories,*' she said. She felt bad for Charlie and wanted me to tell him she didn't blame him for anything."

Ruthie consoled her husband, now beside himself.

"Did you tell my dad what she said?"

"I told him in a letter."

"Did you tell him you bought her house?"

"No. I didn't have to. When he was discharged from the service he came home for just one night, then he was off to start his new life. He had a plan. And let me tell you something about your father. If I had told him I bought that place...he would've wanted to pay me back and I wanted nothing to do with that."

"Why didn't you sell it?"

"I tried. Nobody wanted the place. They found chemical spills from mining in the well water north of there on that side of the lake. People were getting sick from it."

Charlie wanted to go out into the front room to be with his dad, but Ruthie stopped him, whispering to him, *it's too late*, and they went to bed.

***

The next morning at the breakfast table, Eldon told his family that he'd *like* to go with them to Elmdale

127

tomorrow. Charlie was concerned about his dad being up there *in the dead of winter*. JT lobbied his dad on behalf of his grandfather, telling Charlie how much Joe would love to see his old friend; and, "Before I left, Ronna asked me if Eldon was coming. She said there's plenty of room in Moe House."

"Alright," Charlie consented. "We'll have to get his winter clothes in his room, a warmer coat for sure."

"My coat's plenty warm!" Eldon snapped at his son.

A bit later, Ruthie wanted to give Charlie some alone time with his dad in the cabin while Johnny drove her across town to Grampa Tower's apartment to pack some things for his winter visit to Elmdale. Ruthie was good at giving space to people. It was in her nature to keep things running smooth.

Alone Time

Charlie watched JT drive away with his mother, on their way to get some clothes for his dad, who sat in his chair thinking about going back home, where he'd spent over 70 years of his life. Ruthie hoped their alone time would be good for both men, especially Charlie, who wasn't getting *good sleep* of late. Charlie told Ruthie in bed last night that he realized his dad had bought The Pink House to help Mrs. Mueller move on with her life after losing her only child. Then Ruthie made a good point, telling her husband that *"Maybe your dad thought you'd never return home if Betsy lived in that house."*

After overhearing Eldon's conversation with JT last night, Ruthie asked her husband if there was anything he'd like to say to his dad regarding their upcoming visit to Elmdale. He couldn't think of anything...until now. Charlie brought over a kitchen chair and sat close to his dad, who was sitting up straight and alert as ever.

"Dad, that time I came home after I was discharged, when I told you I was moving to North Woodbury...?"

"Yeah?"

The old man had a good memory.

"It took me four days to get there," Charlie confessed. "I showed you that aerial map of the water route that Karen's body had to take to end up in North Woodbury. This computer geek friend of mine in the Air Force figured out the route she had to have taken... Do you recall what I told you the odds were for Karen's body to end up where it did?"

The old man wasn't sure.

"A million-to-one. That's like the odds of Grama Tower getting killed by hailstones. So, I followed Karen's route from here with a couple cases of beer, a cooler, and some junk food..."

"Some *what?*"

"Junk food, you know: candy bars, cookies, chips... I'd find myself parking my truck and walking this incredible route along ditches with culverts, all over southwest Minnesota. After her body left the Minnesota River a few miles south of Milan, that's where it got crazy for me. This route got so convoluted, Dad, and I was drunk... But all I kept thinking was *odd is left*. So, for most of that time I kept thinking something *real special* was waiting for me whenever I got to North Woodbury. I honestly believed *that* with all my heart. When I reached that Big Sioux bridge where they found Karen...I was tired and smelled like a river rat. I hadn't bathed since I left the farm. I remember I left my truck parked near the bridge and started walking and asking Karen's Spirit to show me where to go. The first thing I saw was this black and orange banner in front of this bar that said: *Ruthie's Taverns*. And *right when I walked in*

130

I saw this cute little redhead behind the bar. You know I like redheads...I've told you that before. Anyways, I was dead-tired and I took my usual seat at the end of the bar near the back door. I picked up that habit overseas. Anyway, I found out her name was Ruthie, so I figured she *owned the joint*...after I'd seen that banner out front..."

Charlie paused a moment to enjoy his dad's big/quiet laugh that he'd seen a thousand times, when his whole face lit up with joy. Then Charlie continued:

"We hit it off right from the get-go, Dad. And I owe the life I've had with Ruthie to Karen and that damn water route I followed for *four days*."

They sat together in silence enjoying their time together. Charlie could tell that his dad was looking forward to going home.

"Dad, other than when Mother died, what was your *most important* odd is left?"

"Raising you alone," Eldon smiled. "In those days it was rare to see a man raising a kid alone."

"Dad, why didn't you ever re-marry?"

"I didn't look. Well, I did have a few dates with women friends... It's like what Ruthie said when I asked her if she'd ever get re-married if she lost you. She said she wouldn't *look*."

Winter Visit

Eldon made up his quiet mind to have the time of his life during this winter visit back home to Elmdale with his family. The drive north proved to the old retired farmer – nearing his century mark – that life once again was going back 'round to the place where he'd spent most of his days; and, where the Moe family –was part of his family. Jerry and Ronna believed the return of Eldon and Charlie to Elmdale was a reunion that deserved their utmost attention.

The trio of Tower men - during their drive to Elmdale - talked about Charlie's upcoming visit with Betsy Mueller. At first, Charlie was vacillating over wanting Ruthie to go with him when he met with Karen's mother. Then he wanted only JT to go with him. By the end of the discussion, Charlie decided he'd meet with Mrs. Mueller alone, *"but I want you to drive me when I go,"* he said to his son in the rear-view mirror.

***

Jerry and Ronna were happy hosts, considering their winter visitors *family*. Old Joe and Eldon stayed up late talking in the Moe parlor with the younger generations listening to every word while Ruthie and Ronna chatted away at the kitchen table. Even their sons learned things from the elder men that neither Charlie or Jerry heard about until now. For example: Joe and Eldon talked about a Minnesota man north of here from Starbuck, who'd recently returned home after surviving *"The Great War"* as a decorated war hero.

"He was struck by lightning when he was gettin' gas at the store!" old Joe pointed in the direction of his store.

"Really?" Charlie was surprised that he'd never heard of that until now.

"I was pumpin' his gas and he got hit standin' by his radio antenna. Dead just like that," Joe tapped the arm of his chair.

"That's back when irony still existed," Jerry jabbed his meaty elbow into Charlie side as JT watched Jerry slap his thigh and throw back his head and laugh that goofy laugh of his that Charlie said *hasn't changed a bit.*

Then Charlie asked Jerry if he remembered the time Kenny Krane was caught smoking a cigarette by Mrs. Kellogg outside her 6th grade classroom window.

Another slap on his thigh and Jerry's chest convulsed as if trying to get air into his lungs while laughing as Charlie continued:

"She went after that kid *so fast...* And she made him *eat a cigarette* right there outside her window. We could hear Krane coughin'... That poor kid was so red-faced we thought he was *gonna die!*"

***

A few days into their winter visit and the Towers from California were well rested, and Eldon seemed to be enjoying himself, spending much of the day sitting and talking with his old friend.

Now, JT was driving his dad over to Prairie Home to visit with Mrs. Mueller, a meeting JT set up yesterday with the retired music teacher. Anxious Charlie wanted to stop off at an Ortonville bar to have "*just one*" before this long overdue reunion with Karen's mother. JT suggested they stop afterwards and Charlie agreed absently, obviously in his head about what he would say to Mrs. Mueller today, some fifty years since Karen died.

Up the hill they went, to the top, where Prairie Home came into view. JT parked the SUV not far from the front entrance of the retirement home.

"Dad, she's really a loving old lady. She's not the type to cause any bad scenes."

"Uh huh. Well…let's do this," Charlie opened his door, thankful he'd changed his mind about going alone.

They walked together to the Prairie Home front entrance.

"Why didn't Grampa Tower live here instead of Yankton?" JT asked his dad.

"So, you could visit him. That's why we bought the cabin."

"Why wouldn't he want to live here?"

"I just told you. We all knew he'd get more visits living in Yankton," Charlie said as they entered the double doors that automatically opened.

***

Inside the Prairie Home dining-room they waited for Betsy at the same front table. JT and his dad stood up when they saw Betsy approaching with her walker.

"You sure you want me here, Dad?"

"Yeah. Apparently, you need to hear this as much as anyone."

Charlie was lost in the mother/daughter resemblance, seeing perhaps an old Karen, if things were different. Her gray head was wound high into a bun, her head bent down watching each step carefully as JT warned his dad to, "Let her take her seat on her own. She doesn't want help."

JT had set the stage, placing his dad's chair between his and Betsy's, making sure it was close enough for her to hear him. She smiled at Charlie, "How are you, Charlie?"

"I've been thinking about what I would say to you for over fifty years. And all I can think of is…I'm so sorry for your loss…and for not telling you about the hole in the ice sooner."

She extended her hand and he took it. Charlie cried.

"I've missed her too," he put his other hand on her hand.

She told him it wasn't his fault; and that all three of them played a part in Karen's tragic death, telling Charlie, "I had to stop blaming you, me, God… I prayed every day that you and I would find peace and forgiveness."

135

Charlie cried harder than JT had ever seen him cry, letting go of more and more of the pain until Charlie put his balding head on her hands while his son rubbed his back. Then, Charlie raised his head; he looked straight ahead while recounting:

"I've only told my wife these things about Karen. I want to tell my son now, with your consent…how I remember it," he was asking his old music teacher.

She smiled her approval and he held her hand on the table while he talked to them, looking out at the winter scene through the big dining room window, a vast void of whiteness he stared at absently while recalling:

"In March of sixty-nine, Karen and I were confused about our relationship, unsure about our future. We were getting to the point where we had to commit or break up. For a week or so, we'd been on one of those I-need-some-space separations. One night I decided to walk over to her house while the lake was still frozen; I wanted to talk to her about us. On the lake that night it was scary because I could hear cracking here and there, so I really went slow. I could see her bedroom light was on and there was a car parked beside the house. I knew *you* were in bed because you went to bed early on a school night…"

Betsy nodded that she understood every word Charlie was saying to her, even when he told Betsy that she and Karen had been arguing lately about *"us running off to Canada and you wanted Karen to go to school."*

"This is the part I didn't feel I should tell you… I used the spare key under the doormat and went up to Karen's room. This wasn't the first time I used the key. I went up to Karen's room and I could hear music coming from behind her closed door. I opened the door without knocking and there was Karen slow-dancing and making out with Elizabeth Snow Bear. I couldn't *believe* what I saw, and I stood there frozen like this wasn't real. Karen saw me and I ran out of your house. I fell on the lake and hit hard on my shoulder and I could hear the lake crack when I hit. I was so upset I pounded my fists on the ice until I broke through and punched a big hole in the ice. I stuck my face in that hole, in that awful-cold water and I screamed my head off until my face was numb and frozen. I went home, took the phone off the hook, because I knew Karen might call and I didn't want her to wake my dad. I went into my room and started to pack some of my clothes. I felt like disappearing in my truck, driving somewhere...anywhere. Anyway, I went to sleep in my bed. The next morning, you called when me and my dad were having breakfast.... You remember that?" Charlie asked Betsy.

She nodded yes and Charlie continued:

"You asked me if Karen was there. I said I hadn't seen her since last night in her bedroom. Of course, I didn't want to tell you I'd seen Karen and Elizabeth *making out.* I told you to call Elizabeth Snow Bear, since she was with Karen when I last saw her in Karen's bedroom. I told you I'd call you if I heard from Karen. I told my dad everything about last night, and it wasn't long until we both had the same fearful thought. I ran outside to the lake...and...I saw the spot where I'd fallen and broken the ice with my fists. I saw Karen's footprints following my tracks and ending right there at the break in the ice I made last night. She was coming to see me after I saw her with Elizabeth. I dropped to my knees

137

beside the place where I knew Karen went in. I was in shock that this could happen...to Karen...this crazy girl I was nuts about. And it was clear that *I had caused it*. It was as if I had set a death trap for her...and I couldn't live with that. My dad, if he hadn't been there... I would've joined her. My dad stopped me. He held me down, crying in my face, screaming at me over and over, *'Charlie, odd is left.'* That's what stopped me from jumping into that lake, the same thing my dad said to himself when my mother was killed by hailstones. He kept saying, *'Charlie, I can't lose you, too.'* He kept telling me over and over that we'd get through this together when he walked me back home. He said it's not for certain she fell in, that maybe she'll show up. So, I waited for two days, a time I know had to be torture for you..."

Betsy squeezed Charlie's hands on the table while JT was beside himself trying to imagine this awful tragedy that had been a part of his dad's life for over fifty years. Charlie continued talking to Betsy.

"I was hoping Karen had run off with Elizabeth or would call you from somewhere... And now, I think of how small I was to judge her for being bi-sexual. I should've stayed and talked to Karen..."

Charlie lowered his wet face onto Betsy's hands and looked at her:

"My dad drove me over to your house and was there when I told you what I knew about Karen falling into the lake...and that her footprints ended at the break in the ice that I made. I know she was following my tracks."

138

Betsy lowered her head a bit to say, "I called Elizabeth Snow Bear after I called you. Elizabeth told me when she left *my* house that night Karen *told her* she was walking across the lake to see you. I was hoping she was with you. And when you told me about the break, her footprints...I knew that's what happened. At the time, I didn't appreciate your situation, Charlie. That awful five weeks before they found Karen's body was unbearable."

"I *know,*" Charlie cried, his visible grief causing Betsy and JT to reach for and touch the retired bartender, a man who obviously needed permission from Betsy to forgive himself. "And I'm sorry, but I couldn't go to her service. I was so guilt-ridden I told my dad I'd rather die."

Charlie waited so long for this, and now he had to continue:

"I joined the Air Force to get away. I tried...but Karen and you *were there* on the other side of the world *with me.* I started drinking in the service...and when I was discharged I took a four-day trip along the water route Karen's body had to have taken to end up in North Woodbury. In the service, I'd made up my mind to live my life in the place where they found Karen. I met Ruthie, my future wife, the first day I arrived in North Woodbury. She knows that Karen brought us together...and we will always know that."

Betsy had to tell Charlie how thankful she was that Eldon bought her house, so that she could go back to St. Paul.

"I had to get away too, Charlie...to heal. Thanks to your father, I could. And I know he did that for you."

Charlie nodded in agreement, letting go of more grief.

***

Charlie and JT escorted Betsy back to her room; that's when Charlie asked her if he could bring "Ruthie here to meet you."

"That would be nice," she smiled from her doorway, then both Tower men hugged her goodbye.

Outside Prairie Home, JT could see that his father's face had lost that pinched look from stress he had ever since arriving from California; his eyes and brow were now noticeably relaxed as if a load had been lifted. Charlie stopped near the SUV rental and thanked his son for setting up this reunion with Betsy. When they hugged, more tears; but now they were tears of gratitude for Charlie.

"I can never thank you enough, JT."

"You already have, Dad."

God Knows What

That same evening after Charlie's visit with Betsy Mueller, Ruthie could see and feel that her husband had been awakened to an aliveness she hadn't seen in a very long time.

"You look terrific," she told her husband after dinner in the Moe dining room.

"Betsy showed me that she'd forgiven me, and that allowed me to forgive myself. I must've been carrying a bucket of tears in my head all these years. But I dumped the whole bucket there with Betsy," Charlie laughed.

Ruthie or JT hadn't heard that laugh in a long time.

Charlie sat down on the sofa next to his dad in the Moe parlor while Ruthie and JT helped Ronna with the dishes. Charlie told Eldon all about his visit with Betsy Mueller, including:

"She told me how you bought her house so she could go back to St. Paul to her old job. She really was grateful, Dad…and so am I."

Again, Charlie broke down, his head resting on his dad's shoulder while alone in the parlor.

"It seemed like the right thing to do," Eldon patted his son's head.

"Odd is left, right Dad?"

The old farmer nodded in agreement, then he said, "I kept asking what I could do. One day I was in the bank and I heard that Betsy wanted to sell her house so she could return to her old teaching job in St. Paul."

"You mind if I ask what you paid for the house?"

"She owed the bank ten thousand on a second mortgage, and she wanted twenty thousand on top of that. She paid thirty thousand for it and wanted to at least leave with that much. My banker, Arnie Kohler, told me she was willing to sell all her assets to pay off her mortgage. She was desperate."

Charlie knew that was a lot of money for his dad to spend on a house he never used or sold, and so he asked his dad why he bought the house.

Eldon's cloudy-blue eyes were lit with joy when he looked at his son and said:

"*Your mother* told me to buy the house."

Eldon cleared his throat and continued:

"I left the bank, not even thinking twice about buying that house. Arnie told me it needed a new roof and too many repairs for me to get involved. You were in the service and I was driving your truck that day. I started driving home and it started to hail. I pulled over and covered up best I could while I hit the floor. Your windshield was shattered, but I was okay. I drove right back to the bank with no windshield and glass all over

142

the place. I wrote the bank a check for ten thousand to pay off her mortgage and another twenty made out to Betsy Mueller. I had Arnie put the deed to the house in a safe deposit box. I listed it and not one offer. I couldn't give the place away. That time when we went to John's last football game in Watertown and that girl Iris was with us? She came to the farm and opened your high school yearbook..."

"Yeah," Charlie remembered.

"I could see that Iris reminded both of us of how Karen was. She had Karen's wild and free spirit. And I knew right then that John had to find out what happened to Karen, and that he'd do something good with that house. So, I paid the taxes and assigned the deed to John and hoped for...God knows what."

Charlie sat there, amazed at all this back story revealed by his father, recalling that time he ran to the lake from the farmhouse that night and fell on the tractor lane where Iris found him. He was upset with Iris for going to the lake at night after he'd told her all about Karen during their drive to Watertown. *"Why did I tell Iris about Karen?"* he'd asked himself a thousand times since then, not even telling Ruthie (at the time) that he'd talked to Iris about Karen. *"Was I looking for sympathy from a girl like Karen, someone wild and carefree?"* Just then: Ruthie came into the parlor with a cup of peppermint tea for Grampa Tower; that's when Charlie remembered finding a copy of a money order made out to Libby Prescott for five thousand dollars in Ruthie's jewelry box several years back when he was looking for a ring he wanted to clean. The money order was dated August 3rd, 1995, not long after Charlie and Ruthie retired to California. When he asked her about it, she dismissed it as a loan she gave Libby to move into a house she wanted; and, *"She paid me back right way."* When he asked Ruthie why she didn't mention the loan to him, she said, *"Iris didn't want you to know about the loan...for some reason."*

Top of the Sun

J oe Moe sat ramrod-straight in his favorite chair in his attic apartment watching the sun come up above the little church he and Eldon built when they were young. Winter whiteness was everywhere; 2 inches of fresh powder salted the trees and the land he and Eldon called "home" over two lifetimes, spanning a combined 160 years. *"General Joe"* was a nickname Eldon gave his friend after Eldon helped Joe build the general store. Today, Joe doesn't remember birthdays, holidays, or even know what day it is; however, he still remembers the day Eldon lost his new bride in her garden to hailstones.

"June eighteenth, nineteen fifty," Joe whispered as the top of the sun now rimmed the church steeple.

Old Joe was thinking back to the time he drove his little Farmall Tractor to the Tower place so that Eldon could till his young bride's first garden. It was Joe who told his friend to move the location of Ellie's garden so that drainage from rain didn't flood the entire garden. Not long after the hailstone tragedy, Joe remarked to Eldon that he wished he hadn't played a part in the garden's location, *"and maybe she'd still be here if I hadn't."*

145

"Nonsense," Eldon fired back at his friend. *"That's hogwash lawyer talk. It would be like blaming myself for having my birthday dinner. That's why she was out there. Ellie taught me to stay clear of the blame game, Joe. It's no good. 'Odd is left,' she'd always say, whenever I'd complain or had a problem to deal with. Then she'd tell me to do something positive that was against my nature, to act without fear or judgment. Then she'd get right in my face with her blue and brown eyes so bright and alive and say, 'That's how you'll live to be a very old man, Mister Eldon Charles Tower.'"*

When the sun's light became too bright for his sensitive eyes, Joe reached for and put on his sunglasses. The General faced the sun's morning light, keeping his eyes closed behind his dark lenses; then, he swallowed hard, his hanging neck skin a hideous sight to him in his window reflection now picked up by his prescription shades. He reached for one of his handy water bottles Ronna and Jerry kept supplied in several places around the 2,000 square-foot attic apartment with its wood flooring that didn't impede his walker.

Eldon was due to arrive any minute, since last night, Joe's old buddy mentioned he'd like to see The General's living quarters. Just then: the familiar *sound* of the climbing chairlift approached with Eldon riding up to the attic with Charlie and Jerry following. Joe got up to use his walker, wanting to greet his guests. Charlie helped his father out of the chairlift, then escorted him into Joe's place with the aid of his cane. The host greeted his friend with a big smile, then Eldon remarked, "I guess there's money in dry goods."

146

"C'mon, I'll give you the nickel tour," Joe said, then turned his walker around and led the way.

Charlie escorted his dad around the attic apartment, following Joe's smooth-moving, soundless stainless-steel walker as fastidious Jerry checked the apartment for low water bottles and plants needing watering. Before he made his father's bed, Jerry moved and angled a chair close to his dad's chair so Joe and Eldon could look at each other and still see the view out the east window, which reminded Jerry to adjust the blinds to keep direct sunlight off their faces.

After the tour, Charlie and Jerry stood behind the seated founders of Elmdale, listening to their conversation; they were ready to serve these elder statesmen. Soon, Ronna entered the apartment with Ruthie, both women carrying trays holding fresh coffee and Ronna's walnut coffee cake. They served Joe and Eldon first, waiting on these first settlers of Elmdale.

"This is nice, Joe!" Ruthie exclaimed as Ronna showed her around the apartment.

From his seated position, Eldon could see the church where his beloved Ellie is buried and remarked to his friend, "You know *why* I put my tombstone beside Ellie *early*?"

The General knew something funny was coming, so he made sure his hearing aid was turned all the way up when Eldon leaned toward him and said:

"Because I didn't want *you* to go there *first*."

Joe laughed his silent way and started coughing, prompting attentive Ronna to get him a water bottle.

Only Joe and Eldon knew this inside joke between them, regarding that day Eldon first met Ellie at the Moe lunch counter and Joe had remarked later to his friend, "*That girl's a catch.*"

"You ever think we'd live to be this old?" Joe asked Eldon.

"My grandson, John, wants to know how we live so long. He wants to put it in his book," Eldon said.

Joe's palsied hand pointed to the view beyond the east window as the four standing adults listened in.

"It's just outside the middle of nowhere…and we prefer it that way. We grow our food and we share with our neighbors. When we were coming up…the water was good…and we looked after each other."

Eldon nodded in agreement, adding, "I think it's in our German/Russian genes to live this long. Most of us old rubes came from a good stock of people. I can recall my mother talking to your mother about how old the people lived to be back in the old country. I remember her saying that a hundred years was about the average."

More positive nodding from Joe as Ruthie told her husband, "Johnny should hear this for his book. He's writing in the cottage now."

"When did John start writing?" Ronna asked Ruthie.

Charlie telegraphed that look to his wife that said, *Oh no. Here we go. You asked for it, Ronna.*

"It was in Johnny's junior high creative writing class…" Ruthie answered proudly, as if she had something to do with her son's interest in writing. "Seventh and eighth

148

grade were the years he started getting noticed by his teachers…"

Miguel Champa and Baby Ruthie

Pimple-faced 8th grader Johnny Tower began his daily closet-writing habit from watching his mother's daily entries in her journal she'd make at the bar when business was slow. Ruthie was always interested in her son's writing, displaying his early assignments from his 8th grade creative writing class magnetized on the fridge for all to see the bold red letter 'A' grade he'd received from Mr. Southland, Johnny's *first* encouraging English teacher. His first assignment from Mr. Southland was: "*What would your penname be if you could choose one and why?*"

"*I would choose my penname to be Miguel Champa. I choose Miguel because my dad's best friend in the Air Force was named Miguel. My dad said Miguel knew all the best bars to meet girls, and they had a lot of fun during the Viet Nam War. I choose Champa because that's the fragrance my mother wears ever since her hippie days in California. It comes from the Champa Flower, and my dad says it reminds him of the girls who wore Champa in the bars Miguel took him to. Miguel Champa, that would be my penname."*

***

This is what JT wrote in the cottage, explaining his mother's back story:

"My whole issue about seeing Iris again is a genetic thing –on both sides of my family. My mother's biological father wasn't even alive when red-headed 'Baby Ruthie' was born in the old Methodist Hospital in Woodbury in 1952. It's a tragic story that could never be the big family secret like my dad's past with Karen, since my mom's birth and circumstances were headlined in the Woodbury Tribune and TV news after my mom's biological mother (she calls b.m.) dropped off 6-day-old Baby Ruthie in a basket just inside the front door of Sisters of Mercy Daycare in Woodbury. A note pinned to Ruthie's blanket made front-page headlines: 'Sisters of Mercy, her name is Ruthie Pangburn and she is 3 days old, born in the Methodist Hospital. Her biological father is deceased, as I'm sure you all know. I don't believe in abortions and I would not be a good mother.'

Sister Mary Beth found Baby Ruthie and soon placed the local celebrity baby in Good Shepherd Orphanage, where she was raised there until she was 16. My mother ran off to be a hippie in California for a few years after researching newspaper archives and discovering the truth about her 'possible' biological father. Dane Pangburn was a distraught deputy police officer for Woodbury County when he hung himself in one of the county jail cells. It seems Pangburn was distraught over the breakup with his pregnant girlfriend (my mom's b.m.) who had lost a considerable amount of weight,

151

looked stunning, then dumped the deputy for a married man. My mom never cared to find out her mother's name or if the deputy was her biological father. When you know Baby Ruthie's story —no way could Baby Ruthie ever resist a man like my dad, Charlie Tower."

"It was chemistry," Miguel Champa wrote in his 2nd creative writing assignment: *"Who do you most admire and why?"* Miguel wrote:

"I most admire my parents, Charlie and Ruthie Tower. It was chemistry that brought them together, a mixing and blending of two separate lives coming together from so far away with one common denominator that shines whenever they are together: 'real love.' That's what my mother said when I asked her to describe their life together. I'm lucky to have parents who really love each other and allow me to be this writer I call Miguel Champa."

***

Meanwhile, later in the Moe cottage, and still writing at the antique desk, the same desk Jerry said he used to write love letters to Ronna when they were *courting,* JT wrote:

"After our last visit with Betsy Mueller in Prairie Home —I resist the urge to go find Iris now. It seems that ever since our time with Betsy, both my dad and I have been sleeping better. We sleep sound and wake up rested with more energy than before our visit with Karen's mother. My mom told my dad at the Moe breakfast table, 'Honey, your face looks twenty years younger.' My dad, ever the salty bartender, looked at her and declared, 'Hey, don't look at me like that. If it puts more lead in my

pencil...you'll be the first to know.' Of course, everyone laughed and we enjoyed breakfasting on Ronna's banana French toast with strawberries and Jerry's prize-winning smoked sausage, along with the best coffee I've ever had. Today my mom is going along with my dad to visit Betsy in Prairie Home. I'm not going this time because I think it's best that my dad is alone with my mom in case he has more emotions to release. My mom won't be a hindrance as I possibly could be for him. 'That's okay, three's a crowd, Johnny Three,' my dad laughed his old laugh. Again, it was so good to hear my dad laugh often and real, not some forced half-laugh we'd all gotten used to. I'm wanting to write Iris a letter and plan to get her address from Mary Parrot, the organizer of our 25-year reunion on June 18th, such an important date for the Towers. Nevertheless, my dad's emotional healing with Betsy means I can go live in the Yankton cabin when I take Grampa back. And that's fine with me, since I have no place I want to go. This way I can visit Grampa more often. I want to talk to my parents about the reunion with Iris and show my mom a letter I wrote to her. My mom is so smart about these things. I don't want to hear negative things about Iris, how she's not the 'right girl' for me. Iris could be married with kids for all I know. Either way, I want to express my feelings to Iris about seeing her with Blodough and how I allowed that to affect my relationships with women. Yes, I'm taking responsibility for my past. The way I feel, since my dad met with Betsy, I want Iris to see that I've forgiven her for something that seems to be trifle in comparison to what my dad and Betsy went through."

Earth Angel

No way was Charlie letting a whiteout blizzard keep him from seeing Betsy as planned. Ruthie knew not to even ask her stubborn husband to reschedule their visit tomorrow with Mrs. Mueller for another day.

"It's too important to me," Charlie told JT after dinner last night when earlier Jerry mentioned that *"blizzard conditions are forecasted for tomorrow."*

"I'll walk if I have to," the stubborn retired bartender told his son.

Later last night when Charlie was alone with his son in the Moe parlor as howling winds blew the top layer of old, crusted snow into a winter scene that reminded JT of a shaken glass snow globe, Charlie confessed in a quaking voice that matched his moist brown and blue eyes:

"My heart wants to see Betsy again."

JT understood and wondered if he'd be smart to park the SUV overnight at the store in case snow drifted too high on the Moe driveway as it had earlier when he first arrived. He asked Jerry about it, and Jerry agreed, saying *"Our driveway is the last place to be cleared."*

"That way," JT added, *"as soon as Moe Road is cleared I can park at the bottom of your driveway and pick up my mom and dad."*

Jerry agreed, knowing how important this 2nd visit with Betsy was to his friend.

***

That night after parking the SUV on Jerry's parking spot near the store's back door, and during his walk back while being face-blasted by wind and stinging snow crystals –a lost scene with Iris came to him, something he'd never thought of until now. He wondered if this was like the dreams his father experienced recently in California before seeing Betsy. And, as Charlie told his son on their drive to Yankton from the airport: *"I feel like these memories are coming back...to be seen...then released, freeing me somehow."*

As JT neared the long Moe driveway, he dismissed the weather, wanting his unconscious mind to release this stored memory of Iris now while oblivious to the scrub pine trees, their dull red-brown bark coated with silver frost and swirling powder that made him turn his face left, where he could see the old church across the road. He turned back to the wind, closed his watering eyes until he could see more and more details released from the vast space of the unconscious where he knew such things are stored. For an instant, his thought was to hold it back until safe in the warm cottage where he could write it down. But he couldn't wait...since his legs became weak when making his first step up the

155

snow-caked driveway, whereupon winds blew harder from the west and forced him to stop in his tracks to see what his unconscious mind was bringing out of deep storage:

It was in wintertime, and he had driven his mother, Libby and Iris to the Woodbury Mall to do some Christmas shopping. JT and Iris were now juniors, walking in the mall atrium with the song "Earth Angel" playing for shoppers as his mother and Libby went in one store and he and Iris continued walking, to look for stores they wanted to shop in. He could smell the smoke from cigarettes and weed on her old denim jacket...and that bothered him.

"I hate that song," Iris scoffed.

"Why?" JT asked.

"Listen to the lyrics, they're about a guy who thinks this chick is perfect. Give me a break. He thinks this girl is like...like some mythical angel from heaven. This dude is just a pussy-whipped *loser,*" she then let loose that yokel *loud laugh.*

He watched her swerve off into a novelty store, Iris unaware that he was watching her while she sorted through and sniffed boxes of incense until picking one she liked. Then: he could see her open the familiar bottle of the Champa Flower fragrance oil, passing the top of the tiny kobold-blue glass bottle under her nose to take in the familiar scent his mother has worn his entire life. Upon returning the cap to the bottle –he saw her fisting the Champa in her closed hand before putting it in her coat pocket at the register, only paying for the incense. When she left the store, and walked over to

156

him, he wanted to say something, to tell her he would buy it for her. But he didn't. Instead, when she slipped outside to have a smoke, he went back to that store and bought a bottle of Champa to wrap later and give to her at Christmas. When she came back into the mall she was chewing gum, and he could smell the Champa on her, its unique fragrance clashing with the stench of second-hand smoke on her hands and jacket like the interior of a smoker's old car. He had to get away from her then, away from this *"Wild Iris"* who his mother predicted would get pregnant and never graduate. Just then: walking toward them like 2-legged hyenas laughing and cackling; they were Karl and Ed Haynes, brothers who dropped out of school to work in their dad's sheetrock business. They spotted Iris and waved. She hurried over to them while JT stood waiting for her a safe distance from them. He'd seen them visit Iris in the Airstream when Libby was at work; and he'd seen her smoking weed in their truck while parked at Burger Barn during school lunch period. Iris came back to JT and told him she'd catch up with him later at the mall entrance they came in; she was obviously heading for the parking lot to smoke weed with her friends in their truck. As he watched her leave the mall with them –he was jealous, jealous over her leaving him to be with those two flunkies. He wanted to go after her, yet he knew that each one of those pinheads could kick his ass. *Then*, as now, he imagined seeing Grama Tower's grave near the little church…and he thought of *oil* as if it was time to act. And there it was: *oil* came to him without consciously seeing the manager from the novelty store approaching him and while looking for that presumed shoplifter she had seen on her store video cam monitor in the back office. This no-nonsense woman asked JT

157

where *the girl* was that she saw him with. Without thinking, JT showed the woman the Champa he'd bought, and his receipt, explaining that Iris had brought the Champa out of the store for him to pay for, which the receipt proved.

"I'm so sorry for the misunderstanding," the manager apologized while backpedaling back to her store.

It was one of those moments forgotten until now, as JT opened his eyes at the bottom of the drifting Moe driveway and started his climb on stronger legs while muttering "Merry Christmas Iris," the same words he now recalled saying to himself in the mall right after *rescuing* Iris from an embarrassing situation.

After Karen

By morning the roads were cleared, so JT dropped his parents off in front of the Prairie Home front entrance; then he drove down the hill to a nearby coffeehouse to begin working on his letter to Iris. Now: he felt like seeing Iris as soon as possible to perhaps *break the ice* with her after so many years without contact. He wanted to avoid any possible awkwardness a *cold meeting* at the reunion could bring and words said they might regret.

This was another *oil* for Johnny Blue Eye, to go see Iris before the reunion, and possibly give them both a chance to recapture that time in May when they were young and romance was new (at least for him). That's what he saw: that Iris had loved him and yet dismissed him by delivering the worst of blows: her betrayal with Blodough. Perhaps if he saw her again he could show her he'd forgiven her and at least be free to move on and break this vicious Tower pattern of a lost first love...never recovered.

Yes, this was another oil for JT, to go see Iris asap; and a new letter to her had to work, as he sat down with coffee and a scone at a front window table. He wanted to write as Miguel Champa, the penname she thought

159

was *"hysterical"* and *"dead-on like Johnny Three!"* she'd shout across to him from her bedroom window whenever she knew he was in his room writing: *"You go, Miguel!"* Then: he'd catch that *loud laugh* of hers that he loved, traveling across their open windows.

Now: he turned to look out the front window of the coffeehouse at the bleak winter scene on the main drag where county salt crews left their tracks in both directions. Then, he put his pencil in motion, moving his 1st draft of his letter, not knowing for certain what he would say to her now after 25 years of nothing. He wrote:

"Iris Jean, this is your old neighbor Miguel Champa, Johnny 3, and your favorite: Johnny Blue Eye. I can't help from telling you how often I think of you…in a good light. I saw your name on our 25-year reunion list and look forward to seeing you there. I went to our 10-year & 20-year reunions hoping I'd see you. I think you'll remember I'm a hopeless romantic, first discovering that about myself when you and your mom would play all those sad torch songs about lost love. Over the years I've come to know that I've inherited this crazy Tower trait of lost first loves. After a Billie Holiday or Etta James song, I remember hearing Libby talking to you about her first love, your biological father, and then I'd hear you telling her to 'get over it and move on.' That's what I need to do. I believe seeing you before the reunion would be good…if you can. Otherwise –I'll see you at the reunion. Your friend and neighbor, Miguel Champa."

***

Betsy Mueller welcomed Charlie and Ruthie into her cozy one-bedroom kitchenette in Prairie Home. The Towers flanked the retired music teacher's favorite chair while looking at old photos from Betsy's album, *"one of the few things I kept from The Pink House after Karen,"* she told her attentive guests. Then, Betsy showed Charlie a black and white picture of Karen in her bathing suit taken on the dock in front of her house around the same time Charlie had swum across the lake to meet her for the first time. Compassionate Betsy could see how Charlie looked fondly at her daughter's image and told him she wanted him to have it. When Charlie handed the photo to Ruthie, she was touched by it, telling Betsy how *beautiful* Karen was. Both of her guests had to be consoled by their host, a strong woman who *refused* to play the sad role of a mother who lost her only child over a half century ago.

For Ruthie, she was moved by other things the photo of Karen reminded her of; it reminded *Baby Ruthie* of all the times over the years she had wondered if her biological mother had found peace for giving up her baby; and for playing her sinister role in the death of that poor deputy who could have been Ruthie's biological father. When Ruthie told Betsy her *Baby Ruthie story*, she also talked about how in California in the 60's she'd learned to see her *b.m.* in a positive light.

"That's true," Charlie jumped in. "Ruthie's always said that she believed that her mother *believed* she was doing her baby a favor by leaving her in good hands with the Sisters at the daycare, and that was a *choice* Ruthie has to believe was best for all. Some women have no business having children…and we're pretty sure she knew that she was one of those mothers."

Then Charlie added, while he hugged his life partner, "I always told our son that many women can be a mother, but you have a great mom."

"This is my best friend," Charlie declared to Betsy's smiling face. "And her name is Baby Ruthie."

***

JT picked his parents up in front of Prairie Home after Ruthie called him at the coffeehouse. On the ride to Elmdale in the SUV Ruthie and Charlie talked from the back seat about their visit with Betsy and how much they enjoyed it.

"We mostly talked about our lives after Karen," Ruthie said to her agreeing husband.

"Yeah, it was great," Charlie chimed in. "I didn't feel the urge to say *anything* about Karen. It was all about our lives and what we are doing these days. None of that *past stuff*. It was great."

That's when JT said he wanted to go see Iris asap, "before the reunion."

River Walk

January was cold as usual, yet warmed a bit in late January, enough for Jerry and Ronna to convince their guests…that they were not guests, but rather, *"family: that big reason Elmdale was in this 'longevity belt' my dad researched while in the service,"* JT wrote in his journal. Two Tower lost first loves have shown these two united families that each visit may be their last. This reunion has been so good for Joe and Eldon that the Towers decided to extend their stay into February.

"What's the hurry?" Eldon asked The General.

Joe looked at his friend and asked him, *"We took our time to get here, didn't we?"*

Eldon nodded in agreement.

***

It was in early February that the weather had warmed a notch to 20 degrees with plenty of sunshine.

"Good walking weather," Charlie told his happy wife at bedtime after turning off his bedside lamp.

"I think it's time to tell Johnny about Iris," Ruthie sighed after turning off her light.

Charlie then told Ruthie he was thinking about going for a walk on the lake tomorrow with JT. "Last night I told JT I *need* to do that."

"That's a great idea," Ruthie said. "And if you tell him now...he'll have time to process it before he sees Iris."

Charlie reminded his wife that she'd promised Iris and Libby 25 years ago that she'd *never tell* JT about the abortion and the two checks totaling eight thousand dollars that Ruthie loaned to Libby and Iris.

"Well, I didn't, did I?" Ruthie snapped back after turning her back to her husband.

***

JT and Charlie started the 19-degree morning with another great breakfast by Ronna in The General Store. Then they took off on foot with ski poles to their river walk. Charlie and his friends always thought of Big Stone Lake as a river, because of its length and the narrow width at Elmdale.

Charlie hadn't climbed to the top of Tower Hill via his dad's tractor path since he lost Karen.

"I have to do this," Charlie told his son as they neared the summit with considerable help from their ski poles they would use to test the ice.

They stopped on the summit to catch their breath and to take in this view Charlie had been avoiding for over fifty years. Charlie wore brown-tinted shades, and his son wore blue-tinted sunglasses to protect their eyes from snow glare.

"What are you feeling right now?" JT asked.

"I noticed I'm not bothered by it…like I imagined I'd be."

"That's good."

JT could see that his dad was staring at The Pink House when he told his son that he'd like to see the inside of the house.

They made their way down to the lake, pausing at the Minnesota bank to stab the ice with their poles before safely making their way out onto the ice, sliding along toward the Mueller dock, all-the-while jabbing the ice ahead of them while listening for sounds of cracking ice that never came. The lake was frozen solid; they both felt good about that until suddenly Charlie stopped his cautious slide at the spot where Karen had fallen into the lake. He stood near the place Karen had fallen in. He talked to his son absently while looking down at the ice.

"Because of my anger, it happened. I *knew that* right away, and ever since then I know I've beaten myself up a million times for making that *stupid choice* to be angry at Karen for being *who she was*. I know that anger with myself was there …until I talked to Betsy. So, standing here now doesn't hold the emotional punch I always feared. I owe this all to you," Charlie smiled at his son, then they continued sliding toward the old Mueller place, while up ahead near the rotting dock, a crow and a squawking blue jay in a stand of field pussy-toe stems fought over territory.

Fifty feet from land, they stopped on the ice to watch the birds fight as Charlie revealed to his son:

"Until now, I could never see living a long life like Grampa. Like walking up that hill... I feel like I have more energy."

They made their way through knee-deep old snow to the front door, where JT hid the house key above the door ledge.

And again: while standing in the old Mueller parlor, Charlie said he felt no emotional charge here; he didn't even care to go upstairs. Not because he feared seeing Karen's room –he just didn't feel like seeing something from his dead past. Instead: "Let's walk south on the river to Ortonville and get some of Ted's Chicken."

Off they went, talking about how they could unload that *"damn white elephant';* that's what Charlie called Betsy's old house as they slid south on the lake, adroitly using their poles for balance and thrust.

Charlie said, "Grampa paid thirty thousand bucks for that house and lot, and won't get anything close to that, JT. And I think anything you get for the place should go back to Grampa. I know he'd like that."

"Sounds good. But who would buy that place?"

"We'll stop in the real estate office near Ted's and list it low... Let's give the damn place away!" Charlie barked while they focused on the ice ahead of them.

"Yeah, let's do it," JT agreed with his mentor and old coach.

166

"JT, I wanted to say something about me *not* having you practice free-throws or even painting a free-throw line on the green heart. *My fault.* It was hard as hell for me to see you go through that, and I really screwed up bad on that...and I'm sorry."

"It was Iris that made me see how lucky I was to be that Johnny Three, and to prosper from Mom's plan for her sandwich. Hell Dad, *I wasn't good enough* for college. To tell you the truth...I never got over Iris."

"When did you start having sex with her?" Charlie was curious and happy to have this lead-in to Iris. "No, wait. Don't tell me now. I want to sit down for this." Then, he surprised JT by asking him if he could have a hit of that Creative stuff. When JT slid west, headed for a boulder on the west bank, Charlie yelled out: "Not in South Dakota! Let's find a spot on the Minnesota side!"

"Why the Minnesota side?" JT was curious as he followed his dad toward a cluster of big rocks on the east bank.

"During the day, if the lake was frozen, Karen would smoke her pot on the Minnesota side, out of respect for her mother being a teacher in South Dakota. Sometimes she'd go down to her dock and smoke...mostly at night..."

Charlie picked out a flat rock to sit on, turning his back to the gusting west winds that had chapped his lips considerably since his visit here. JT sat down next to his dad, each facing Minnesota's western border that Joe Moe called *"The Bulge...that place in 'the river' that snaked west for ten miles."*

167

As JT filled his screen with a pinch of Creative, Charlie was into his head about how to broach this abortion thing with his son as he watched sparrows flitting around the bank as if they weren't used to many visitors around here. JT handed his pipe to his dad, offering to light it for him, so his dad could cup his hands around the pipe to shield against these gusts of wind blowing and swirling now from two directions. Charlie took a big hit...without coughing, surprising his son, who also managed to get a small hit from the orange glow of Creative.

"That's smooth," Charlie smiled, as JT put a bit more in his bowl. "I think I'm good...but you go ahead," Charlie said, now busy with his new thoughts about telling JT about Wild Iris.

Then: as Creative does, Charlie thought about something he'd long forgotten, and told his son about that time when he'd been discharged from the Air Force, and he and Grampa stopped for a couple beers.

"And I asked him if he was proud of me. I don't know why I asked him that. I guess because I had served my time and got out with an honorable discharge. There was a bunch of anti-war sentiment then, and anyway I flat-out asked him if he was proud of me. You know what he said to me?"

"What?"

"He said, *'Pride is a negative feeling.'* Then he told me he's *happy* for me."

"I've heard you tell that to Mom before. Like when she ever said she's proud of me."

168

"Yeah," Charlie recalled. "And the older I get…the more it's true for me. I had no idea – until these visits with Betsy - that my wounded pride was killing me. I've spent fifty years masking Karen's death with work, prosperity, drinking, doing everything but what I feared: finding a way to forgive myself. You got me there and Betsy gave me permission to forgive myself."

After JT put away his pipe, Charlie was ready to tell his son:

"JT…I need *you* to forgive me and your mother for something we did for Iris. And I say *we* because I knew about it for a long time and didn't say anything to you. Your mother and I made a judgment call…for our eighteen-year-old son who had a *fling* for a few weeks. Call it your first love," Charlie smirked at his silly thoughts.

Charlie could see that his son was into his head about Iris; and, the retired bartender felt *that now* was the time to clear things up after smearing his dry lips with cherry lip balm:

"Libby called your mother a couple months after we retired. She told your mother she needed five thousand bucks to help pay for Iris's abortion. You know how Grampa didn't tell us he bought The Pink House?"

"Yeah."

"Well, your mother didn't *tell me* about helping Libby until years later. People don't tell loved ones some things…to protect them. Like how we didn't tell you or Grampa about the abortion."

169

"Mom was pro-life, I know that much, from the Baby Ruthie days..."

"Yeah, that's right. That's what I asked her. Then I understood...*after* your mother told me that Iris said the kid could only be yours ...or Blodough's."

Charlie winced a bit, knowing how much his son despised Blodough.

"Did Grampa tell you about Iris and Blodough...and how I saw him *with her* on Blodough's *science table* right after she got her diploma?"

"Yeah, we heard about it. It had to be awful for you. You know we used to see you and Iris hanging out a lot in May, the month before you graduated. We just thought you were buddies. The point is...whether it was you or Blodough...Iris was *not going to have that baby.*"

"So, Mom *paid for it?*"

"At first it was five-grand, then Iris called your mother and bumped her up three thousand. Iris said she wanted to take Libby with her to this *safe clinic* in Mexico to have the abortion done by this well-known doctor, whatever..."

"So, Mom *paid for the abortion?*"

Charlie looked right into his son's stoned eyes, eyes that matched his as no other eyes could, and repeated "*You...*or...*Blodough.*"

Charlie could see that he had to do what his dad had done for him at the lake, not long after Karen was lost. He had to feed his son words that he needed to hear.

170

Again: "No matter what...Iris did *not* want to carry that baby. Your mother tried to get her to change her mind. And...your mother loved Iris...and didn't want her to get some *hatchet job* from some unlicensed *quack* in Omaha or Mexico."

JT was into his Creative thoughts upon hearing this news about the abortion. He thought of the letter he'd written Iris, and was glad he hadn't shown it to his mother, or even worse...mailed it.

Absently, JT remarked how *this changes everything about the reunion.*

"Why does it have to go negative?" he asked his son while getting to his feet and standing in front of him. "It's *ancient history.*"

"Not with me, Dad!" JT was obviously upset about this belated news.

"I know, I know. So, let's process through this, okay?"

JT nodded positively.

***

When they could see the main downtown area of Ortonville, up ahead on their left, JT had pretty much processed everything important...and told his dad he would think about his next move with Iris, "the *right* move," JT emphasized. That's when Charlie stopped on the ice, planted his poles confidently in front of him, and said, "What is that Creative stuff you smoke? I hadn't thought of *this* until now..."

"What?" JT was curious.

"I could *never remember* why I used to hate that Patsy Cline song, "She's Got You." I had Bernie take that song out of my jukebox. But I'll be damned if I knew why...*until now*...when I just remembered *that was the song* Karen and Elizabeth Snow Bear were slow-dancing to and making out to when I opened the door to Karen's bedroom. I had forgotten that until now. I wonder if Elizabeth still lives around here?"

"Let's get to Ted's. I'm hungry," JT said.

She's Got You

Outside the realtor's office –the sun broke through a wall of gray. Charlie stood facing the sun, his eyes closed and relaxed...until he saw that his son was on the phone after calling one of the *Snow Bear*s listed in the local phone book that the realtor gave to JT. As JT listened while scribbling down information while on a call, Charlie couldn't think of anything he wanted to say or ask Elizabeth if he met with her now. A thousand times Charlie wished he'd stayed there in Karen's bedroom doorway, and had fun with it, instead of some unconscious threat to a selfish ego that led to and caused Karen's death that night.

After JT snapped his phone shut, "She still lives here." He pointed across the lake in South Dakota, "In Big Stone City. I got her number and address right here," he showed his dad.

"I don't know what I'd *even say* to her," Charlie shrugged.

"Ask her about the song," JT smiled, his blue-tinted shades looking right into his father's brown-tinted lenses.

"Patsy Cline?"

"Yeah," JT kept smiling at this upcoming possible Creative oil situation he was handing to his dad, and his dad didn't like it.

"You're the one that *plays* that song now," Charlie returned. "Iris...*she's got you...and bad.*"

Charlie looked around for a place, asking himself where could they go now to get Creative.

***

It was a 10-minute walk to the other side of the viaduct to Big Stone City, South Dakota. Charlie led the way, down to a spot under the viaduct where he would smoke cigarettes and drink beer with buddies, including Ted and Jerry.

The Tower men planted their walking sticks and sat back against an angled concrete embankment that faced the frozen lake. Charlie was thinking about earlier with Ted, outside Ted's back door when Charlie smoked one of his old friend's Camel lights that tasted good after chicken, beer, and earlier Creative.

"I told Ted that he was the one who got me started smoking. I asked him what was the first cigarette I ever had. I was testing his memory. Ted looked right at me and said, 'It *had to be* a Lucky Strike...because that's what my parents smoked...and *so did I*.' Ted laughed so hard –I saw his denture plate drop from the roof of his mouth. I asked Ted if he remembered Elizabeth Snow Bear from Milbank. And he said she comes into his place all the time."

174

After sharing a bowl, Charlie said about Karen's girlfriend:

"I still don't have a clue what I 'd say to Elizabeth."

JT asked his dad if he wanted to call her.

"No, no," Charlie waved off that idea, explaining, "I just don't *know* what good it would do to talk to her *now* about Karen."

"You can talk to her about the great visits you've had with Betsy..."

"Yeah, I guess...but it's this whole thing about me reacting the way I did when I saw them together. I really don't have anything to say about that. I think Elizabeth is one of those dead past people, *things* that come and go, and are better off *gone.* "

"Yeah, that's a good point. And I *don't* feel that way about Iris."

"Yeah," Charlie agreed. "You *have* to see Iris again. She's got you, JT, that's for sure."

JT nodded in agreement.

"As far as that song...I'm over it. I can't say the same for you," Charlie teased his son, and glad to be off his sore feet. "I think I should call your mother...have her pick us up. You and your mother need to talk."

JT agreed, and his father called his mother. That's when JT realized that he had the key to the SUV and showed the key to his dad to let him know.

175

"I guess JT has his key…so, we walk back. And my feet are killing me."

That's when Ruthie told her husband that Ronna said she could use her car anytime, and so Ruthie told Charlie she'll pick them up.

"Meet us at Ted's," he told his wife.

***

They walked back across the viaduct with Charlie informing his son:

"It wasn't just that song by Patsy that bothered me. I have a couple others."

"Yeah?" JT was curious because he had the same sentimental connection to certain songs that Iris played.

"That Hall and Oates song, 'She's Gone'…used to drive me nuts."

"Uh huh," his son could relate. "What was the other one?"

"America's 'Ventura Highway.' Two more songs I had Bernie remove from my jukebox," Charlie chuckled as they reached the Minnesota side of the viaduct.

"Why did 'Ventura Highway' bother you?"

"Two reasons for that one. Karen *loved* that song. She always talked about us running off to California *to cruise* Ventura Highway."

JT asked his dad what the other reason was.

176

"Your mother lost her virginity to that song when she ran off to California to be a hippie. Some surfer dude on the beach had a cassette player."

"How do you know that?"

"She told me. Your mother tells me everything. She can't keep a secret, even about her past."

"How come she kept Iris's abortion a secret from you?"

"You'll have to ask her."

"Come to think of it…I never did see those songs on your jukebox," JT realized.

"Now you know why," Charlie smiled.

Ventura High Way

Ruthie parked Ronna's car and walked into Ted's Chicken, where Charlie and his buddy Ted were having a beer and a lively conversation in a far corner booth, a spot where two old friends could laugh and get loud without bothering any customers. Ruthie greeted Ted and saw 2 pair of ski poles leaning against the wall near Charlie. She asked Charlie, "Where's Johnny?"

Charlie slid over and told his wife that JT had an errand to run, and "he'll be back soon."

Ruthie didn't want to sit now; she told Charlie she was going for a *power walk.* Then, before she left, she asked Charlie if *all went well* with Johnny.

"Oh, yeah, he's cool about it."

"Good," Ruthie was relieved.

***

Ruthie was two blocks into her power walk when she saw her son come out of a retail store across the street. She called out and waved to him. She could see that he was surprised to see his mother, as they met in the middle of the quiet street with no traffic in sight.

During her drive to Ortonville, Ruthie had given her next move to *oil*. She also had a secret in her past that would help explain this news about Iris to her son. However, Johnny surprised her first as they walked on the sunny side of the street.

"Dad told me about Iris and the abortion. It's strange to think that it might've been my kid."

"I know, sweetie... Ever since I knew we were coming here, I thought it would be good to give up a secret I have... Something I've never told anyone, even your father. It might help you understand *why* I did what I did."

"Does it have anything to do with 'Ventura Highway?'" Johnny again surprised his mother.

"The song?"

That's when Johnny removed a CD from his back pocket and handed it to his mother. She laughed at the America CD and asked him if his father told him about her days in California after she ran away from Good Shepherd Home in Woodbury.

"He said 'Ventura Highway' was *not* his favorite song after you told him that was the song playing during your *first time.*"

"More like three words: Ventura high way," she admitted with a bit of humility as they crossed the desolate street. She was thinking how to tell her son about this brief yet crazy time in her youth. "It was more than my first time. I got pregnant and had an abortion in Mexico, the same place I referred Libby and Iris to."

"Why didn't you want Dad to know?"

"Baby Ruthie was my identity. And...I didn't *want* your father to know anything about it. What *good* would it do? If I had the baby, who knows where I'd be or if I'd even have you and Charlie. I was sixteen. The kid that knocked me up took me to Mexico and paid for the abortion. We were *not* parent material. We didn't have a clue from day to day...*believe me.*"

As they walked, they were both into their heads about the conversation; JT was aware that this was a big deal in his mother's past as he continued to listen without judgment.

"Before I got pregnant I'd tell *anyone* that abortion was wrong...because of Baby Ruthie. I'd been doing pills with this kid, all kinds of drugs...even LSD. He had this dive apartment by the beach. I'd heard all kinds of stories about women born with birth defects because of the drugs they took. I was really scared because he was doing more than I was...and I *did not* want to bring life into this world with our track record for abusing ourselves."

Now, Ruthie waited for her son to say something. He surprised her again:

"Does Ronna have a CD player in her car?"

"I don't know."

***

Soon, mother and son were listening to America's "Ventura Highway" in Ronna's car. All-the-while JT kept thinking how Iris Prescott's life was like his mother's in many ways. Their glaring common denominator was abandonment. And then: it came to him, in a rush-tingling wave from head to toe as he turned to Ronna's front passenger window to conceal his emotions that the music helped him release. He realized he was like his father, a male rescuer who found the perfect woman who needed a steady man, a man who would never stray and be her lifelong partner. *"That's what I wanted to do for Iris,"* he told his mind again and again until the song was over and he ejected the CD.

Ruthie knew when something was bothering Johnny, so she asked him what it was. That's when JT asked his mother:

"Did you talk to Iris after she got back from Mexico?"

"Libby called me collect from Mexico and told me Iris was recovering well. And then she thanked me. I haven't talked to any of the girls since then."

JT nodded his head unconsciously, until his mother had to ask:

"What is it, Johnny?"

"Those sad torch songs Iris and Libby played…and *Iris*…her *life*… I was this hopeless romantic sap when it came to her. Mom, I don't kiss and tell…but I've never come close to being as *alive* as I was when I was with Iris. Ever since Dad told me about the abortion I keep seeing that framed inscription of Grampa's: *What we do not grasp…is lost forever. When all is lost…odd is left."*

"How do you feel about Iris now?" Ruthie asked.

181

"The same. Like I've been *lost* without her for twenty-five years."

"John Eldon…you *are* a hopeless romantic," she said before asking him what he was going to do about Iris.

"I'm ready to see her *now,* Mom. I don't want to *wait* for the reunion."

"Then…you've *got* to follow your heart."

"I was thinking I could write her a letter, telling her I know about the abortion…and it's all just the dead past…and…I want to see her before our reunion."

"Write from your heart…and let me read it *before* you send it," Ruthie forced a smile.

Heart of Mine

On Valentine's Day, the Tower family left Elmdale, all agreeing that this had been the best visit ever. Yesterday Charlie went to Prairie Home alone to say goodbye to Betsy, and to let her know that her old house and lot were finally sold at an auction for ten thousand dollars. Betsy was confused when Charlie handed her a cashier's check made out to her for ten thousand dollars. Charlie said:

"JT and I tried to give it to my dad...but my dad wanted *you* to have it. And there was *no arguing* with him about this. It's yours."

The music teacher and her one-lesson *student* held hands in the Prairie Home dining room. They loved each other in a way as survivors of any tragedy are forever bonded. Betsy and Charlie had endured a combined century of living *after Karen*. Betsy told her visitor, "*It pleases me immensely...to see the difference in you, Charlie.*" They were now able to laugh at stories they told about Karen, things they alone could only know and appreciate.

This same *subtle feeling* of Charlie's, that he was cured of something at the very core of his being –was

183

also happening for JT. It wasn't something anyone would understand as the Towers do. JT made good thoughts about Iris, choosing to think of good memories only.

***

They picked up JT's van at the Watertown car rental agency, whereupon Ruthie rode with her son while Charlie and Grampa Tower followed in the SUV they would drop off at the airport before Charlie and Ruthie's flight back to California. Grampa Tower was impressed that JT saved over two hundred bucks in airport parking fees by parking his van at the Watertown car rental location. As with Iris, unable to let go of her emotionally, JT told his mother that he decided to trade-in his van and get a new vehicle before he saw Iris.

Baby Ruthie the writer and her son Miguel Champa had planned this part of their trip when Ruthie would read the letter her son had written to Iris. They agreed this was the time to read the letter and discuss it before he even tried to get her address and send it. It was Miguel who realized while in the throes of his letter that Iris had the *real* hard part compared to his self-imposed head games he chose to play, all in the name of resisting intimacy. Then, it was Ruthie who told her son that *"Eldon did the same thing. It skipped a generation with your father. You and Grampa shut down...and your father didn't."*

While writing his 2nd letter to Iris, it was all so interesting to Miguel the writer, these genetic personality traits skipping a generation. And yet, Charlie told his son during their visit that he doesn't know for sure whether he *ever* would've been in a relationship "*if I*

184

hadn't run into your mother when I first arrived in North Woodbury. I was like my dad in that way, a one-woman guy. I've always been that way. Finding your mother...was my oil."

***

JT handed his mother the letter to Iris that was folded inside an unsealed envelope as he drove his old van south on I-29, its salt-covered surface framed by dirty snowbanks from recent plowing. She put on her orange-tinted reading glasses to diminish the snow glare, then began reading Miguel's letter to Iris:

"Dear Iris, I saw your name on the list of attendees for our 25-year reunion on June 18th. I wonder if you remember that date after visiting Grampa Tower's farm? It's the same day Grampa Tower turns 100; and, it's my dad's birthday. Remember the hailstones in the garden?

I'm on my way back to Yankton, where I plan to live in the cabin. My parents and Grampa Tower were with me in Elmdale for a special family reunion. It was more like a healing fest kind of thing for all of us, since my dad had these wonderful visits with Betsy Mueller, the mother of his girlfriend Karen, who my dad told you about when you rode with him to my game in Watertown.

Betsy allowed my dad to forgive himself for Karen's death. It was wonderful to see, Iris, this big positive change in my dad's health. It's as if their reunion transformed our family, which in turn, my parents were compelled to tell me about your visit to Mexico with your mother. I was shocked and confused when I heard about

185

it...at first. Then, my confusion cleared, and I could see how you must've had the hardest time while going through that, Iris.

Iris, I wanted you to know that I am most anxious to see you again -even if it's before the reunion...if that's possible for you. Whatever is going on in your life, I am still your friend from a long time ago, and will always be your...Johnny Blue Eye. -JT."

Ruthie folded the letter back into the envelope and thought about her words carefully, as such things told - to another writer - about his work, requires careful considerations. It reminded JT of the *careful feedback* his mother would give him before turning in his paper. Her remarks were always spot-on and much more encouraging than a busy teacher's scribbled notes. Still waiting, he quick-glanced into his rear-view mirror to see the SUV following at a safe distance on this isolated stretch of I-29. His mother's words surprised him:

"You *can't* send this."

"Why?"

"It doesn't *feel* right to me. It's a well-written letter. But...you're missing something *before* you can see her...or even *send a letter*..."

"What do you mean, Mom?"

She handed him back his letter and tried to explain:

"This dynamic between you and Iris has a *blockage*...just as *real* as your father's resistance to forgive himself...for fifty years. You've done the same thing with Blodough..."

186

He knew she was onto something, because *fear* was
upon him now as he kept his old van between the lines
of his lane, even though that sucking black hole named
Blodough was pulling him into this orbit of dread as his
father must've felt before seeing Betsy.

He had to raise this inchoate question lodged in his
throat, two words to his wise and compassionate mother:

"Why now?"

"*Because*...you're afraid to. It was such a damaging
blow to your developing ego, you couldn't even tell us
about Blodough and Iris..."

"Maybe I thought Grampa would tell you..."

"You *know* who told us? Libby. When she called me
about Mexico and needing more money...I told her I
wanted to hear *every sordid* detail before I'd even
consider sending more money. And I told Libby flat
out, '*If* you don't know the details...then you better get
them from Iris. Or you can go 'f' yourselves if this ever
hurts Johnny.' That's *exactly* what I told her. Then she
told me how you saw Iris doing the nasty with Blodough
on his science table...and *right after you graduated.*
That girl. Do you think I wanted Iris in your life after I
heard about that scene? And the more I thought about it,
the more I realized that Blodough was a way to deny that
it was even your kid. *And,* just as I learned to forgive
my b.m. and b.f., so would you, *if* you ever found out.
Yes, your mother took care of everything. Just like the
Johnny Three Plan. I wanted you to live your life
without a mistake like Iris...ruining it."

"But I never thought of her as a *mistake* when I was with her."

"Blodough was *her* mistake…and you let that decide whether you ever love again. That was *your* mistake. And Johnny, there's one person *you need* to confront. Blodough might show up at the reunion for all you know. That would be too awkward. You have to clear the air with that asshole before you see Iris."

He knew his mother was right, that he had to do *this thing* he feared before seeing *Iris* again. JT had *this feeling* that his mother wanted him to find out something about Blodough…that she didn't want to tell him.

***

Saying goodbye at the airport, Ruthie hugged her son and told him what she always told Charlie:

"Use things…and *love* people. This is your opportunity to grow. If you don't confront Blodough…it'll come back 'round to bite you on the ass. Johnny Three can do this."

He watched his parents rising then vanishing on the airport escalator. He hustled back to the van, where Grampa Tower was waiting on the front passenger seat. John was anxious to talk to his grandfather about confronting Blodough.

Confronting Blodough

Strange weather came to Yankton in late February...again. For three years in a row the gray starkness of winter was gone in February, replaced by green budding trees that framed the Missouri River for a thousand miles in both directions. With these changing weather patterns JT felt this desire to change his life by *oil* more than ever before.

His mother had opened his eyes about confronting Blodough. During the drive to Yankton with Grampa Tower it became crystal clear to JT that confronting his old coach and nemesis was the key to seeing Iris again...if only because he feared that more than anything, even more than seeing Iris again after news of her abortion. And he knew he had to stop smoking Creative before seeing Dowd Blodough. JT wanted to be lucid and clear-eyed, even though he couldn't think of anything he really wanted to say now to the randy science teacher. It was Grampa Tower who told him on the return trip to Yankton, *"Let it come to you...then act on it."*

189

***

Cold-turkey Creative gobbled up February and mid-March with 3-mile power walks every morning and every evening. He'd hit *The River Trail* with Mourning Doves moaning and Pheasants fleeing on his first weeks of herbal abstinence. The look and feel of it all, this Blodough/abortion thing; then throw in these crazy weather patterns he was denying with the rest of the world -he missed Creative.

He liked walking on the trail beside the river; it reminded him of his dad and what he must've endured. It was clear to JT that just as his father needed Betsy to forgive himself, Johnny 3 had to confront the man he's hated for nearly three decades. Except now, John Tower and Coach Blodough had one thing in common: lost fatherhood for one of them.

Since there was no internet at the cabin JT went to the library and discovered that there was also no *Blodough* listed anywhere in Superland. So, he looked in a Watertown phone directory and found 3 *Blodough*'s listed.

Outside, his first call to *Walt Blodough* surprised JT. Walt answered the phone and JT told Walt he was one of his brother's players at North Woodbury. Turns out, Walt is Dowd's brother, a rather nice man who wanted to give JT his brother's phone number in Elk Point, South Dakota, a town maybe 20 miles north of N. Woodbury off I-29.

"I want to surprise him," JT was truthful, and in the throes of a new oil.

190

"He's retired now. He's got an acreage near Elk Point, about a mile east of the Phillips 66 on Broken Kettle Road," Walt said slow and deliberate as JT wrote down the easy directions.

"Thanks for that. I'll find it. Bye."

He started walking toward a coffeehouse in downtown Yankton. He was into his head about finding Blodough so fast...and so near. But still, he thought staying away from Creative (as he has) would bring him clarity as far as what he would say to this guy that he's hated for so long.

Step after step on the clear Yankton sidewalk –he felt his addiction to Creative pull him to and into his van, ever so anxious to see if it could help him with Blodough...*now that I know where he is*. His recent abstinence had increased his energy, yet didn't release any new thought patterns that Creative did naturally.

Now, on the carpeted cargo bed of his old van, he filled his pipe's screen and asked himself again if he *really* wanted to do this. Someone said *yes*, and he took a quick hit...holding the sweet smoke in...before exhaling and sitting back against his rolled-up sleeping bag, ready to see something new and different. Right away: he thought of the *5th Truth* Grampa Tower asked him to recite from memory during their drive back to Yankton. Quickly he got out of his van, locked it, and walked down the sidewalk recalling this maxim his grandfather lived by: "*Pushing through fear is less frightening than living with the underlying fear that comes from a feeling of helplessness.*"

Just then: he stopped walking on the sidewalk with his thought, *"What am I waiting for?"* He turned around and went back to his van, ready to begin this impulsive/long-overdue confrontation with Coach Blodough. He drove his van east, headed for Elk Point, to that acreage on *Broken Kettle Road.* He knew he'd been to that area when he worked Elk Point businesses, dropping off 2-for-1 Johnny 3 business cards to about every single business in Elk Point. He did all that personal legwork, handing out every card himself to promote Tower Tavern's Johnny 3 Sandwich, the lone outlet for South Dakota. In those days, he'd introduce himself as *Johnny Three,* promoting his mother's creation, a popular sandwich sold in only 3 Superland locations. He recalled that Phillips 66 station on Broken Kettle Road that was less than 20 miles from him now. As he drove he kept telling himself to relax, to go with the flow and see what happens.

I'll surprise him and we'll talk, he reasoned, resisting his mind's rising fear that lobbied for *more time* before going to see Blodough.

He continued driving, safe in his Creative state, until he reached the 29N rest area, where he wanted to stop, rest and write a bit, to see if *Miguel Champa* could help bring *something* out of him that would make this surprise visit a positive opportunity to grow; and, to get closure like his dad did with Betsy Mueller...*somehow,* he hoped.

He parked his van on the same spot he always parked. Nearly every monthly trip to Yankton to visit Grampa Tower, he'd stop here for a writing break each way; this was Miguel Champa's writing spot at the end of another

192

Zen-like month of handing out 2-for-1 Johnny 3 Sandwich business cards. These were Superland's small-business owners and managers, most of them had heard of this local Johnny 3 legend who would stop in to drop off his cards a few times a year. Besides that: they loved Ruthie's sandwich. It seemed like all the men knew on sight that JT was Johnny 3, and that he still held high school basketball scoring records in Superland considered by all to be *"untouchable."*

Now, once again in the throes of a new oil, he took a quick hit of Creative before peeing in the restroom, a clean bathroom break oasis for travelers moving up and down this I-29 corridor that stretched from Kansas City to Canada. This rest area never failed to remind JT about where he was, just outside the middle of nowhere, as he first would power-walk around the massive parking area framed by this stop on the prairie that was akin to visiting an old friend for Miguel Champa. He was ready to write on the bed of his cargo van, with the back curtain closed and the dome light on. He wanted to write something that would help him confront Blodough. Miguel wrote:

"The time has arrived. I must face my biggest fear: Blodough. I could be minutes away from seeing this man, this last person on earth I'd ever want to see or run into, let alone seek out on my own. Right now, I feel like calling my mom to ask for her support. But then, she could talk me out of seeing Blodough. I want to discuss the abortion with him, and that could lead to Iris on his science table. And the rest of the stuff...about Blodough never playing me in games...who cares? Not important now. Now that I'm writing about this I can see that I DO want him to know that he didn't get away with being

with Iris without any consequences. At least that's what I feel he deserves, some level of responsibility for being this unknown accomplice...like I am. Not that I feel guilty about something I was unaware of. Somehow, Universal Laws come around again; and besides that — I'm not certain I wouldn't have done the same thing if I were Iris or my mother. And yet: Blodough showed no discretion, because he had graduated from North Woodbury that day too with Iris, after taking a teaching/coaching position for next year with Jefferson, South Dakota, some ten miles south of his acreage in Elk Point. He didn't break any laws by being with Iris. They were consenting adults. And, if Blodough had played me like I wanted...I wouldn't have been motivated for the Johnny 3 Plan. It's all so confusing why I have to go see him."

***

He parked at the Elk Point Phillips 66 station and walked around the parking lot thinking about what he'd say to Blodough when he saw him. Never had he conversed with this man; not even in his boring science class. He knew one thing he could do. He went to his van's console and grabbed a few Johnny 3 business cards to hand out in the station/convenience store.

It was automatic for Johnny 3, just as his 3-point shots had been, to walk into this place where they had to know *Coach Blodough.* JT got a large carry-out Coke at the fountain before handing his 2-for-1 sandwich offer cards to the young clerk at the lone register, letting the young man know, "That's good for anytime at Tower Tavern in North Woodbury...or the other two locations."

"You're Johnny Three?"

JT nodded positively, then asked if *"Coach Blodough's place is a mile that way?"* JT pointed east.

"Yeah, it's on the right…you'll see it. One of those manufactured homes."

"Wasn't Coach Blodough the head football coach here? Or, No, it was Jefferson, right?"

"Yeah, it was Jefferson," the young man was certain.

"He was my football coach at North Woodbury," JT said. "That was before you were born."

The friendly clerk nodded positively as JT explained how he wanted to surprise his old coach, and that Blodough's brother told him he lived here. Then JT asked:

"Do you know Coach Blodough? I mean, is he married or…what do you know about him?"

"I'm not sure," the kid shrugged. "I don't think he's married."

"Is there anything Coach Blodough is known for around here? Was he considered a good coach or science teacher?"

By the kid's reaction, JT could tell that he was about to reveal something, so JT pressed with a discreet tone, "I heard he liked to flirt with the girls."

Then the clerk told JT that his brother's girlfriend was a cheerleader, and she told his brother that Coach Blodough sat next to her on the bus coming home from a game, adding, "She said he put his hand on her leg and it creeped her out," the clerk laughed his goofy laugh.

195

"Did he ever get in trouble for that?"

"She didn't tell anybody for a long time."

Then, the clerk surprised JT:

"I hear he moved up to college girls. He's a personal trainer at Fitness Universe in Vermillion."

"Fitness Universe?"

"Yep," the clerk nodded.

***

JT saw the *Blodough* mailbox and parked his van on the shoulder of Broken Kettle Road, where he could see Blodough's rather modest beige-colored manufactured home. There were no parked vehicles near this place that looked like a breadbox with a porch to JT. It appeared as if Blodough lived here alone. After his recent conversation with the clerk at the gas station, JT had a bad feeling about this guy he was trying to *confront...about something.* To see him here, at his home, seemed dangerous now, since the clerk's comments about Blodough were as if nothing's changed about this jerk in some ways since high school.

He took a quick hit of Creative to change his thought patterns now. Then, he found a pair of binoculars under his seat he'd stored there since his move out of the trailer. He scanned the front of the Blodough property from his front passenger seat after adjusting the lens. To the right of the house he scanned an open shed, whereupon he could see a rusty football blocking sled for linemen that he recognized from his playing days. Then, against the wall of the shed his binoculars

196

revealed something strange/familiar under stacks of
lumber and pallets, and yet it was too blurry to know for
sure what it was. He had to go there, on foot, leaving the
binoculars on the front passenger seat. Just then: a
vehicle approached from the west. JT feigned a tire
inspection on his van until the car passed by.

He hurried to the Blodough shed; the closer he got –
the more he couldn't believe what he saw was real. He
stood there in a Creative stupor looking down at his
stolen basketball target with the backboard still attached
to its sawed-off foundation; and there was the
fluorescent golf ball, dust-covered but glowing a bit
under the pile of lumber in this shed that smelled of
gasoline and grass-caked lawn mowers. When he tried
to pull out his old backboard...it wouldn't budge; then
he was startled by flitting barn swallows residing in the
rafters. He could see the rusty-orange spring-loaded
lever attached to the golf ball along with the counter his
dad created. He thought about driving his van down
here and loading his stolen property into the van, but he
didn't feel like moving a ton of junk to get at it, let alone
try to load the thing himself without being seen. He
could feel his heart racing as if he was in a fight-or-flight
situation, which gave him an instant THC headache at
the back of his neck. He walked back to his van in a
daze, playing that memory in his head of that night when
he *heard the chainsaw* outside his trailer and then saw
the thieves drive off with a Johnny 3 souvenir. Back
then: he was glad to see it gone; it was a bad memory
after his humiliating misses at the free-throw line. But
now, after getting behind the wheel of his van and u-
turning out of there, "That bastard ripped me off." Then
JT reasoned that Blodough could've bought it from

someone. Either way, it was all so strange seeing his Johnny 3 training target rotting in Blodough's shed.

On his drive home to the Yankton cabin he realized how Creative had failed him at the Blodough shed, giving him dry mouth and paranoia instead of a creative solution to handling this experience. This wasn't high school; and yet Creative made him feel like an insecure stoned teenager who was so protected by his mother –he couldn't be told about Iris's pregnancy or her decision to abort it. And all the while he thought he'd made an impulsive adult decision to go see Blodough in person… It was Creative that made him go.

Driving through Vermillion his busy mind was telling him to go to that health club now, to confront Blodough about his stolen property in his shed. Instead: he headed for home, tossing out the window his stash, watching it in his side-view mirror scatter across the South Dakota prairie at 60 mph. No more impulsive moves of a stoner, *"It's time for another oil,"* he thought. *"One that comes from a clear mind without a smokescreen."*

***

He didn't sleep at all that night…because of Blodough. The next night was the same, partly because of Creative withdrawals. In the past, he'd stopped smoking for periods of time and had these nights of insomnia. He still couldn't come up with a good reason to confront Blodough. In a few days, he'd pick up Grampa Tower for a visit at the cabin. *"Grampa will help me,"* he believed.

High Time You Went

That first weekend in March was Grampa Tower's first visit to the cabin since returning from Elmdale. Birdfoot violet and black-eyed Susan were in bloom early and lining the front sidewalk of Yankton Manor as Eldon watched for his grandson's van to pick him up. Standing tall in his faded blue overalls with his butterscotch cane planted under his fisted strong grip, he could see a brown-headed cowbird hopping across the parking lot in front of him, pecking at granulated stones and causing a 70-year-old memory to appear:

It was that day he'd first met Ellie in Joe's store, when she consented to letting him walk her back home. They'd talked most of the way to her house in Ortonville. Closing-in-on her house, she spotted a dead bird on the road, and with her handkerchief she placed it gently on the grass, a safe distance off the gravel road to prevent the bird from being pulverized by traffic. Not a word was said about it during the remaining walk to her front door. On his solitary walk home he stopped to look at the fallen bird and realized right there he was falling in love for the first time in his life. He'd walked home without recalling one step of his journey. That bird, motionless in the prairie grass, that was the same image he saw when he ran to her still body in the garden littered with hailstones.

Eldon blinked his wet eyes clear…to the present as a new silver Camry parked in front of him. JT got out from behind the wheel of his new car and hustled over to his grandfather.

"I traded-in the van this morning!"

The old man was surprised as JT opened the front passenger door for him and helped him onto the front passenger seat, an easier move compared to the van. After taking his cane JT helped his passenger with his seat belt.

During their drive to the Hy-Vee store, JT pointed out all the new features; he even played one of his old CDs to show the improvement in his sound system. Before their slow walk to and into the store Eldon remarked wryly with his Eisenhower grin how he *liked the smell of this one*, alluding to the constant odor of second-hand pot in the old van.

"I quit smoking weed, Grampa," JT stated with confidence, knowing the old farmer would like that news.

"That's good," Eldon said as JT handed him his cane and they made their slow walk toward the store.

***

Seated at their usual front-window booth in the dining area of the clean store, an empty snub-nose grocery car parked nearby, JT told his grandfather everything: about seeing his stolen basketball target in Blodough's shed in Elk Point. Then, against his dad's advice –he told him all about Iris and Mexico and that Iris told Ruthie that only he or Blodough could've been the father.

"How do you know that's true?" Eldon asked.

"Well, I know the timing fits the conception for both of us."

Awkward silence until JT told his grandfather that Blodough works at a fitness club in Vermillion. But the old man wasn't clear why JT even went to Blodough's house in the first place.

"I wanted to let him know I saw him with Iris on his science table…and let him know about Mexico…"

"Didn't you say that you saw two men in a truck drive off with your target?"

"Yeah, and I didn't see Blodough. I saw the back of them at night and heard them laughing like they were drunk."

"Blodough could deny it and say he bought the thing," Eldon made a good point.

"I think Blodough paid those guys to do it."

Eldon told JT that he couldn't prove that Blodough took it, "and prob'ly won't admit it anyway."

"I *just* want him to know about Iris and what she did in Mexico…and I want my stolen property back."

Eldon removed a checkered handkerchief from his overalls and blew his nose into it before asking, "Do you really want the thing back?"

"Yes. I don't want *him* to have it."

"Well...he'll probably give it back...since everyone in town knows it was yours. And if he doesn't...you can sue him for it and press charges."

"Uh huh," JT agreed absently.

"Since you got rid of your van I'd have him deliver it to you."

"Yeah, but I don't want that jerk to know where I live."

"Go to his work and talk to him. That'll light a fire under his ass. I'd stay clear of his property. No witnesses."

"That's a great idea. I could go there as a potential new customer. Get a free pass."

"Now you're talkin'," the frugal retired farmer grinned.

"I could call the health club and find out when he's working..."

After Eldon reached into his overalls pocket for a short shopping list he handed JT:

"Sounds like it's high time you went... But *get* our groceries first," Eldon chuckled.

As JT pushed the shopping cart on his way to do their shopping, Eldon turned to look out the front window of the store to watch the world go by. He was feeling better after talking to his grandson. When he got back from his visit to Elmdale…he heard that two Yankton Manor friends had passed while he was away. They died on the same day. After he'd been back for a couple days he finally asked one of the staff about them after not seeing them for some time in the dining room, where they often ate together and chatted. Both men were in their late 80s and knew that Eldon was one of the oldest Manor residents. Reaching the century mark wasn't a big deal to Eldon Tower, for he'd been given *more than my fair share of days,* he'd often say. Behind Eldon's good-naturedness was the incredible fact that he'd outlived Ellie by 70 years, about an average lifetime. He'd never failed to see his young wife whenever he put his imagination to it. As now, he could find some piece of her profile in the scudding clouds moving across his window; or, he could make out things in clouds she had knitted for them every night before bedtime. He used her oil to feel grateful that he could raise Charlie by himself. And there, in a space of blue between moving clouds –he saw her *blue eye* looking at him, not as if she was watching over him; but rather, he saw it as a reminder to be grateful for what he has; and *never* –for what he's lost. He could see her whenever he looked at Charlie and JT. *"I'm lucky,"* he'd tell himself every day, thankful for what he had. He'd known other men who had lived long lives with their mate, lose her, then die shortly thereafter as if unwilling to live without her. Not Eldon Tower; he knew she'd never go for that.

Meanwhile, JT was looking for Eldon's denture cleaner when the store's sound system started playing Anne Murray singing "I Just Fall in Love Again," the same song Iris played for him the night before his big game, helping him let go of his built-up stress. And now: he started to let go, shielding his face with the box of denture cleaner, releasing streams of toxins streaming down his face, the *poison* Iris said that had to be released. And it had worked for him too, a thousand times in his solitary darkness when he thought of her and how he missed a life with her and now: *possibly* their child. And he knew she had played this very song for him, for she knew that we all must let go of the poison, the poison of a world chasing greed and lies and a thousand betrayals. Yes, he loved her...no matter what she did.

"It's high time you went," he repeated over and over to himself as the song ended and he tossed the denture cleaner into his cart and moved along the aisle feeling better...*much better*, he knew.

The Longest Night

*"*Tomorrow, after I take Grampa back to his apartment –I'm off to see Blodough. It's near midnight and I'm too restless to sleep. Part of my restlessness is because I have more energy now since letting go of Creative. I have no plan when I see Blodough, except to go with the flow. I called the fitness club and found out that 'Coach B' is usually in the club around noon. I didn't schedule with him to take a training session; I said I wanted to talk to Mr. Blodough and the receptionist suggested that I just stop by. Grampa said I should call the local cop in Elk Point, to get his name and find out what my options are for recovering my stolen property. That way, Grampa said, I'll have some leverage. I believe my restlessness is not fear. It's more like I'm anxious to clear the air about Iris and finally confront him man to man, something I was incapable of in school."*

That night, after writing a bit, JT put on his coat and walking shoes and went for a 15-minute power walk to the bait shop, about a half-mile from the cabin. Returning home, he could see that Grampa Tower's bedroom light was on. One of his nightly trips to the bathroom, JT presumed.

Inside the cabin he could see that Grampa Tower's bedroom light was still on under his closed bedroom door. JT wondered if he needed anything, since usually if he got up to use the bathroom or to get a drink of water from his bedside table –he'd turn the light off right away. *Could he have called out to me?* JT wondered and went to the bedroom door and listened. Nothing. He knocked lightly and pushed open the squeaky door, whereupon he saw that the old man was sitting on the side of his bed in his pajamas, the few fine silver strands of hair at the back of his head were fluffed out as if he was in this sleepy state of confusion as he was staring at Ellie's bedside photo, the same one he keeps on his bedside table in his apartment.

The sound of his grandfather's voice startled him; it was this raspy kind of whisper that was weak and halting when he said, "Oh…I just got up…to get a drink of water… I got dizzy when I tried to get up…"

He sat down beside his grandfather and asked him if he needed to pee or wanted a glass of water.

"No, no, I'm fine."

"You think you should lie down?"

He watched the old man lie back down; when JT tried to pull the covers over him:

"No, I don't want to be covered."

JT watched him from the foot of the bed while scolding himself for even bothering his grandfather with his Blodough situation. Then he let Eldon know that they were just five minutes from the nearest hospital if he wanted to go get checked out. After a while:

"Feel better?"

"I'm okay," Eldon whispered.

"Should I turn off your light?"

He nodded yes.

"I'll leave your door open. If you need anything, let me know."

***

There was no sleep for JT that night. He was on the couch listening for any calls for help. Every so often JT would get up to look in on him, checking his breathing, which *sounded* like the old man was sleeping. Just before dawn JT started to doze off, flinching himself awake and listening for sounds of trouble coming from his grandfather's room. Unable to sleep, he got up and made a pot of coffee since the old farmer would normally be up with the sun.

When morning light came, JT checked to see if Eldon was getting up without trouble for his morning bathroom ritual. Grampa T was sitting up on the side of his bed putting on his slippers. JT helped Eldon put on his purple robe that was draped over a chair before helping him stand.

"Did you sleep well?" JT asked.

"Uh huh."

"How do you feel? Any dizziness?"

"I'm okay," Eldon said, sounding more like his old self now.

207

"Coffee's ready."

"I can smell it," Eldon smiled, taking his cane from JT to make his way into the kitchen.

***

By early afternoon, after he'd returned Grampa Tower to his Yankton Manor apartment, JT knew he'd be too haggard to go see Blodough, since he wanted to be rested for that encounter. He'd stayed with his grandfather until the head nurse at the retirement home had checked Eldon's vitals, which were close to normal and no dizziness.

Upon returning to the cabin he bathed in infrared light while hanging upside down on his inversion table. Then, after his light therapy he picked up his journal from the floor by the sofa and read his last entry he made this morning while Grampa Tower took his bath.

"Last night was the longest night. Grampa wasn't feeling well, and that's unusual for him. I can't recall any health issues he's had or recall ever worrying about his health as I did last night. This has put Blodough and Iris in a different light for me. It feels more like the dead past and something I should let go of. Or, as my mom said, I could be avoiding something I should do to move on with my life. Whenever I think about my stolen Johnny 3 target and Mexico –I want to pound these walls until my fists are bloody and this overwhelming feeling of cowardice is gone. Last night I went for a power walk in the early March night that felt like summer. Later, after Grampa complained of dizziness I wondered if these crazy weather patterns with wide temperature swings could cause his dizziness. For 90-

208

plus years he's been living in 4 distinct seasons with time to adjust for each season coming and going. Are older people having more trouble adapting or coping with these erratic weather patterns? Even my relatively young body seems out of whack just from missing one night's sleep. When I asked him again over coffee if he'd slept well, he said he did, and yet, I had this feeling he was just telling me that so I wouldn't worry about him."

Pinheads, Reunions, and Mercy

I t took JT a few days until he felt like Grampa was in the clear without recurring dizziness spells. Going to see Blodough was on the back burner for now, contributing to a series of lost memories that poured out of him, spilling onto his journal pages as if these were important things he needed to be conscious of before meeting with his old coach and nemesis.

Over the years, JT had attended both of his class reunions since graduating in '95, each time hoping to see Iris. Iris never showed. His 10-year class reunion turned into a brief encounter with Blodough and a one-night stand for JT and former classmate Mercy Palmer. He found the journal entries in his cabin closet where he stored all his writing, things he'd forgotten and yet seemed important now when nearing a meeting with Blodough.

"What a waste of time that was! I was bummed out because Iris didn't show. I don't know why I thought she would; perhaps my ego hoped she would. Greg Barnes, a friend and teammate, had a flask of Jack Daniels and we polished it off on a picnic table in Riverside Park where about 50 of my classmates gathered. About half the guys were single and looking for girls to hook up with. A couple of them were still

210

pinheads I never liked in high school. One of them knocked up one of the hottest girls in our class during our senior year. He asked me if I could make a free-throw now. And I asked him if he'd learned how to read. We laughed it off, and yet I was ready to punch his lights out after a couple sips from Gary's flask. Then that pinhead asked me if Iris was good in bed. I told him to watch his mouth before my fist found it. When I was ready to go I saw Blodough talking to a group of guys; just seeing him made me approach Mercy Palmer and we ended up together all night at my place. He was still getting to me after 10 years. Now, I wish I hadn't gone."

North Woodbury's Class of '95 20-year reunion was another no-show for Iris Jean Prescott. That reunion was at least more enjoyable for JT since Blodough didn't show either. Mercy Palmer was now Mercy Holtz, attending this reunion with her new husband Ralph. It was an awkward moment for JT when Mercy brought Ralph over to JT's table to meet *Johnny 3*.

"I've always wanted to meet you," friendly Ralph gushed after their introduction by Mercy. *"I played for East Woodbury and was one of the scrubs put in to intentionally foul you. I fouled out of the game in three minutes,"* Ralph laughed with Johnny 3.

"Did I make any free-throws?" JT winced at Ralph.

"Nope. You missed 'em all. And that's why my coach named me player of the week!"

They all had a good laugh and joined JT at his table. Somehow, Blodough's name came up and Mercy was also glad her old science teacher wasn't there, since she revealed to JT how Mr. Blodough *"gave me extra credit work after school. Which meant comparing the size of his hand to my breast."*

"She didn't even report the perv to the principal," Ralph nodded with disgust.

"I needed to pass his class," she shrugged.

JT could only offer an understanding nod without explaining why he understood.

***

That night after his 20-year reunion, *Miguel* wrote about the event in his journal; now, sitting in Grampa Tower's chair under his reading light, his last two sentences in the old journal entry gave him pause for thought:

"How in the hell did that perv get away with sexually assaulting his students? He probably will do that wherever he works."

Which Hunt

A nother storm brought snow; then a bizarre week of 70-degree sunshine before more snow. JT was allowing the weather to maintain his vacillation about going to see Blodough. By late March he'd run out of excuses to delay seeing Blodough...until out of the blue he got a phone call from a former teammate named Mark Dudley, who'd become a Tower Tavern regular a few years after his parents sold the bar. It was one of those freaky things that seem to force things to move forward when you're looking for a sign or a reason to do so. At first, Mark explained how he happened to get JT's phone number from one of JT's 2-for-1 Johnny 3 Sandwich cards that a friend gave him in South Woodbury. The rest of Mark's reason for calling went like this:

"I stopped to have a beer in Bud's Bar in Pender after workin' all day layin' sewer pipe for the county. A basketball game was on the TV and your name came up. I told Bud I played with Johnny Three for North Woodbury. The bartender told me that two of his customers, Daryl Hunt Sr. and Daryl Hunt Jr. bragged about stealin' Johnny Three's basketball setup. They said it was the easiest hundred bucks they ever made."

After this stunning revelation JT asked Mark if he heard those guys were paid to steal it or did it on their own and sold it for the money.

213

"He didn't say. He said they were drinkin' and laughin' about it…until someone in the bar told 'em it was worth ten times that much."

"So…do these Daryl Hunt guys live around Pender?" JT asked his ex-teammate.

"I don't know for sure, JT. I could prob'ly find out for ya."

"No, that's okay, Mark. No big deal."

There it was: another clue and another excuse to delay seeing Blodough. *But at least,* he reasoned, *I'd have more leverage if I find out the truth.*

***

This was JT's first road trip in his new car, driving south on Highway 81 about 70 miles into Nebraska before turning east at Norfolk for 25 miles to County Road 9 for a few miles north. Pender is a farm community near the western borders of two Native American reservations, the Winnebago and Omaha. This part of the country is a blatant reminder that America's bread basket is near-empty in these pockets of rural poverty in a state known for its good economy and low unemployment rate.

Pender is like a hundred other towns spoked out from Superland –dependent on agriculture and weather. It was easy to spot Bud's Bar on Pender's mud-stained main street, where he parked between mud-splattered pickups much like the one he saw driving away with his target. He removed from the inside pocket of his jacket the Micro Stick voice-activated recorder he bought in an electronics store in Yankton yesterday for this trip, perfect for a writer who wanted proof or leverage when confronting these rubes who stole his target. JT was aware that that these "suspects" might not care much at all about a theft that happened some 25 years back, and no witness to identify them.

Now, still behind the wheel of his Camry he pushed the *record* button, knowing both Daryls or one of them could be in the bar now for all he knew; and –more evidence might be forthcoming from Bud or any bartender who knows these father and son thieves. From his glovebox he grabbed a few Johnny 3 Sandwich cards and left his new-car smell for the sweet smell of silage mixed with cow shit and mud coming from the cargo beds on both sides of him.

He entered the busy dark bar's plaintive atmosphere drowning in Patsy Cline's "Stand by Your Man," a song he'd heard a thousand times in Tower Tavern. Flush-faced men and women looked his way from barstools, all facing the bar's stock of colorful glass bottles lined 4 rows deep on both sides of the antique cash registers. Above Patsy and the *din of chatter* he could hear a *loud mouth hag* on a barstool barking obscenities about how *Obama Care* ruined her life, finding sympathetic nodding ears on both sides of her. From growing up in his parents' bar –he was certain that the old man behind the bar had to be Bud, the owner, the same man who told Mark about the two Daryls who bragged to him about stealing the Johnny 3 target. JT used his dad's wisdom now; it was on auto-pilot, reminding him in his dad's voice to *"take a seat away from the bar. He'll see you. He knows tips are better with distance."* To his right were high/round cocktail tables lining the wall near two pool tables that were in use. A banquet table held hot dogs and buns in a steamer with plastic bottles of ketchup and mustard standing beside uncovered trays of relish and diced onions. He took a seat on a barstool at one of the high tables and kept his blue/brown eyes on Bud, knowing sooner than later he'd come over to take his order. This was the best spot for him, because he knew he couldn't explain to Bud anything above Patsy's wailing at the busy bar where he could see Bud scrambling to catch up. And now: he could feel his hand sweating on the Johnny 3 Sandwich cards as drops of perspiration trickled down his chest while his running/silent voice recorder captured every sound in the joint. When Patsy finished her anthem –trouble came out of the jukebox when Anne Murray began singing "I Just Fall in Love Again," that same plaintive love song Iris played before his first big game as Johnny 3, the sound that helped him cry and release the stress he needed to.

"Not now, for God's sake," he groaned inwardly just as the old aproned bartender draped a bar towel over his shoulder and headed his way. Now, sentimental JT struggled to keep his eyes from welling over.

He wished he had on his sunglasses when Bud stopped to wipe down a nearby table, rebuking himself for being a pathetic romantic sap. With no plan –he handed the friendly bartender one of his cards and swiped his eyes clear when Bud read the card.

"You're Bud, right?"

"You're Johnny Three?"

JT nodded yes and shook Bud's extended hand as the owner said he "was just talking about *you* the other day."

"I know. My friend was in here and told me I should talk to you about the guys that stole my Johnny Three basketball target. I was hoping you could tell me where I could find these two Daryl Hunt guys."

"One of them is right over there at the end of the bar," Bud pointed to the burly back of an older man on a barstool wearing a black cowboy hat with black cowboy boots.

"Which Hunt?" JT asked after a shot of adrenaline widened his eyes and dried his mouth instantly.

"Senior!" Bud answered above Anne's sweet voice.

"I just want to know if they stole it on their own or if someone paid them to do it. I don't want to press charges. How do you think I should approach him, Bud?"

Bud put the card inside his apron, scratched his chin and said, "Let me think on this a bit," then placed a cocktail napkin on the table.

"I'll have a draft beer."

As Bud walked away, that song caused JT to shield his face and cry behind his hand, letting go of his tension faster than if he got up, left the bar and ran around the block a few times.

Then: he watched Bud draw his beer from the tap...then another one, carrying them both to the end of his bar, whereupon he placed one of the beers in front of Daryl Sr., along with the Johnny 3 card, telling his customer, "Johnny Three bought you a beer." When Hunt Sr. turned to look at Johnny 3, JT raised his hand and fake-

217

smiled at the big-bellied man right when Anne finished and John Anderson began "Swingin'" from Bud's jukebox. Hunt Sr. got off his barstool and followed Bud over to JT's table. JT handed Bud a ten-dollar bill and told him to keep the change after delivering his beer plus one of the two thieves who stole his target. Bud stayed close-by as Hunt Sr. explained:

"My kid was paid a hundred bucks for takin' that thing. We were drunk that night," Hunt appeared to be blaming it on alcohol.

"Who paid him?" JT had to know.

"I don't know *who it was*."

"Where'd you take it?"

"To this place in Elk Point. Nobody was there. We just dropped it off."

"Was that the same person that paid your son?"

"I can't say for sure. It was a long time back."

Then Bud helped JT by asking his customer to call his son and ask him. The man didn't hesitate to speed-dial his son on his cell phone.

"Hey…who paid you that hundred bucks to take that basketball thing we took to Elk point?"

JT was on the edge of his stool, unable to hear the voice at the other end of the call.

"Uh huh," Hunt Sr. repeated twice before relaying to Johnny 3:

218

"Some chick named Iris...*Wild Iris*," the man repeated his son's words to JT's gape-jawed face.

"Can I talk to him" JT had to ask.

"This guy wants to talk to you... No, no, it's cool. Just talk to him."

The man handed JT his cell phone.

"Hey...Daryl...so this Iris paid you a hundred bucks to take it?" JT plugged his other ear with his finger to block out the music.

"That's right," Hunt Jr. answered in JT's ear.

"What did she look like?" JT wanted to be sure.

"Oh, I don't know...we were partying... She lived right next door to the place in an Airstream."

"Uh huh. Did you know the man who you delivered it to?"

"No. She wrote down directions to get there. We dropped it off in the driveway and drove off."

"Did she say *why* she was paying you to do this?" JT asked.

"Like I say, I was pretty wasted. That's all I know, man," he sounded sincere to JT.

"Okay...thanks for talking to me."

JT handed back the phone and thanked the elder Hunt and Bud for their help and exited the bar in a daze just as Ronnie Milsap asked: "Am I Losing You?"

***

219

JT's drive back to the cabin was a blurry shock-filled journey of thoughts that didn't make sense to him. A thousand times during his unconscious drive back home he kept asking out loud: "Why would she *do that* for Blodough?" He kept trying to recall anything he might've said or done that would cause Iris to do this for Blodough. *"Why would Blodough pay her to do that? And...why would he even want my target?"* Searching his memory of things around that time before his target was stolen:

***

He recalled one Sunday morning, when he was sleeping more, because he was depressed about his free-throw misses that made him the joke of the school. He came out into the kitchen and Libby was there having coffee with his mother at the kitchen table. After he got his cereal and sat down to eat at the table, he was upset with his mother because he overheard her whispering to Libby how *bad* he was feeling lately, and that *he even stopped writing in his journal.*

"Go ahead and ask him," his mother said to Libby while JT ate his cereal with his head bowed, not wanting to talk to anybody.

"Ask me what?" JT said without looking up from his cereal.

Libby said, *"I know it's a couple months off...but JT...would you consider taking Iris to your prom?"*

"Prom?" he stopped chewing and looked at his neighbor as if she was crazy.

"I don't even know if she'd want to go, but if you were to ask her…maybe…? Libby winced at JT.

"I don't feel like going to the prom, Libby. Right now, I'm the big joke at school. I'm doing everything I can just to stay in school to graduate. I don't want to be around any of those people at a prom. Iris told me she might not even have enough credits to graduate."

He could see that he'd made his point clear, and that Libby was fearful of her daughter not graduating.

***

Now, on his hazy drive back home, unaware of his surroundings since leaving Pender, he thought back to that period in May when he and Iris were dating, and they had made their own plans for the night of their prom.

Prom Night with Chris Rea

It was a Saturday night in late May, close to the end of that period when Iris and JT were dating. Iris was standing outside Tower Tavern's back door having a smoke. The bar was busy as usual on a Saturday night, the perfect time for JT to sneak out the back door with a six-pack of beer from the bar's cooler. When he came out the back door with the sacked beer, Iris took his hand and they hurried away like happy children, going around the long way, headed for her secret spot under the train trestle to celebrate their own prom night away from the crowd.

They sat close to each other on the cool slab of concrete sharing a joint and sipping their beer. The May moon-lit night was spring-perfect. JT had good news:

"I started writing again."

"*Miguel's back*!" she laughed. "What did you write about?"

"*You*, mostly," he said with his exhalation.

"Really? Tell me about it."

"It's about how you helped me get out of my depression…"

"How'd I do that?"

"By being my friend...after...you know...the Johnny Three disaster."

She laughed. "You were bummed out for a long time. I noticed you started getting a little better after your target was stolen...don't you think?"

"Yeah. I tried not to look at it. I was glad they took it when they did."

"One day you'll laugh at the whole Johnny Three thing. Ruthie says she sold more sandwiches *after*...the disaster."

"I know. It's like my failure made sales sky rocket."

"If you're smart, you'll stay positive about your *failure* and have fun with it. That's how you make Johnny Three worth all the work you put into it. You're a celebrity around here. Everybody's heard of Johnny Three."

"I got caught up in my head... Every practice shot I took for two years I shot from my heart...like my dad said to. And my goal was to get a scholarship so my parents could sell the bar and retire..."

"And they *did*! But *you* made it happen!"

JT changed the subject: "Your mom said you might move back to Omaha after you graduate."

"You mean *if* I graduate. I'm not goin' back to school here. If I flunk...I'll feel stupid every minute I'm there. My mom says we might move to Omaha either way, since she doesn't think she wants to live here when Charlie and Ruthie retire to California."

Then, she had to say, "I think my mom knows we're foolin' around."

"Is *that* what you call it?" he watched Iris butt her roach against the concrete, take a sip of beer and light a red, apparently not wanting to talk about their relationship or moving away.

"Even if your mom moves to Omaha with the Airstream...you could live with me. I'll have the trailer."

"I *don't* think my mom would go for that."

"Why not? You're eighteen. We're both eighteen," he said.

She didn't want to talk about this stuff, yet assuaged it by telling him she could drive up from Omaha to visit him after she gets a car.

"Or..." he suggested with a shrug after crushing an empty beer can in his hand, "I could drive to Omaha."

At the time, he didn't think he sounded needy, and yet it had turned her off to a point that she could only nod in agreement, as if that was an option too. Then: she watched him remove his little cassette player from his back pocket as he asked her if she missed going to their prom. She shook her head no, wary of his next move, for she always knew he was a romantic sap, a trait she really wasn't attracted to.

"I brought some music for *our* prom."

She watched him turn on the cassette player and place it on the ledge; he stood up facing her as Chris Rea's "Fool If You Think It's Over" began playing. She giggled, took his extended hand and stood against him as he began turning clockwise, slow-dancing under the spring-damp trestle where the sweet scent of the Champa Flower on her neck made him close his eyes and wish this moment would last forever.

***

Back at the cabin: he hurried to his stored journals and found the one that held his words from their prom night. In Grampa Tower's chair and under his reading light he began reading Miguel words:

"That sweet fragrance of Champa was in her hair as we slow-danced to Chris Rea under the train trestle on our prom night. At first, she giggled on my shoulder as if she was happy and vulnerable, shuddering from emotion. My eyes were moist from joy and sadness, for I knew this Tower trait of lost love was working its way to my heart and telling me this was the last dance we'd ever have together. We both couldn't look at each other for this reason. I know this to be true, as sure as I know she was withholding falling in love with me, resisting my pathetic romantic Tower trait of loving one woman for life. So, I closed my eyes and wanted to pound my fists against invisible man-made time to protest this dance I would have to hold onto in my brain and on these pages that Iris would never see. I remember slowing our dance even more, both of us listening to the lyrics that soon made her tremble against me. Now, as I write these words in my room I swear I can almost hear her crying in the space between our windows. Again, and

225

again I want to pound my fists through something that would break through this past life of hers that I know crushed her heart and locked it so no other man who really loved her could reach her and hurt her again. I know she plays it safe and settles for one-night stands and boys who steal her body and vanish in the night like those drunken jackals that stole my target. I don't want to learn how to protect my heart like she does. Yes, it's happened to me too; that skinny Wild Iris is closing this Tower heart of first love...and leaving me alone."

He closed his journal and thought it credible that Iris paid Daryl Hunt Jr. to steal his target. Except: Iris paying a hundred bucks on her own to have it stolen? *"No way,"* he reasoned to himself. *"She was always broke. If she ever had that much money –she'd never give it to that redneck to steal my target. And why would Blodough pay her the money to steal it, then keep the stolen property in his shed for twenty-five years? Did she steal it to get her passing grade from him? If so: why would she be with Blodough on his science table after she'd just gotten her diploma? She didn't have to. It doesn't make sense."*

Ready or Not...

J T parked his car in the back row of the health club parking lot in Vermillion. He opened the side pocket of his gym bag and turned on his Micro Stick recording device, leaving the pocket open. Yesterday, when driving back from Pender he had time to memorize the questions he had for Blodough. Late last night he wrote:

"I found out that Iris paid a hundred bucks to have my target stolen. It was mind-numbing, one of those shocking truths that forced me to recall our back story, the things she'd said and done around that time. I'm going to surprise Blodough tomorrow at the health club and ask him to explain why he has my target on his property. I want him to explain everything before I reveal what I know. What really hurts is that Iris and I were together in May –a couple months after my target was stolen. It's possible I will never know all the details, but positive leverage must be used to get to the bottom of this when I meet Blodough. I had a good case of confusion all the way home to Yankton and resisted calling my mother to get her help. I must do this on my own without any help. I'm going tomorrow, ready or not… There's no other way."

***

Johnny 3 entered the health club toting his gym back, its open pocket capturing the metallic/grunting sounds of

227

the weight room; there were background noises: whooshing sounds of stair climbers and tread mills mixed with the sound of a ringing phone and small talk from staff and club members in the open workout areas within view. He wasn't sure if Blodough was working now. This was his *oil* plan as he approached the smiling receptionist.

"Is Mr. Blodough working now?"

"Coach B. doesn't work here. But, I believe he's in the pool now."

She asked a co-worker if Mr. B. was in the pool and she wasn't sure.

"He was my coach in high school…and uh…I want to surprise him… Hopefully get a day pass and maybe he'll give me a tour…"

"It's five dollars for a day pass."

After he paid her, she handed him a towel and a padlock with key.

"Oh, uh, do you have bathing suits or do you sell them here?" he asked.

"No, I'm sorry," she smiled.

***

In the locker room, JT was wary about running into his old coach after stripping down to his boxer shorts and shower thongs. He locked his clothes in a locker and fastened the locker key with the attached safety pin to the inside waistband of his boxers. He carried his gym bag into a shower stall, took a quick shower, and stopped his busy mind by reminding it: *"odd is left."* He wrapped his towel around his waist to conceal his revealing swimwear and followed the signage directing him to the "Pool." Ready or not…he trusted oil as he made his way into the pool area, whereupon he could see that all the cordoned swimming lanes were filled with swimmers. He walked along the edge of the pool unable to see if Blodough was in the pool, stopping at the elevated lifeguard stand to ask her if "Coach B" was in the pool.

"I think he's in the sauna," she pointed to a windowless cedar door on the other side of the pool.

On his way to the sauna he reminded himself of oil, and could sense this subtle shift within as if everything he wanted to know…was behind that door…the same door he could never pass through when he graduated into the real world with Iris. Just before he pulled open the sauna door to slip-in quickly –he put his gym bag down, removed the towel from his waist and draped it over his head to conceal his face.

Once inside the steam-clouded sauna, he could barely see the lone man seated on the long cedar bench at the top tier. The man - to JT seemed too frail to be Coach Blodough - also had a towel draped over his head. *How fitting was this,* he thought, *to be looking for Blodough in such a hot place as this,* as he climbed to the same level and sat down on the hot cedar five feet from this man, placing his bag between him and this rather frail-looking man he still didn't think was Blodough. When JT reached into his bag to remove a bottle of water he turned the open pocket of his gym bag toward the man and matched the man's forward-leaning posture with his towel covering his face. Then: he moved the towel down to his neck to get a better look at this man...until...again: ready or not...

"Coach?"

No response. Again, but louder and more specific: "Coach Blodough?"

The man turned his head to the voice, brushing back his towel to reveal his bald head and that familiar scowl JT could never forget. It was shocking to see this emaciated man who had to be in his early 50's now, and once physically intimidating to JT, now a pencil-neck ghost-of-a-man suffering with some disease. *And why hadn't his brother said he was ill?* JT wondered.

"Is that you, Coach?" JT could see the burning stare of death looking at him.

"Who are *you*?" Blodough shot back in this flinty whisper of a dying man and that dismissive scowl.

"John Tower...from North Woodbury," JT scooted himself and his bag a bit closer.

Blodough seemed to be mouthing the name to himself until JT scooted a bit closer and almost yelled, "Johnny Three!"

Then, Blodough remembered this Tower kid and reached for his water bottle beside him, taking a sip of his water, his atrophied arm trembled as he swallowed painfully as if drinking shards of glass. Now, sitting so close to this emaciated man –JT forgot everything he wanted to ask him.

"I heard you worked here as a trainer," JT had lost any enmity he thought he'd have now.

"Used to," Blodough hacked up phlegm onto the floor and swiped his mouth with his bony wrist. "Testicular cancer and radiation ended that," he admitted with a sense of resignation that JT felt compassion for. And then: Blodough started to talk as if he had things he wanted to unload from his conscience, like a dying man who had nothing to lose now since the cancer had advanced to his lungs.

***

JT lost track of time and 5 pounds of sweat in that sauna by the time he reached his car in the health club's parking lot. After dropping his gym bag into the trunk of his car, he knew he was too weak to drive; he was physically whipped and emotionally drained from the sauna and all those words captured on his recorder inside his gym bag. He felt like a dehydrated zombie wanting a place to go, to be alone with his thoughts in a crowded place where nobody would know him. As he walked away from his car he could feel muscle spasms in his calves like he used to get in August during football practice.

He found himself on the USD campus in a daze, soon entering a cafeteria in the Student Union Building pointed out by a friendly student who thought the man was lost. He was. He was anxious now to sit somewhere alone with a big fountain cup of iced Coke, to sort things out, to get a grip on those words spoken from that dying man who joked that he was on his "*last leg,*" and flying to the Mayo Clinic tomorrow for what he believed to be his last round of radiation treatments.

231

He found a corner window table that looked out to the campus of the only college that offered him a basketball try-out after his Johnny 3 disaster. And now: he even wondered *if that was real* as he looked out at a world that had been unreal to him and changed 180 degrees after his sweltering sauna visit with Blodough. Everything spoken from that dying man had to be true; he felt it in every dripping pore of his body when his ex-coach confessed why he never let JT play, hoping he would quit football, and said that he was glad he did quit after benching him at halftime in Watertown. Then JT asked, *"Why?"*; and Blodough explained in a flinty whisper:

"Your parents bought me. Your dad would come to my office when you were a freshman and plead with me to never let you play. He threatened to sue me if you got hurt because he said he had *this plan* for you…"

"Johnny Three?" JT asked and waited for Blodough to stop coughing.

"That's right. A business plan that he said would be ruined if you got hurt. I don't know how many sandwiches he delivered to my office… And every year, two or three times at least…there'd be a few-hundred bucks in cash left in my mail box in the school office. I knew where it came from… And *I took it."*

"So that game I quit at halftime in Watertown…?"

"Your dad said if you get hurt playin' he's goin' to the principal and let him know about the bribes he paid me. And he was going to blackmail me about my father."

"What about my target? I saw it in your shed."

232

"Your girlfriend paid some guy to steal it and deliver it to my place. I wasn't paid for that. She told me your dad wanted me to keep it for him…and everything would be fine."

"Iris told you that?"

"That's right," Blodough said and took a long drink of painful water. "Your dad paid Iris two hundred bucks to have someone steal it, so I gave her directions to my place. I already had applications out to other schools. I wanted out of there, and no way was I going to mess with your dad after I took money to *not* play you."

"All this time I hated you," JT confessed.

"Your dad was smart. He knew you'd use that for motivation."

Then: JT wanted to know about Blodough's relationship with Iris, telling him that Iris got pregnant and that she said one of them had to be the father.

"She came on to me the day she graduated. I know I'm no saint… And I should never have been with her…"

"On your science table," JT added.

"She *told* you that?"

"No, I *saw* you."

"That girl used me to get a passing grade. Look, I'll admit I was a horny bastard. She was eighteen. It was a crazy thing to do. She even called me to get five thousand dollars to have this abortion in Mexico. I told her it couldn't be me, that I've been sterile since I was a sophomore in college when I got gonorrhea."

233

"What did she say?"

"I hung up on her, and could only hope she didn't make trouble for me at my new job."

"So that was *my kid* she aborted?" JT said to himself out loud.

"I wouldn't bet on it. Did she try to get money from you?

"My parents gave her eight thousand dollars total."

"Serves 'em right," Blodough shrugged, too weak to celebrate the fact his parents were bribed by Iris.

Blodough was right: that JT couldn't believe anything about Iris, especially her claim about pregnancy. The more he thought about his parents manipulating his life in high school –the more he understood it, for they had a long-term plan to provide for his security –and they managed that well. He also understood that the individual past lives of his parents before they even met had sealed his fate as a protected only child who would not be victimized by people capable of bringing devastating losses like Charlie and Ruthie endured.

Now: watching these young students move past his window, he could no longer pretend to have been like them…ever. John Tower's future was always certain. He was a rich kid, protected by loving parents who believed they knew what was best for him. Now he knew his mother had wanted him to find this out for himself, about his parents blackmailing Blodough and forcing his silence by making the coach keep his target…while the sandwiches kept selling.

"And I was willing to go along, to follow their plan," he lamented inwardly before repeating to himself one of Grampa Tower's maxims: *"Nothing grows in a comfort zone."*

Finishing his Coke, he couldn't help wondering if Iris and Libby *had* to move away because his parents knew he was fooling around with Iris. All the enmity toward Coach Blodough had vanished in that sauna. And now: there was nothing to do about his past, nothing important he *had* to know. Today had only opened his eyes about how far his parents would go to protect him, from mendacity to bribery and blackmail. Looking out at these hopeful students, he knew he had been young and insecure as they must be, with no clue how to catch up with a lost past clouded with uncertainties. And yet: unlike 9 out of 10 of these young minds –he had no worries about money.

"Yet, I'm dead-broke emotionally," he would write later that night in his cabin. *"I have to look at today as a new beginning for me and flood this barren island of Me with a new kind of vibration that attracts a 'real' full life of balanced living. I don't look at today as a disaster, as I did when I was a joke at the free-throw line. Like Iris said: 'to turn it into a good thing, have fun with it.' At first, when I left the sauna with Coach Blodough and we shook hands, wishing each other well, I felt like moving far away from Superland, dismissing that reunion with Iris and starting over without telling my parents a word about my plans. But then: what about Grampa Tower? I can't leave him alone or take away my regular visits with him. After our last visit in Elmdale, I know that seeing me sustains him until he can see me again. I can't take that away from him, just to prove that I can*

235

live my life on my own terms. I can do that here, I know."

Just Go Away and Be Happy

Nine weeks until June 18th. JT spent all last week walking the woods around his cabin, vacillating about attending his reunion and seeing Iris. Last weekend during a Grampa Tower visit at the cabin, he played the recording of his sauna meeting with Blodough for the old man. After he listened to the recording (twice), Eldon promised his grandson that he wouldn't reveal any of it to Charlie and Ruthie, admitting that he could understand both sides of the situation. Eldon reminded his grandson that because of his parents' meddling –today he was free to live his life on his own terms.

When Grampa Tower went to bed JT found and read the journal entry he made on the day his neighbors moved away. He tried to *see* that day in early summer, a couple weeks after he and Iris graduated:

Iris was away, saying goodbye to friends when he'd walked over to her spot under the train trestle and sat on the cool slab of cement. He lit his pipe, and was aware he'd purposely avoided the Airstream, where his mother was helping Libby with her moving preparations. He'd managed to avoid Iris since they graduated. Earlier today, he had helped Libby connect the Airstream to a truck Libby traded-in just for this move. He hosed out her septic tank hose and stowed it for her, not asking Libby anything about their plans or where they were moving to, even though Ruthie had told him their tenants were moving back to the Omaha area. Libby was offered a management position at the same casino she'd worked for in Council Bluffs before moving to North Woodbury. Libby hugged JT goodbye and tearfully wished him well, knowing that he and her daughter had *a terrible falling out* ever since the day they graduated.

Stoned, here at *her* secret place, he watched for the Airstream until he saw it crossing the bridge into Iowa…and gone forever.

"Just go away and be happy," he'd muttered.

At *that time*, he was incredibly relieved to have avoided saying goodbye to Iris; he was still in shock for the way they ended —and she knew that. Now he could go home and help his parents pack for *their move* to California, since the bar was sold for more money than they ever imagined, giving their only child a secure Johnny 3 Sandwich income on top of that…as planned.

When he returned home from her spot, it was strange to him to see the vacant space where the Airstream had been parked for years. As he stood on the ground the Airstream had covered, he could see dozens of cigarette butt filters that Wild Iris had left behind. He was aware then that he was holding onto her memory, often returning to her spot over these last 25 years, unable to let her go.

***

Every few days he would go to the library to look for Blodough's obituary in the Elk Point News, expecting to see it any day. Instead, in early May, Ronna called Charlie and Ruthie in California to let them know that Betsy Mueller had died peacefully in her sleep at Prairie Home. Charlie called his son early the next morning to let JT know about his music teacher's passing. Again, Charlie tearfully thanked JT for making their reunion possible. Rather than ask his dad if he was going to fly back for Betsy's service:

"I could go on your behalf, Dad."

Within an hour JT was on the road headed for Prairie Home after Ronna told him that Nurse Dee at Prairie Home had a letter for *The Tower Family* that Betsy had given her.

On his way to Elmdale, he thought about Coach Blodough's recorded words in the sauna when he told JT he could pick up his basketball target whenever he wanted. JT told him that he didn't know what he'd do with it, and that he's never missed it. That's when JT asked the dying man if he needed a ride to the airport. Blodough said his brother was picking him up. That's when the man from Watertown felt the urge to reveal the Blodough family secret, something that might've explained Charlie Tower's leverage regarding approaching the coach about not playing his son. It happened when young *"Dowdy"* was a sophomore stand-out quarterback on the Watertown football team when his father Warren Blodough was the head coach. After a big loss, Warren got drunk and rear-ended Orville Anderson's tractor, killing the 70-year-old farmer instantly. The senior Blodough and father of

239

seven was sentenced to 10 years in the Sioux Falls penitentiary, leaving his wife and kids to struggle with their father's crime until he was killed by inmates after three years into his sentence with a parole possible in a year.

"They beat him to death with a dumb bell," Dowd revealed on the recording.

After Eldon heard the recording, JT told his grandfather that he could imagine his dad knowing all about Coach Blodough's father and using that information against him as leverage for not playing JT. And: it was the dying coach that made a good point about Johnny 3's free throw disaster, telling JT that Coach Bergdorf should've insisted that JT shoot free throws at practice instead of three-point shots, until it was too late.

Spooky and Jenex

His first stop was at Prairie Home, to find out the time and location of Betsy Mueller's service, if any. Walking to the front entrance he noticed what a perfect day in May it was, not a trace of winter's gloom anywhere. Yellow star grass was tall at the top of windy Ortonville Road. He stopped to watch a chipping sparrow riding the waving grass, reminding him of the recent walk on the lake he and his father had.

Nurse Dee was on duty and informed JT that Betsy's private service might be over by now in Ortonville Funeral Home; and:

"She left a letter for your family," handing JT a sealed envelope addressed to *The Tower Family*.

JT opened the letter right there and read:

"To JT, Charlie and Ruthie, I must say that I think of you every day since we've had our treasured visits in Prairie Home. Your kindness and generosity has been with me to start every morning. In case it becomes my time to leave this world I've requested my ashes scattered in Big Stone Lake, to perhaps reach a place as

241

Karen had, where good things returned to me in such a loving way. Love, love, Betsy."

JT returned the letter into the envelope, walked out to his car and drove to the funeral home after getting directions from Nurse Dee.

***

Betsy's service was filled with empty seats that faced a lavender-colored porcelain urn that held the music teacher's ashes. JT showed the funeral director Betsy's letter and JT was given the urn to scatter her remains as she requested. In the service register he saw *Elizabeth Snow Bear* had stopped to pay her respects, along with a few of Mrs. Mueller's many students.

***

The Pink House was nearly gone. The new owner was working on the foundation of a four-plex he planned on finishing before next winter. The friendly man told JT he was welcome to use his dock for Betsy's final request. When JT reached the end of the dock, he could see a couple mallards paddling away from the intruder. Across the lake, he saw the familiar eastern-sloping fields of Elmdale, now green for a thousand rows on both sides of the Moe/Tower tree line. He told Ronna he'd stop by the store for a late lunch and accepted her invitation to spend the night in the cottage. Now, he felt this subtle difference of well-being in *a lightness*, perhaps somewhat how his dad felt after his first visit with Betsy.

He knelt onto the old barn-wood dock, opened the urn and removed the plastic liner that held Betsy's ashes.

He poured them out and away from the dock and watched the gray ashes float then disappear into the cold lake water. He stood up and wondered if Betsy had been holding on, waiting for his dad's visit before she could leave this world. He closed his eyes and faced the sun behind him. There was nothing more he felt he needed to resolve with Iris or his parents. It was time to appreciate this moment. Nothing could hold him in the past now. *"No more mysteries to kill,"* he opened his eyes upon picking up the scent of marijuana wafting from somewhere.

"Creative," he whispered, looking 360 degrees around the dock until he spotted someone across the lake behind a rock. Then: he saw the profile of a woman sunning herself on one of the flat rocks not fifty feet from Grampa's land; and then he could *hear music*, a familiar song his dad would play on their jukebox, "Spooky" by Classics IV. If he drove over there now…it might be too late. Creative mixed with "Spooky" pushed him into oil laced with Grampa Tower's words: *"What we do not grasp is forever lost. When all is lost…odd is left."*

He didn't care how cold the water was –he kicked off his shoes, stripped to his boxers and dove off the dock into the glacier-cold lake water. He surfaced fifty feet closer to Minnesota mixing side strokes with back strokes, aware that he was headed for the very spot where Karen had fallen into the lake. Between States, he stopped to listen for "Spooky." He could hear it ending.

She had to have heard him swimming toward her. By the time he could touch bottom, this woman, perhaps 40, attractive with strawberry-blonde hair, sleeveless white t-shirt and frayed cut-off jeans, was standing akimbo on the flat rock she'd been sunning on. To JT, this woman looked fit and not at all wary of him. She was looking down at this crazy person who just swam across the lake; she thought he was harmless. JT looked up at her, into her green eyes when breathing hard; that's when he noticed her eyes saw brown and blue.

"Are you crazy?" she laughed.

Catching his breath, he said, "I thought I smelled reefer...and like a retriever...I started swimming toward it."

She laughed, sizing up this shivering man to be as she felt: harmless; she opened her fisted hand and he saw her pipe and lighter.

"If you're *that desperate*..." she offered to share.

He took a hit from her pipe and asked her if she was from this area.

"Sioux Falls. My aunt died and I'm her executor. I'm Jenex."

"I'm JT," he smiled back at her. "Like Generation X?"

"Right. My parents were creative."

After she *spelled* her name for him, she asked him:

"What does JT stand for?"

"John Tower. That's my grandfather's land," he pointed.

"I didn't think anyone lived there?"

"He leases-out the land. He lives in Yankton with me."

244

"You're freezing. I could give you a ride back to your clothes."

"No, no, thanks… Hey, you want to get lunch at Moe's General Store?

"Sure. That's where I'm parked."

Before getting back in the water he turned back to her and had to ask:

"What's your aunt's name?"

"Betty Welch."

He nodded and hit the water. She watched him swim back to the dock, whereupon he waved at her and she waved back. She could see him peel off his wet boxers and put on his pants, soon hurrying for his parked car.

***

All the way to Moe's store, JT was high with that rush a man feels when he meets a woman he likes, someone who turns out to be attractive to him after risking himself in oil. He'd lost this *feeling* by playing it safe for too long…and he made this moment happen just like his father had when he walked into the future Tower Tavern. It wasn't dumb luck; he knew his father created Ruthie in his life. Now, after losing his buzz, he was still this romantic sap in the throes of an interesting oil that he was anxious to follow up on. Her name was Jenex, and because of *her* he was feeling confident about his impulsive oil that told him to swim across the lake to meet this woman.

And now: the approaching 25-year reunion with Iris wasn't the only thing in his life he was looking forward

to. This oil had awakened his desire to write as soon as
he was settled into the Moe cottage. *"And just maybe,"*
his mind said, *"Jenex would go to the reunion with me,
instead of this protracted solo act of the good son who
lived his parents' plan and retired young without many
problems. And how can I say they were wrong when I'm
free to swim across a freezing-cold lake on a weekday
when most men my age bust their ass every day knowing
social security will surpass defense funding and the
Federal Reserve will only print more money and
diminish the value of their work. Am I being Gen X with
her?"*

***

When JT walked through the store's back door, Jerry
had just finished slicing ham for a customer waiting at
the meat counter. JT wondered if that old Chevy van
parked outside belonged to Jenex.

"Hey, you!" Jerry smiled with a friendly wave and told
JT that Ronna was in the kitchen. Before going up
front...JT could see Jenex seated at the end counter
stool, the same stool Ellie was on when Eldon first met
her with Joe. Her back was to him; she had on a purple
silk jacket and she was writing in her journal with her
strawberry-blonde head craned down and forward as her
curled left hand moved her words across the narrow page
with this sense of urgency that intrigued him and
reminded him that he hadn't written much since his
sauna visit with Coach Blodough.

The reefer Jenex shared had worn off during those
first few moments of that cold swim back to the dock.
He knew he was going after Jenex, akin to young
Charlie going after Karen Mueller, swimming over to

her while she was sunning herself on her dock. JT was into this oil, and would borrow his dad's sense of humor when he thought:

"She must like me...or she wouldn't be here."

"Hello stranger!" Ronna called out when exiting her kitchen to wait on this customer who said she was *waiting for someone.*

She watched JT and Ronna hug at the other end of the lunch counter, then closed her journal, watching this crazy guy who swam across the lake.

"Ronna, did you meet Jenex?"

"No, she said she was waiting for someone. I never dreamed it *was you!"* Ronna laughed.

"What's on the menu, Ronna?" JT asked.

"Roast chicken, mashed potatoes and gravy with carrots and beets."

"I'm in," JT said. "How 'bout you, Jenex?"

"Me, too. And a Coke please," Jenex smiled at Ronna.

"Two Cokes," JT added, then sat at the counter, leaving a stool between them, ready to play Charlie Tower, a role he knew as well as Ruthie did. She surprised JT:

"So, you're going commando now?" she laughed beautifully loud, a laugh he was instantly attracted to.

Now it was *Charlie's* turn as she seemed really fixated on his *Tower eyes,* back and forth from his blue eye to his brown eye...waiting for his reply. He surprised her:

247

"Hey, that water was ice cold." Then he leaned forward like he'd seen his dad do a thousand times to a thousand strangers and said discreetly: "When my *nuts*..." Jenex started laughing so loud, he had to laugh with her, and finish his thought: "When my nuts first hit that water, it was so cold it turned one of my eyes *blue!*"

After a big laugh, Jenex leaned over to JT and discreetly said, "I can't believe you could smell that reefer from across the lake."

"I've been cold turkey a couple months...and I could smell it. But I couldn't figure out where it was coming from."

After Ronna brought their drinks and went back into her kitchen, JT continued:

"I saw this woman from a distance and figured...what the hell...maybe she'll share."

Then he asked her what she was writing.

"Oh...that's my journal."

"I keep a journal."

"Really?"

"I'd like to convert it into a novel."

"That's interesting," she said.

"Did you write about our meeting today?"

After her hesitation and laugh, he said, "I'll take that as a yes."

***

Enjoying Ronna's terrific meal, JT found out the 2 most important things: she's single; and, she said she'd meet him tomorrow at a coffeehouse in Milbank that was close to her aunt's house.

"How long will you be around here?" he asked.

"If I can get her house listed and ready for showing before her estate sale this weekend...I hope to get back to Sioux Falls by the middle of next week."

He asked her what kind of work she did.

"I work in the kitchen of a retirement home."

"Really?"

"My grandfather, who lived here most of his life, lives in Yankton Manor. He'll be one hundred this June."

"That's incredible."

***

Upon leaving the store she invited him into her van *to share a bowl.*

"There's something I like about you," he said.

***

They talked in her van for 2 hours, then she drove home and JT drove to the Moe cottage, anxious to write in his journal about their long talk in her van.

249

A Better-Feeling Story

"What I like about Jenex - that's so rare these days - is her slow way of living. She explained how she'd gotten her real estate license when Trump was elected, hoping sales would be fast and easy in a growing economy. But then, she said with this visible light in those green eyes, that she ran out of gas. She said the hectic pace was stressing her out. For nearly 3 years she stayed in that American rat race believing she had to suffer through it to get ahead and be this American Dream that came true. She said all she was doing was matching the crazy weather we were all creating in our unconscious chase for money. One day, she had enough, and moved to Sioux Falls to live a slower life. She started to get healthy and took a job in a retirement home kitchen that fit her new modest lifestyle in a studio apartment. I believe her when she says she's never been happier. Now here's the amazing part: When I asked about her family it became clear to me that this beautiful woman was a kindred spirit I want to spend time with. Her parents have owned a bar in Worthington, MN, her entire life...and she said she

wanted no part of that life when she graduated. I told
her about Tower Tavern and my Johnny 3 Sandwich gig
that allowed me to retire last December to the Yankton
family cabin so I could live near my Grampa Tower. We
both agreed how it was "Spooky" how much we have in
common...considering how we met. In her van, we
never shared another bowl. I told her about oil and how
my family has prospered by living in oil over 3
generations. Her eyes were lit with the color of wet jade
while she faced me from her van's driver's seat talking
about being an archetype for change regarding 'slowing
the world down'; and how Millennials must reverse this
trend by creating their own independent political party.
She talked about how technology and the brains that
brought them to consumers are not compatible; and
because of our innate primal fear of other tribes and
nations, we're testing weapons in space, risking further
damage to our ozone. It was all so interesting. I look
forward to seeing this Jenex tomorrow."

***

The next morning JT met Jenex at Margie's Coffee
Cup in Milbank, a few blocks from her aunt's house.
They picked up where they left off in her van yesterday,
until she had to get back to her house for the start of the
estate sale. Earlier this morning, Jenex went door-to-
door reminding Aunt Betty's neighbors about her aunt's
estate sale starting at 10 this morning. When JT offered
to help with her sale –she knew it was time to let this
nice guy from Yankton know that she was not interested
in dating now, for reasons she didn't care to explain.
They hugged goodbye outside the coffeehouse and he
drove away in his Camry, headed home, not at all
disappointed about Jenex. To JT, he had passed another

test of maturity, and more proof to him that his life was already a better-feeling story.

Night Devils and Toothpicks

3 a.m. on May 18th JT was awakened in his cabin bedroom by the ominous sound of city tornado *sirens.* He got out of bed and in the dark made his way to the kitchen portable radio and heard frantic warnings to find shelter now, since confirmed reports of 3 twisters had touched down in the Yankton area. He dressed fast, thinking of Grampa Tower in Yankton Manor as he hustled outside to the increased noise of foreboding weather warning sirens that seemed to be coming from several directions in the ink-black sky above rustling trees in total darkness.

He drove away from the cabin headed into God knows what, on his way to the retirement home, unable to tell whether he was in the path of a funnel as increased winds blew hard…then eerily stopped…right when he turned on his car radio to hear if any of these deadly night devils were on his path. It was all perilous driving on the downtown Yankton streets where all street lights were out, and swaying signal lights blinked red while tornadic warning *sirens blared ten-fold* along with a cacophony of *wailing emergency vehicles* everywhere.

That windy drive to Yankton Manor was the quickest, yet longest of drives. The one-story brick building was in total darkness. On his run to the front entrance...the wind eerily subsided just as he heard it always had before the sound of the freight train. It picked up again upon entering the front door; he stopped to listen for sounds of people near the dark vacant nurse's station. Nothing.

He hurried to and into his grandfather's apartment and could see his empty bed with the covers peeled off and dangling over the side of the bed as if the old man left in a hurry. His favorite bedside pic of Ellie was gone. Just then: he heard *that demonic sound* of an approaching train and he bolted for the dining room, looking out the front door entrance he saw his car rolling toward him like a toy car. The last thing he remembered was diving under a table just inside the dining room, where he curled up and covered his head when the dining room exploded with tables and chairs and glass crashing into him.

***

Yankton Manor, as well as *most* of the high-risk tornadic town of Yankton, were spared a direct hit by one of 2 F3 *severe tornadoes* that ended up doing most of its 180-mph wind damage in the open countryside north and west of the town. JT managed to escape with bumps and bruises and a bunch of toothpicks pierced into his back and arms; one of the wooden missiles was lodged in his cheek and removed when he checked his body for possible injuries. One of the building custodians had seen toothpicks lodged in his back and removed them after JT was informed of their location.

All Yankton Manor residents escaped injury, because of the prudent early evacuation made by the staff, getting every resident down to a basement shelter an hour before JT even arrived. JT's *totaled* Camry was on its wheels and blocking the front entrance of the building. Amazingly none of the glass was shattered so JT started the engine and inched it out of the front entry area before parking it on the debris-strewn parking lot.

JT then went to the basement as *all-clear sirens* were blaring across the town. He found Eldon playing cards with other residents; his standing-framed pic of Ellie on the table, off to his side. After talking with the director, JT escorted his grandfather to his room, where Eldon could change out of his pajamas and spend a week or two at the cabin until repairs to the retirement home were completed. They were both hungry, so JT drove them in his totaled Camry to the Hy-Vee to get breakfast and coffee.

The store was swarming with customers who were thankful their community of 15,000 had zero deaths from those night devils that had stressed them for hours, causing one long night for all. Later this weekend JT would write: *"There was this palpable pioneer spirit over these God-fearing people coming into the store as my relaxed grandfather and I enjoyed a good breakfast with fresh coffee. We sat at our usual window table watching these hearty people really look at each other as they made their way in and out of the store. There were no wizen-faced rats trying to get that last stick of butter in their greasy hands; they were all happy to be*

255

here now. It was nice to experience real people being good to each other after a close call."

While finishing their breakfast at the Hy-Vee, JT asked the old man:

"I don't even know if the cabin was hit... I left so fast."

"If it was all lost...what would you miss the most?" Eldon asked.

"My journals," JT answered without hesitation.

The old man's understanding nod made JT continue:

"I met a girl when I was in Elmdale. Her name is Jenex."

"What?" Eldon hadn't ever heard such a name.

"Like Generation X...Jenex," JT repeated. "She lives in Sioux Falls and works in the kitchen of a retirement home. She moved from Minneapolis to live a slower life."

"Slow is good," Eldon smiled. "Are you going to see her again?"

"I don't think so. She said she wasn't interested in dating now. And...that's okay."

"You still going to your reunion to see Iris?"

"I don't know, Grampa. It just doesn't *feel* that important to me now."

Another positive nod from the retired farmer.

"I know I'll see *you* on that day," he pointed to the old man in his blue overalls, referring to Eldon's 100th birthday. "Do you ever think about turning a hundred?"

"Do I *what?*"

"Ever think about being a hundred years old?"

"People remind me about it so much...I don't have to," Eldon chuckled.

Then, JT asked his grandfather if he believed he'd be with Grama when he leaves this world.

"Nobody knows. We all have to die to find out," Eldon shrugged. "I choose to believe that we'll be together... At the very least, we'll be a few feet apart from each other," he laughed his silent way.

"Grampa, you know this year I've really stepped up my acceptance level."

"High acceptance brings joy," Eldon said after a sip of his hot coffee. "So, tell me...if we go back to the cabin and find that all your journals are gone with the wind...you'll have some accepting to do," the old farmer pointed and chuckled at his grandson.

It never ceased to amaze JT how this lifelong widower had lost the first love of his life just as his son Charlie had. Yet Charlie moved on and managed to find Ruthie. *"That's where I'm headed,"* JT knew, *"moving away from that Tower trait of one-time love. My dad did it. Grampa didn't want to. It's up to me to feel good about who I am right now. I want more than a picture on my bedside table. Life isn't meant to be lived alone.*

257

And yet, my grandfather is a healthy contradiction to that."

"High acceptance brings joy," JT reminded himself as he handed his grandfather his butterscotch cane. Then he watched the strong old farmer stand up by using one hand on his cane, using it for just enough balance and leverage to get to his feet with ease. Both men were having a good day.

Light of Forgiveness

Eldon stayed at the cabin with JT for 2 weeks, until all repairs were completed in the wind-damaged dining room of Yankton Manor. Today, JT returned his grandfather to his apartment in his teal-blue cargo van, a 2010 model with low mileage that left him way ahead after getting paid by his insurance company for his totaled car. He helped his grandfather put away his just-laundered clothes and returned Grama Tower's picture to his bedside table. Then, JT escorted Grampa Tower to the refurbished dining room, where Eldon reunited with residents at a new table in the same spot he usually dined with friends.

The last couple weeks in May were the longest stretch of time they'd spent together in the cabin. JT managed an hour of power-walking every day with long bursts of daily writing in his journal. Eldon relished his independence at the cabin; it was like being at the farm again in many ways. The last thing Eldon wanted to do was impose on his grandson's life. *"It's all good for me, Grampa. No imposition at all,"* he told the old man after Eldon dropped and broke his favorite *DEKALB* coffee cup from the farm.

***

259

JT stopped at the library to see if Coach Blodough's impending obituary was posted. Nothing. Then he called the health club in Vermillion to hear how *Coach B* was doing since his last visit to Rochester. The receptionist said he hadn't heard anything about Coach B since his last trip to the Mayo Clinic.

Instead of calling Blodough's brother in Watertown, JT drove his teal-blue van over to the Blodough trailer to check on the terminally-ill man. When he turned down the Blodough gravel drive he parked by the shed, not far from his target –because he decided he wanted it back after all. He didn't know *why* he wanted it back or what he'd do with the cumbersome relic, except he felt that Blodough might want the thing out of there. *"And, it's an excuse to stop by,"* he reasoned.

No vehicles were parked outside Blodough's manufactured house. As he walked to the front steps that led to the only door, he could see that all the curtains were drawn shut, so he knocked on the door lightly at first…then *louder* after no response. For some reason, the ex-Warrior felt anxious…like he had in football practice around his mean coach.

"Maybe he's dead in there," JT feared while turning the doorknob and opening the trailer door. He sniffed the air for that dead-body smell he'd always heard about. It smelled stuffy without ventilation.

"Coach!"

Still nothing as he then heard the faint sound of *music* coming from the back bedroom. Moving toward the bedroom he then could make out a familiar song his dad

played on their jukebox, *"Can't You See"* by The
Marshall Tucker Band.

"Coach!"

Nothing. Passing the messy kitchen, he saw pizza and
Chinese carry-out boxes on the counter surrounding a
sink filled with dirty dishes. A tall plastic garbage can
over-flowed with garbage that looked like it had been
collecting for some time. Before reaching the back
bedroom, he saw the bathroom of a dying man: the floor
covered with dirty towels; the sink dripped water as if
left on for a cat or a dying man too weak to close the
valve.

"Coach!" he barked before poking his head into the back
bedroom, whereupon he saw a clock radio on the floor,
where Marshall Tucker played for this bare-chested
dying man facing away and lying on his side, wearing
these brown, yellow and orange Yogi Bear pajama
bottoms. JT turned off the music and talked loud to the
breathing skeleton lying on soiled sheets, "Coach, it's
John Tower!"

Blodough rolled over and spoke in this inaudible
delirious whisper, his black eyes lit with this fever of
death like a wet-black onyx that had very little whiteness
surrounding each eyeball. *"How could this be the same
Coach Blodough?"* JT thought while staring down at
this wasted man who used to intimidate him and all his
peers physically.

"Go away…leave me alone," came this raspy whisper
that spewed phlegm onto his chin.

"Coach, you *can't* stay here like this."

261

"I want to die here, in my home…not in a hospital."

Blodough turned his back to this unwanted visitor.

"This is crazy," JT whispered out loud. "I'll get you some water."

He left the bedroom in a state of panic, not knowing whether to call 911 or comply with a dying man's last request to die at home. He opened the fridge that only held a pan filled with water; the freezer was empty with no ice trays. The cupboards were bare, so he rinsed a dirty glass before dipping and filling it from the pan of water in the fridge. Back in the bedroom he elevated Blodough's hairless skull so he could drink from the glass. Then, JT noticed empty prescription bottles on the floor, obvious pain killers.

"I could call your brother."

"No!" the angry voice demanded and reached out, grabbing JT's shirt and holding on with his cold bony fingers. "What are you doing here?"

"I came by to see how you were doing. I thought I might haul away my target in my van…"

"*Take* the *damn thing*," Blodough twisted and snarled his mouth in such an ugly way.

"You want me to re-fill your prescriptions?"

"No! No more pills! Just go away, Tower. I'm not your problem."

"I'm not *leaving you here*, Coach. I'm taking you to my place… Or I'll call 911 and they can take you to a hospital."

"No! No hospital!"

JT went to the bedroom closet and found a hooded
Warrior track & field outfit, a black and orange outfit
that was easy to put on the emaciated Dowd Blodough,
who now had to weigh less than a hundred pounds.

***

JT moved his van close to the trailer steps, placed 3
couch cushions on the floor of the van's cargo area just
inside the sliding side door. He'd propped open the
trailer door with a kitchen chair before carrying the
dying Warrior chief to the waiting van.

***

When JT had parked near his cabin's front door –he
thought Blodough had died on the drive over here. But
he was still breathing. JT carried Blodough into his
bedroom and placed him on his bed, telling him he was
running a bath for him.

"Why are you doing this? Let me die," he pleaded.

"Look, Coach…you *stink*. Until you die…you don't
have to *stink up my place*."

That comment from Johnny 3 gave the grouchy coach a
coughing chuckle before he said, "Suit yourself."

JT ran a cool/tepid bath for this man burning up
inside. Even though the cabin's bathroom was equipped
with grip handles for Grampa Tower –there was no
gripping for Dowd Blodough. It was like bathing a
skeleton whose black eyes would open and close every
so often as if reminding his unwanted caregiver that he
was still alive. As JT washed the top of Blodough's bald

263

skull with a washcloth, he asked his ex-coach what happened in Rochester.

"*This* is what happened," Blodough almost forced a chuckle. "I'm a nuclear disaster on my last leg," he nearly laughed until he began coughing phlegm up that dribbled onto his skeletal chest.

"What did the doctors say this means?"

"It *means* I want you to do me a favor, Tower."

"What's that?" JT stopped washing Blodough to listen to this dying man's "favor."

"I want you to put your hand over my face and push me down into the water until I drown. I won't struggle."

"Are you serious? I'm not Doctor Kervorkian… That's not an option."

Blodough was disappointed that JT was not into a mercy killing.

"Look," Blodough paused to cough, "I can't take this pain, Tower. I showed *you mercy* in Watertown when I pulled you out at halftime. *You* quit the team…*for yourself* and *your Johnny Three Plan*. Your dad didn't want you hurt…so I took your *sorry ass* out of the game before they *killed you*."

This was a chance for JT to confess to his coach:

"I planned on quitting right after that game anyway. I wanted to *win* that game and then quit. I *was pissed* because you pulled me out… You're right. We had a plan. And it worked. One of the reasons it worked was because I wanted you to see Johnny 3 break records. I

264

hated you *that much.* And, it was all a charade... *You were part of the Johnny Three Plan all along.*"

JT drained the tub, dried off the coach while he was still in the tub; and then JT managed to get a pair of his boxers on his dying guest. The *moaning* and *groaning* from Blodough's aching body gave Johnny 3 this instant oil, just like the same impulse when he swam across the lake to meet Jenex. He carried his coach onto his bed and set up his infrared light on the bedside table, shining its red rays onto Blodough, who was flat on his back in JT's boxers and wearing JT's best sunglasses to protect the coach's eyes from looking directly into the infrared light.

JT sat on a bedroom chair, writing in his journal, stopping every fifteen minutes to move the red light around the bed, getting all of Blodough's skin and bones the maximum exposure to light that opens blood vessels, increasing circulation. This was helpful in wintertime for JT, an experiment to diminish the winter doldrums of prolonged grim grayness for weeks on end; it worked to lift JT's mood. Miguel wrote:

"Maybe it could work for Blodough. I've begun this oil and haven't told him. I'm driving Coach B to Colorado tomorrow to get some Creative for him. It will help this terminally-ill ghost manage his pain. I've heard of cancer side effects, and Creative will diminish the level of pain somewhat. He's getting red light now to help with the pain since he refuses any medication. He wants me to kill him. I won't. It's all so strange to have him here like this, so sick. The law and the repercussions of doing such a thing scare me into just wanting to make his final days or hours comfortable. It's amazing how

forgiveness began with Betsy Mueller. That's what Coach Blodough and I are going through. I think he feels that I'm already there. I hope he can make it to Colorado."

Go... Went... Gone

Dowd Blodough had never been to Colorado, or smoked weed, except for some Watertown ditch weed that gave him and his brothers headaches. JT made the teal-colored carpet of his van's cargo bed *"comfy as hell,"* the grouchy retired teacher/coach admitted after riding for 12 hours to Boulder on JT's futon with a bamboo pillow that the terminally-ill passenger said cradled his head just right.

Now: JT was coming out of the Boulder Weed Shop with a supply of Creative and a new pipe for his passenger. JT was anxious for Coach B to try Creative, believing it would change the dying man's thought patterns and diminish his physical pain and nausea. That's why Blodough agreed to go, telling *"Tower"* after the infrared light treatment in the cabin, *"I'm open...let's go!"* Dowd moaned and groaned while being dressed in his Warrior track suit for his trip to Colorado.

Unlocking the van's side door, JT wondered if his passenger had croaked while he was in the weed store. He slid open the door and was surprised to see Coach B propped up and listening to his classic country music on Blodough's iPhone; he was wearing the same track suit with his Jefferson *Hawk* baseball cap on, and still

267

wearing JT's shades ever since his infrared light treatment. Before their trip it was JT's idea to stop at Blodough's house to pick up a few things the retired coach wanted; and, JT thought it best to take out the garbage piled in the kitchen and strewn throughout the trailer.

Now: JT left the van's side door open, to let in the fresh mountain air and the majestic Rockies that were close and *"awesome"* to this dying man as he faced the eastern slope of a mountain range he'd never seen until now. *Tower* scooted over to his ill passenger, showing him the stuff he'd bought while filling the new pipe's screen with a pinch of Creative.

"It's so strange to smoke this stuff legal with the door open," JT remarked before putting the pipe close to Coach B's chapped lips and lighting it.

He watched the retired coach take in a little hit, then inhale and hold it in…with zero coughing after exhaling.

"Smooth huh?" Tower said after loading and having a bowl himself.

As they both stared out at the mountain range, its snow-capped peaks cooling the very air they were now breathing, JT was happy with this oil he'd come up with in the cabin just yesterday when he was bathing this man who he'd hated for most of his life. JT said to his old coach:

"It's strange to be smoking weed with Mr. Blodough… Or even stranger: Coach Blodough."

The track suit was so baggy on Coach B that JT couldn't tell if he was breathing or not. He could see that straight-lipped scowl of the man who Johnny 3 hated more than anyone for over half his life. And it was all staged...for the Johnny 3 Plan that worked perfectly. Now: JT could see and appreciate how this terminally-ill man had played a leading role in aiding his early retirement and the long-term economic security for his parents.

The effects of Creative on Blodough were rather immediate: he started talking, literally spitting out more words in the next five minutes than he had since their sauna meeting in the health club. In that raspy whisper:

"Tower, I have to admit I admired your first Johnny Three game when you shattered every scoring record against Watertown. I grew up around most of those people who drove down to see that game... They expected to kick your ass like they did in football. I was really impressed. Well...you were there...when the whole gym went crazy with your shooting. It was truly...amazing."

JT nodded positively, while recalling that awful August day he quit the football team his sophomore year.

"Coach, I always wondered why you put me in *bull in the ring*? That's not something you do to a QB."

"Your dad wanted you to quit. He catered lunch to my office, as well as a few choice words. Your dad was a persuasive man. He started talking about my dad. Charlie Tower knew everything. He said how he played against my dad's team when my dad coached eight-man football for Watertown. With the subtlety of a knee to the nuts he started talking about my dad's DUI and manslaughter conviction, telling me how *hard* it must've

269

been on my family after my dad was murdered in prison. I've had plenty of parents come to me wanting me to play their kid more... But *never* anyone like this Charlie Tower who wanted me to *stop* playing his kid...to make you quit...before he gets hurt..."

As he started one of his awful coughing spells, JT handed Coach B a tissue from a box he'd grabbed earlier in Blodough's place along with his water bottle, which JT retrieved off the trailer floor along with his charger and iPhone. The thirsty man emptied the bottle of water down his burning throat, causing JT to re-fill it from the 5-gallon jug strapped to the side near the back doors of the cargo van.

Already, JT could tell that he'd made the right move by bringing Blodough here. And, as Creative does:

"Coach, how 'bout we climb into the Rockies?"

Blodough almost smiled; another good sign to JT that Creative was doing some good.

***

They went to Nederland, a mountain village nearly 3,000 feet higher than Boulder's 5,430 feet above sea level. They parked in an isolated area that still had snowfall piled high in shaded places. The van's side door was open and looking out to a panoramic view of a deep canyon, a blue-black shadowed gorge that dropped to below sea level in places. The temperature was 20 degrees cooler and wind gusts rocked the van. JT could see that Coach B's breathing was more labored up here. The once-salubrious fitness freak liked the workout his lungs were getting, waving off the notion to drive back down to Boulder. Then:

"How 'bout gettin' *creative*?" Blodough asked his driver.

JT was happy to load up Coach B's new pipe and help him indulge…before helping himself. Again, Creative seemed to open this flinty flood gate of words that this dying man thought fitting to say after JT covered him with his favorite blanket, another item JT took from Blodough's house for this oil run to Colorado.

Listening to this man go on and on about anything that came to his mind, JT realized that Blodough's mind was killing the retired science teacher by giving him this final run of soft babble that was nothing more than a smokescreen for a dying man…induced by Creative. There was no point asking Coach B if he liked Creative, this green herbal anodyne that was diminishing the pain of a body on fire from cancer, from drugs, and from powerful radiation. Tower continued listening while also in his Creative-induced brain babble that was telling JT loud and clear that Dowd Blodough's life had been sick and on fire long before the young science teacher and coach came to North Woodbury High. Tower listened:

"I came to North Woodbury to escape my past in Watertown, eventually paying off that lot and *cracker box* with my teaching salaries. It's all I own in this world. I'm leaving it to my brother, Walt, all twelve thousand dollars-worth, *if that*," he raspy-chuckled. "Oh, Tower, I should tell you that Elk Point Funeral Home will handle my cremation. It's paid for. They'll scatter my ashes…wherever."

271

About this time when listening to this morose ramble, JT said they should get a motel here.

"Or in Boulder if the elevation here bothers you?"

"Here's fine," Blodough whispered.

***

JT carried his passenger into the motel room, placing the dying Warrior chief on one of the two mushy queen-size beds in the rustic Nederland Inn. Right away JT turned up the heat in the chilly room and brought in his passenger's blanket from the van before loading and assisting Coach B with another requested bowl of Creative.

Soon JT fell asleep, for he hadn't slept much since bringing Coach B to his cabin.

***

The dream JT had, was too quick to recall, and gone forever…like Dowd Blodough when JT awoke in the middle of the night in the stifling-dry room to use the bathroom while Perry Mason was on the tube. Heading back to bed, he turned down the heat and slid open one of the front windows. In the dim light of a black and white re-run –he looked over at his roommate still propped up with pillows and covered with his blanket; he could see the TV screen reflection in the brown lenses of his sunglasses. He went to the side of Coach B's bed, turned on the bedside lamp and could see no signs of breathing.

"Coach?"

272

JT sat down on the sagging mattress, removed his borrowed sunglasses and saw those dead black eyes open, confirming that his passenger was gone. JT closed the eyelids with Perry Mason his witness.

He carried Blodough's dead body into the cold cargo area of his van and covered the body totally with Blodough's blanket, leaving the a/c on, for fear of that dreaded dead-body stench from decomposition. An hour after a quick gas fill-up in Boulder, JT took his first Creative break at the Colorado Welcome Center not far from Nebraska's I-80E, a trip he'd made dozens of times.

All the way to this point and while parked at the expansive welcome center, JT stopped his busy mind by recalling some of his dad's boyish pranks. This was his mind's way of protecting itself from the reality of driving through 4 States…with a dead body; and in 3 of those States -Creative isn't legal. He locked his van, leaving the a/c running on high, his pipe filled and hidden in one of his hooded sweatshirt pockets. He felt silly, *again* forgetting that Creative is legal here while walking to a distant picnic shelter.

After a legal/discreet hit from his pipe, it wasn't long before he held the image of his dad never failing to ruin every Xmas morning by waking him in the middle of the night to show his bleary-eyed son all the gifts Santa was bringing.

"You mean things that Mom hid," young JT recalled whispering to his kid-like dad.

Somehow, the bartender always managed to make Xmas Eve ever so thrilling, pouring them each a shot of Jim

Beam with eggnog on ice with a sprinkle of nutmeg.
Then little JT would find himself in bed half-drunk and
wide awake with hours to go before morning…before
Santa. Soon…the smell of his dad's cigarette wafting-in
from his bedroom window from the north and westerly
winds that would blow hard every December. His dad
was like this excited boy after showing his son what
Santa brought Mom:

"You mean what you got Mom?"

"Yeah, wise guy. *Get to bed… And not a word about
this to your mother."*

Now: JT hustled back to his idling van, reminding
himself, *"No tickets. No speeding."* He knew he had
one long Creative drive ahead of him before reaching the
Elk Point Funeral Home, some 10 hours away he figured
from his experience on I-80. It all seemed so strange to
JT to be hauling Blodough's dead body across these
never-ending plains. There was no time to try and find
Walt Blodough's phone number in Watertown now. He
would call Blodough's brother when he got to the
funeral home.

"How did I get here?" he kept asking his mind, while
wanting to believe this was a life-changing event that
would serve him well.

He resisted calling his parents in California, not
wanting to hear any more *reasons* or *explanations* for
their Johnny 3 Plan that was still affecting his life, like
Iris and that *damn reunion* just two weeks away.

"Is this what I've been doing, clearing all the subterfuge and hidden agendas just so I can live my own life today? And now...Blodough's gone."

Bully and The Beast

"*Still no appetite*," he wrote at a Lincoln Cracker Barrel table, getting several re-fills of coffee from the friendly server, "*and my van now idles at 66 degrees inside. No smell from Blodough...yet. 170 miles to Elk Point. I'm clear about telling the funeral director I found his customer in his trailer, already dead. No sense in trying to explain this Creative run to Colorado. Like Grampa T always said, 'The Lord doesn't send the Law.' To me, that just meant that a bunch of unnecessary story is more trouble than it's worth. After my last Creative break at a rest area that included a good power walk close to the Platte River, it's strange how a dead body in your vehicle can bring back to life these repressed memories with such clarity. It shows me that something strange/wonderful is coming when I go to my reunion in just two weeks from now. My memory showed me this dance hall in North Woodbury, not long after Iris and her mother moved next door to us. A band made up of N. Woodbury high school guys played to a pretty good crowd. As I sat on this folding chair I saw my new neighbor dancing like this wild beast with this bully-asshole guy who intimidated most everybody wherever he went. I don't remember his*

*name, but I do remember how jealous and envious I was
to see that creep dancing with this sexy new neighbor of
mine. I watched them leave the dance floor after a
grinding slow song ended. It was awesome to see her
dance. I became aroused on that folding chair just
watching her. I was glad it was dark when I followed
them out of there. As I write this I realized I was
following her with this same sense of dying dread – as
when I'd followed her to Blodough's classroom. When I
followed her out of that dance hall I was in one of my
early oils, for Iris Jean Prescott was the first girl I'd
ever chased...discreetly. The last time, when we
graduated, I'd followed her to that room of science
where she killed the mystery of us with a man I hated,
the same dead man in my van. I recalled when I was
outside that dance floor I could see that bully's ego
inflated to the max; and he had that alcohol-flushed face
I'd seen a million times in the bar. I watched from a
distance as they shared a cigarette outside his car. She
saw me and waved. I waved back and walked away from
her in the wrong direction to go home. Eventually, by
the time I'd walked home I'd played that image of that
bully burying his face into her curly-brown hair and
talking to her while they slow-danced. He made her
laugh. I made her wave."*

Hard Things First

After 12 hours of hard sleep in his cabin bed, he felt re-charged and hungry after 2 days of no sleep and no eating. He wanted to shower quickly, craving a big breakfast before a much-needed power walk downtown before his drive this afternoon to North Woodbury. Yesterday, the Elk Point undertaker had removed Coach B's body out of his van before any serious decomposition left its mark. For 3 hours…JT waited at the funeral home until Walt Blodough showed up with another brother; they were pulling a large U-Haul trailer with *Dowdy*'s pickup truck, a vehicle given to Walt by his dying brother a week ago. Rather than explain Colorado and Creative to the executor, JT told Walt that he found his brother dead in his house when he stopped by to pick up his target.

JT ended up helping the brothers load some of Coach B's stuff into the U-Haul after they'd helped JT load his target into the van. When JT gave Walt Blodough his brother's blanket, water bottle and iPhone –JT was glad no questions were asked.

Later last night, leaving his van's cargo doors open all night to air it out, he wrote in his journal while relaxed in his Grampa Tower's favorite chair:

"I'm tired now. It was all so strange and comical to hear Coach B's brothers haggling over their brother's things they would distribute to the family: 'Mary gets this, Momma gets that; I want that shotgun; You ain't gettin' that shotgun 'cause Dowdy said I could have it.' Back and forth the Blodough brothers squabbled over nearly every item they carried into the trailer as I stood in the trailer to help them load. They were not mad at each other in a real angry sort of way; but rather –in brotherly combat, each brother making his point then moving on…to the next item. I couldn't see any sign of palpable grief having just lost their brother. There was no talk of fond memories they alone knew. As one brother said to the other, 'Let's get this shit loaded so we can eat.' They reminded me of ten thousand like them, prospective Johnny 3 Sandwich customers I'd talked to when working the Johnny 3 Plan…that I will never complain about again. Sure, I'd been manipulated a bit, to 'stay the course,' as my mother would often say during the early years of their retirement."

***

Recently, JT kept asking himself, *"Now what?"* After this bizarre experience with Blodough, his upcoming reunion with Iris paled in comparison to what he would do with his life now…*after* the reunion…and *where*? During his last extended visit at the cabin, Grampa T had told his grandson that he should travel, go to places he's never been. *"Go to places other than*

Colorado," the old retired farmer smiled before asking John if there was any place he'd like to see.

"Not really. I've thought about that a lot...and I can't come up with a place. Maybe that's because of that damn reunion. Besides, if I went some place new I'd be going there to see if I'd like to live there. And there's no other place I'd like to live right now."

The old man's worn face said, *suit yourself.*

***

Now: he checked his open van, smelling no sign of death in his cargo area that was now covered by his basketball target that had weathered considerably over 25 years in Blodough's shed. During his drive home from Elk Point he had a great idea about how to *unload* his target, an excuse to go back home to North Woodbury to visit two high school friends, Marty Gunderson and Mary Parrot. Mary was part of a new oil he came up with after stopping at his favorite rest area to take a Creative/bathroom/writing break. This was a time when he was so relieved that Blodough was history for him, and he felt like celebrating *"for some odd reason,"* he wrote at one of his favorite writing sanctuaries.

***

Next day at 5 p.m., JT parked his van near Tower Tavern's back door, opening the cargo area's back and side doors to air out his recent writing break. He stood looking at the old Tower trailer on this side of that familiar tree now shading the vacant space where Iris lived. And then: the green heart. He walked over to the lime-green concrete landmark, noticing how faded it looked to him. The stump of wood from his target's foundation was still sticking out of the earth in the fold of the heart, reminding him of that night those rednecks chain-sawed it into their truck…and drove off. *"Now it's back with me,"* he mused, and walked over to the bar's back door, forcing this memory of when his dad was standing by his butt can having a smoke; it was the time when Iris and Libby first moved away and his dad was aware that his son was hurting over Iris after their mysterious falling out when they graduated. Charlie was smart enough to know that Wild Iris was not the girl for his son. That's what Ruthie kept telling him.

"She's not the right girl for you, son," Charlie tried to console JT. *"What goes 'round comes 'round. She'll get hers. Trust me."*

***

Marty Gunderson, the 2nd owner of Tower Tavern, was happy to see his old high school idol, calling JT *"Three"* ever since his record-breaking first game. The Johnny 3 Sandwich was Tower Tavern's only food item they sold in his bar: (another smart move by Ruthie to include this *"food exclusivity"* in all 3 distributors' contracts). If you were hungry in any of these 3 outlets –Johnny 3 Sandwiches…that's it.

Marty followed JT outside his back door, on his way to see *"somethin' I picked up for your bar."*

JT and Marty stood outside his van's open back doors.

"How'd you get this?" Marty was flabbergasted to see this piece of Johnny 3 original memorabilia in front of him.

"Never mind. You want it?"

"Yeah! How much?"

"Take it," JT shrugged. "I'll help you unload it now."

Marty and JT carried the Johnny 3 target into the bar, leaning it against a wall near Charlie's old jukebox. Gunderson was elated about mounting this piece of local sports history next to the glass-framed Johnny 3 orange and black basketball jersey that Johnny 3 wore the night of his first big game. Charlie was the one to tell Marty to go into the locker room after the game (Ruthie's idea) and fish out the jersey in the tub of soiled uniforms, securing #3 for their plan to provide security for their son.

Even now, Marty liked to tell JT how Charlie and Ruthie were in the throes of selling the bar to Marty when Charlie said he'd throw-in his Johnny 3 jersey (hanging in the same spot) with the deal. Before good-natured Gunderson could respond, Ruthie said to him, *"But you have to keep it where it is…displayed here."*

Marty, the team's manager/towel boy had no problem leaving the jersey of his idol right there above Charlie's old jukebox, for he was *"Three's"* biggest fan when JT broke all those scoring records in one game that are untouchable after 25 years. Marty Gunderson was the perfect buyer for Charlie and Ruthie, a nice young man who loved to market the Johnny 3 Sandwich and the Tower Tavern legacy to locals who appreciated nostalgia.

Standing over the target near the jukebox, Marty was admiring something he thought he'd never see again.

282

Again...*Three* had to tell his friend he didn't want to talk about *how* or *where* he got his target. No way was he even mentioning Blodough this close to a reunion.

Soon, reunion organizer and class gossip Mary Parrot walked in the front door, greeting JT and Marty with hugs. Mary was the biggest reason JT wasn't going to mention anything about Blodough. Marty ushered his friends to a private corner booth where JT and Mary could visit without the bells and whistles of slot machines going off. JT called their class reunion organizer last night and set up this meeting to *"catch up on things,"* JT said over the phone. *"Big-mouth Mary"* was a real snoop dog on gossip, knowing more about their classmates than anyone else on the planet.

Soon Marty was behind his bar filling their order of Johnny 3 Sandwiches and frosted Mexican Cokes in beer mugs That's when JT broke the ice with Mary by recalling their homecoming date their senior year, a *painfully*-awkward experience for JT since he'd recently quit the football team at halftime during the recent season-opener at Watertown.

"You're the one that *asked me* to go to homecoming," JT corrected his old friend. "Jake was in boot camp in San Diego, so I was a safe date for you."

Mary laughed, recalling how Charlie and Ruthie always said she was like this *Phyllis Diller character telling dirty jokes all the time.* But now Mary wanted to jump in and tell their *homecoming story*:

"We were in your dad's car on our way to the homecoming dance when the oil light came on. Not that baloney *oil stuff* you talk about...the *real* oil light came

283

on and you *freaked,* had to get to a gas station *right away...*"

"Right, right, but you left out those pics your mom took of us when you wrapped your leg around me and grabbed my crotch and your mom took the pic because you said it was for Jake...that he'd think it was funny. Did Jake think it was funny?"

"Yes," Mary laughed her *big-mouth laugh* that Marty could hear above Charlie's jukebox on his way delivering their order.

"What *happened?*" Marty wanted to know as Mary slid over on the booth and JT caught Marty up to speed on their homecoming date, a story Marty hadn't heard before:

"I pulled into the Sinclair Station, checked the oil and put in a couple quarts..."

"He left *his door open!*" Mary injected. "It was *freezin'* outside and I moved over and closed his door..."

"Yeah she did! And she nearly pinched *my pecker off!*" JT laughed with Mary.

Mary explained to Marty that JT was washing the windshield and when she closed the door he had his crotch right there in the hinge of the door.

"Ouch," Marty winced.

"Marty, I'm not kidding when I say it hurt so bad...I had to go right into that filthy bathroom and check out the damages."

Mary had a good laugh: "There was *no dancing* that night."

Then JT recalled something he'd never told anyone before, and knew Mary would find it funny:

"The next morning my dad asked me why I was walking funny. I told him my pecker was sore. My dad yells out to my mom, 'See! I told you he'd *screw* that Parrot girl! Her boyfriend's in the service and…there you go…! I blame this on *you*, Baby Ruthie!' Man, did they have the biggest fight I ever heard them have."

All three friends had a good laugh and caught up on their lives without any drama, all positive talk. But Mary and Marty were interested in hearing how Charlie and Ruthie were doing. Anything new with that couple really was of interest to regulars Marty Gunderson and Mary "*Big-mouth*" Parrot.

Then: Marty had to excuse himself to attend to his bar, leaving Mary and JT alone. She was about to surprise JT like she'd done when she grabbed his crotch for the homecoming pic going to Jake, a guy that could kill most anybody if he wanted to, and known to be one of those non-jocks not to be messed with. Mary affectionately calls Jake - her husband of 24 years – "*Crazy Jake,*" an excellent Marine, and one of Baby Ruthie's biggest fans.

Mary knew what JT wanted to know right now:

"I don't know *where* Iris lives or *how* to contact her. I sent the rsvp note to her grandmother's address in Omaha. It came back with a positive reply to attend and there was only an Omaha postmark on the rsvp."

"How'd you get her grandmother's address?"

"Ruthie gave it to me when I called her about our ten-year reunion. I think she had been given the address by Libby…if I recall."

"You *always* recall, Big-mouth," he said, then laughed.

"Look JT, I know guys like you. You want to play it safe, be *all-prepared* for this possible *big rejection* from Iris…*Johnny Tower,*" Mary purposely calling him by the name his mother always called him.

"Are you saying I bought into their parental protection?"

"You *had* to. Back then, you didn't *have* to do the hard things first like the rest of us had to. You were the good son, Johnny Three. God, JT, we were *all* so jealous of you and your *dream life* while we were payin' the bills and raisin' our families. Ruthie told my mom all about how you never got over Iris. She must've been your *first,* right?" Mary laughed, wanting to hug this guy she loved like a brother.

When Marty came back to their booth he asked Mary if he should get a banner for the front of the bar, 'Class of '95 Reunion' in black and orange lettering.

"That's a great idea," Mary said. "It'll keep away your regulars so we have enough room for the attendees…"

"My customers know *all* about the reunion here. You still think two hundred will show for the reunion?"

"Pretty close."

"That's our maximum capacity," Marty warned Mary.

"Don't worry Mr. *Maximum Capacity*! Bet nobody's ever called you *that before*!" Mary face-laughed into Marty's face. "Don't worry, I'll keep a count on the name tags given out at the front door."

"What about the ones *like me* that come in the back door?"

"I've heard that about you, Johnny Three!" Mary laughed her devious way.

"I'll be behind the bar and send them over to get tagged," Marty waved it off as a trifle thing.

"Tagged or shagged, Martin?" another face laugh from Mary, a laugh that Charlie and Ruthie loved over the years whenever Mary stopped into the original Tower Tavern to unload the latest gossip on them.

***

Later that night, JT wrote in the cabin:

"I told Mary that I've done the hard things last, because I wanted to do what my parents wanted me to do. How could I not, when they'd worked so well together, putting me in their retirement plan. How can I resent them? If Blodough and I could reach that space of forgiveness like my dad and Betsy Mueller, everything else seems easy. And Boldough was all imagined rage against a guy who had been blackmailed by my parents...for my security. Mr. Blodough and Iris were in a low phase of self-esteem. It's no wonder they hooked up."

287

One Long Birthday Present

By June 10th warm late-spring weather had sprung all over Superland for 300 miles in every direction as he drove Grampa T north on I-29. It had been a busy morning for JT getting his grandpa packed for their 10-day birthday celebrations in Elmdale for Eldon and Charlie. The van's cargo bed carried Eldon's favorite chair from the farm, along with enough clothes to last them a few days beyond 6/18.

From the van's front passenger seat, Eldon was thinking about JT's resolution with Blodough during his Creative run to Colorado and the words he'd told John:

"This will be one long birthday present for you, too. Ever since Charlie and Mrs. Mueller...now you and Blodough. I predict you and Iris will have a good reunion."

"I'm not sure I want to go now. What do I say? I forgive you for Blodough and the Mexican abortion?"

"You don't have to say anything about those things...do you?"

"I guess not," JT agreed.

***

Ronna was expecting them for dinner at 6 in the Moe dining room. JT had never felt better in his life. Which meant: he'd never felt this good around Iris and all her drama. Something inside of JT was shifting. It's been subtle, this shift, ever since his Blodough past vanished with the sealed bag of ashes given to Will Blodough by the Elk Point funeral director. Back when JT was helping Coach B's brothers load their dead brother's things into the rental trailer, JT told them that their brother mentioned to him that he wanted his ashes scattered on the 50-yard-line on the Watertown football field, where they all played for their first coach, their father. Each brother nodded solemnly, since they were aware that their father's ashes were secretly scattered on the same field at night...after their father was murdered in the penitentiary.

***

Last weekend, right after JT had his last meeting with Mary Parrot, he and Grampa Tower were finishing their Hy-Vee breakfasts when JT speed-dialed his mother's cell phone number. Johnny 3 was taking over with *his plan* for 6/18 that Eldon was hearing for the first time:

"Mom, instead of you and Dad flying out here to stay at the cabin, why don't you call Ronna and see if I could drive Grampa up to Elmdale a week before the

289

eighteenth. And we all stay in Moe House. That's the best present we could give Grampa and Dad."

"You're right, Johnny. Absolutely. I'll call Ronna and get back to you. But what about your reunion with Iris?"

"I can do both."

"Call you back soon," Ruthie said from California.

JT put away his cell phone and asked the old farmer, "How does *my plan* sound?"

Eldon was visibly pleased to be going home again for another visit with his family, to God willing, reach the century mark. This time every year when close to another birthday, Eldon wondered what his life would be like if Ellie could've had some of his years. There's no balance or fairness to it. So, he let it go…and he didn't think about it again until the next birthday, after another year of out-living her. *"The missing her, never goes away,"* he told Joe Moe. *"And we don't want it to,"* old Joe fired back, referring to his wife Edna of 54 years who died from pneumonia in 2005 at the age of 85. They were married a few months after Eldon and Ellie were married.

***

Halfway to Elmdale was when Ruthie called her son to let him know that Ronna said he could use her car to pick them up at the airport instead of a rental. JT liked that idea since he knew his dad wouldn't like riding in the cargo area like Blodough did, especially since JT *told* Charlie the whole story about Blodough. Charlie thought it was *creepy* how Blodough's ashes ended up on that football field in Watertown. JT had zero desire to ever bring up Blodough's part in the Johnny 3 Plan.

***

By 6 p.m. Eldon was seated at one end of the Moe antique cherry wood dining room table with JT seated to his right. General Joe was seated at the other head of the table with Jerry and Ronna flanking him, ready to serve any need. Ronna's meatloaf dinner was a favorite dish for Joe and Eldon. The conversation moved to 'the weather' when Jerry asked Eldon about the recent tornado that damaged Yankton Manor.

"John was the only one injured," Eldon remarked. "He was there right when it hit."

JT explained to his hosts that he only had "a few cuts and bruises, that's all."

"I have my own theory about climate change," Jerry said to his guests, since Ronna and Joe had heard Jerry's *theory* before, "about once a day," Ronna sighed, adding: "Hardly a day goes by without hearing it."

Jerry went on to explain in his deliberate folksy way:

"The planet is changing because of resources we've taken from its core. It's going to force us to change…for the better. We will all *have* to get along as one tribe on *one* planet…or we don't survive."

"I can believe that," JT agreed with his friendly host. "We *have* changed the weather."

"Not only *changed* it…we've accelerated it," Jerry said.

***

Later that night, after Grampa T was asleep in his comfortable guest room, JT wrote at the cottage table, *"This visit will be one long birthday present for Grampa and my dad. This gathering was my idea, my plan, and I'm glad I'm here. In Yankton, I kept wanting to drive down to Omaha to find out if Iris is there or wherever. First, I was going to stop into the C.B. Casino to see if anyone knew where Libby was living. But now, up here in Elmdale, I don't have the mind garbage. My ego can take a few awkward moments at the reunion when I see Iris Jean again...cold. I realize she helped me become Johnny 3 as much as anyone did; and I was fortunate to live off that reputation. It's good for all of us here, especially Grampa. He and Joe enjoy each other's company. It's good to see."*

***

On the 14th JT picked up his happy parents at the airport in Sioux Falls in Ronna's car. Right off, Ruthie and Charlie wanted to know *all about* the Blodough experience. JT was ready for them, refusing to say a word about anything related to the Johnny 3 Plan, including his recovered target and the blackmail payments that controlled his playing time.

"Nothing good can come from bringing up the dead past crap," Johnny 3 reasoned.

Then, when Charlie asked his son if Blodough talked about his Watertown family, JT just said, "Not much."

During their pleasant drive to Elmdale, Ruthie asked her son from Ronna's back seat if he talked about Iris with Blodough.

"No, he was too ill to have any conversation about that."

"That's awful," Ruthie said. "He's still a young man...and to be so ill..."

For some reason, JT thought he'd test his parents by telling them he believed Blodough's life was pretty much ruined in Watertown. But there was no response from his parents, no queries at all, convincing JT that his parents didn't want to talk about the dead past either.

***

Later that evening after a grand reunion in Moe House, JT wrote from the cottage desk while evening showers came down in a steady stream of noise he managed to ignore.

"We're all here now. I could see them all so happy to be together for this Tower holiday that everyone in Elmdale knew – 'all 63 of them' – so says Jerry. My parents look great; I can tell they love their life in Julian. I'm so happy for them, these people who provided me with early retirement. I'm getting a haircut tomorrow since I plan on going to my class reunion. The weather is pleasant here."

***

Next morning, at the Moe breakfast table in the summer house attached to the kitchen, Ruthie served Grampa Tower coffee in a new *DEKALB* coffee cup, replacing his old cup he broke at the cabin. Eldon was elated to get the cup, for that was his seed company for most of his life.

293

"It's just a little birthday gift *early*," Ruthie kissed Eldon's bald head.

That's when old Joe had to say from the other end of the table, "At his age...*early* is good."

***

On the early evening of the 16th JT and Charlie walked up Moe Road to the old Tower farmhouse where Charlie was raised. Jerry gave Charlie a key to the front door of the long-empty house where Charlie was raised.

Upon entering the old house, Charlie could smell the linseed oil his father always used on the pine floors. Charlie walked into the bare kitchen, where he noticed the worn markings of the four legs from their table-for-two that stood there for as long as he could remember. As Charlie opened and closed cupboards, JT stayed in the front room watching his dad. Charlie moved to the kitchen window and talked while looking out at the green rows of corn.

"Just being here with Grampa is the best present I could have. I'm glad you came up with this plan," Charlie said without moving his gaze. "One time I asked him why he stayed here all these years after my mother died. He said she loved it here. That's all he said. And I think that's a big part of why these people live to be so old. They stay connected to the spirit of the people they love. I never saw that in other places like it is here."

***

Later that night, JT wrote about their visit to the Tower farm:

*"I watched my dad go into his old bedroom, walk to the
window and open it. He was breathing in the June air
and joking about his 'no play list' on the bar jukebox.
He told me he remembered another song on his list:
"For the Good Times" by Ray Price. Then he told me
about how he used to open this window to let Karen in
when his dad was sleeping. Then he closed the window
and turned to me, and said in this real and passionate
way that I've got to go to the reunion and tell Iris
everything I can...get it out...and leave in love, leaving
nothing left unsaid. I could only nod that I would...and
now I'm afraid again...afraid of that girl's ability to
reach me and hold my attention for a lifetime...like
Grama had done for Grampa."*

***

On the afternoon of the 16th JT covered his recent
haircut with a baseball cap and walked from the cottage
to the lakeside rocks where he met Jenex. He wanted to
have his *last* bowl of Creative before the reunion.

Across the lake, through his blue-lensed shades he
could see that Betsy and Karen's pink house was history.
The roof and framework of the new 4-plex were up amid
sounds of hammering and electric sawing that drowned
the soft waves lapping against the rocks. He turned his
back to northern wind gusts and 2 boys fishing off the
bank across the lake and north of the construction site.
One good hit of Creative changed his direction of
thought to how good it would be to see Iris Jean
Prescott. He wondered if she still smoked weed and
whether she was married or in a relationship. Possible
images of their reunion flashed across his mind, visions
of dancing slow together under the train trestle followed

by a hand-holding walk to the river, to the same spot Karen sent Charlie, a place where lives would cross paths.

Now: it was time for an oil, something to swerve his safe, comfortable ride of conformity into the lane of the unbeaten path, where every man alive today must go…before it's all gone. Science can't save every man. Disease can leave him alone in a *cracker box* in Elk Point, where a man named Dowd Blodough held onto his past like any boy facing death, afraid to let go of his young life that was just getting started, a life so hard to figure out.

What Have I Done?

" *June 17th, 2020, in Elmdale. Creative is a smokescreen for things I don't like. So, I can't smoke tomorrow –unless Iris does. Tomorrow's the big day. Ronna's having a birthday brunch for Grampa and my dad so that I can be there for Ronna's famous double-layered chocolate cake and a double-candle blowout for the two birthday boys.* "

***

By late afternoon on the 17th JT again had walked up then down Tower Hill to the lakeside rocks where *again* he got Creative for *the last time* before the reunion. Then: impulsively he called Jenex. He was surprised she answered her phone and sounded friendly and glad he called. Before he could think - during his Creative stupor - he'd asked Jenex if she wanted to go with him to his reunion tomorrow.

"I'd *love* to," she said. "I went to my twenty-year reunion and had a *blast*."

JT asked if he could pick her up at a coffeehouse that was familiar to him instead of the complicated directions to her apartment she tried to give him. After his impromptu call, he said out loud, "What have I done?" and stared absently at the old Mueller lot across the lake. It was clear that bringing Jenex to his reunion was for his ego, to protect himself from Iris. Later he wrote:

"I wanted Jenex as a buffer, like a sister going along to help out her brother. And I think Jenex feels that way about us, like it's some sibling friendship. I would almost welcome Iris being in a happy relationship rather than being single and free and open to trying us again after 25 years. Only a real coward brings a relative stranger to a reunion. What have I done? I blame it on Creative...and the total fool I am."

***

After dinner, JT wanted some advice from his dad; he knew what his dad would say after he told him about his Creative/impulsive call to Jenex. Charlie's advice was predictable:

"Call her *now* and cancel. Tell her that one of your classmates you haven't seen in twenty-five years...called you...and wants a *private* meeting with you...*before* the reunion."

JT was impressed by Coach Charlie's astute advice. Charlie Tower, the career storyteller went on:

"Then you can tell Jenex the truth...that Iris Prescott was a very good friend who helped motivate you in some powerful way during the early days of the Johnny Three Plan. You can say this was a big part of your security that allowed you to retire young. You can tell this Jenex that you have to be alone with this Iris with no distractions."

Within 10 minutes JT had erased his date with Jenex, telling her almost word-for-word what his father suggested he tell her: the truth.

Charlie was thrilled about his son's quick action, saying, "Funny how most problems are handled with words…traveling at the speed of sound. And *that* was one mature phone call you just made."

"Thanks," JT shrugged. "And no more smoking that dope until *after* I've seen Iris."

"I think that's a smart idea," Charlie agreed on his last day to be 69.

Tower Holiday

Birthday bread with coffee was a meal by itself when Ronna served her thick Dutch rye bread right out of the oven to her guests, her family, the only two families on earth – the Moes and the Towers – who could truly appreciate this Tower holiday. Ronna's homemade jams and butter spread over thick slices of warm rye bread was a big hit with all assembled for this special day in Elmdale.

A bit later, Charlie drove his dad in Ronna's car the short distance to the little church across Moe Road. JT followed them on foot while Ruthie and Ronna prepared for the birthday brunch. JT arrived in time to see the old farmer in faded-blue overalls make his way with his butterscotch cane to his wife's grave beside the small church cemetery. At Ellie's grave, Charlie and JT flanked the old man. All three generations of Tower men were surprised to see that Eldon's flat unmarked grave marker beside his wife was now inscribed (except for the date of death).

"Who did your marker, Dad?"

Eldon kept looking at his future resting place and said, "Joe had it done. Last time I was here I told him I couldn't remember if I paid for my engraving," Eldon chuckled at his best friend's thoughtful gesture.

Then: as 3 generations of Tower men stood looking down at Ellie's grave, the Tower custom for 6/18 was for each generation to say something to Ellie's Spirit or to recount a memory of her in Eldon's case. Eldon went first, after JT asked him if there was anything he wanted to say now to Grama Tower. They waited for this man who today had lived a hundred years of days and nights, most of them on this land, and most of them without his beloved wife. Finally:

"I'm a hundred today, Ellie. How 'bout that? For seventy of those years I've been right here on this very day... I thought about what I would say today...if I ever lived this long... And I got nothin'," Eldon chuckled with Charlie and JT.

Then it was Charlie's turn; with this palpable look of joy on his face he looked down to his mother's grave as he talked to her Spirit:

"Mother, I'm here to tell you on our birthdays...we are healthy and happy to be together. I was thinking on the way over here what I would say. Or what I would *wish* for on my birthday... I wish you could've met my wife, Ruthie, and your only grandchild, John Eldon. Thank you for giving me life on this day, Mother."

Now it was JT's turn. To Grama Tower's Spirit:

"A long life of missing someone like Grampa has missed you...*must have* the oil you told Grampa about. Grama, the oil you passed on to Grampa has been your greatest gift you left with us. We've all used it. It's given me a better-feeling story to live in. Oh! And thanks for bringing my dad into this world on this date seventy years ago. He's a good man. He and my mother gave me an important kind of security that I appreciate more and more every day. That was their plan."

Charlie appreciated his son's words and gave JT a big hug.

"Dad," Charlie said, "let's get you back to the house so JT can get ready for his reunion."

Eldon planted his cane in front of him, his big hands covering the worn butterscotch handle. They watched the old man dip the bill of his cap below the morning sun and stare down at the shaded blue violets Ronna had scattered randomly around Ellie's grave over the years.

"John, I have a birthday wish. I want *you* to go to your reunion…in the spirit of love…without expectations."

Love and No Expectations

No music. No thinking. Grampa Tower's *birthday wish* made the 3-hour drive from Elmdale to Tower Tavern a quiet drive for JT. Whenever a fearful thought about seeing Iris voiced itself between his ears, *"Love and no expectations,"* was JT's reply. This was his *oil* on this special day. Not an easy thing to do, unless you do it for someone else, someone you love. Anytime one of those negative thoughts or images came to mind, *"Love and no expectations"* made it vanish. In his Creative-free birthday wish zone he could imagine his grandfather working alone in the field all day, seeing Ellie's garden growing day after day, seasons coming and going without her. The retired farmer said he'd learned to control his mind on a tractor, and when doing chores over 60 years, some ten thousand days and nights…of missing her.

JT stopped at his favorite rest area to write…as planned.

"And now I'm here…on my way to seeing Iris after twenty-five years. Getting at least a chance to truly see

her this time. Something Grampa and my dad never will have for the rest of their lives. And don't I know how they feel...if only because I'm a Tower. When I drove past Watertown there were no thoughts about Coach Blodough or the ass-kicking trampling delivered by those brutish Buffalo. That game, I was beaten down into snot and dust; then behind me was Iris Jean looking down at Johnny Blue Eye. She knew about Karen then. Now I understand that look in her green eyes was Wild Iris, the girl who would forever decide on her terms what boy or man would hurt her. And now I know exactly what my dad had told her about Karen when they drove to the game. Now: in those dim jade-green eyes of hers I can see that secret about Karen my dad made her keep from me. My dad was using Iris to protect me from myself. From there on —my life was planned, all laid out for me. Not so with Iris Jean Prescott. She had her life to herself, something I admired and was attracted to. That's just one of the good things I want to tell her at the reunion."

***

Johnny 3 parked his van behind Tower Tavern. He didn't want to go inside the bar now, feeling weird about being one of the early arrivals. Now he was resisting the urge for Creative after changing his shirt in the back of the van. Before closing the side door —he had this flash of an image of the dying Coach Blodough right there on his cargo bed that time the dying man was so mesmerized and stoned in Nederland and taking in the majestic Rockies for the first time. Then, another image: of Johnny 3 dodging last New Year's Eve here, "*a no-show. Maybe she won't show. Love and no expectations,*" he reminded himself.

After closing the van's side door and locking it, he turned to look at his green heart, more faded than ever. He walked around to the front of the bar and saw Marty's banner covering the Johnny 3 Sandwich banner in orange and black letters with white background: 'Class of '95 Reunion.' He crossed the road on his way to her secret spot, a chance to kill time and this thrilling romantic notion of his (with no expectations) that he would find her there under the dark trestle with a burning candle on the ledge…waiting for him…at that private place where they would smoke and have sex and talk about her fear of not graduating.

Summer weeds and prairie grass were high. JT had outgrown his allergic reaction to pollen, just as he had outgrown his dead past. In the shadows of her secret place, he could now see scattered empty beer cans and cigarette butts near the concrete ledge, a sign that others come here to get away from the world. He stepped back out from under the trestle to look across the road, whereupon he could see vehicles arriving in dust clouds when turning onto the bar's front parking area. Then: he looked to his right at the building of the old casino where Libby used to work, a place that had changed hands several times since Libby and Iris moved away. He wondered if Libby would be with her today, then dismissed that notion when his mind kept leading him to some Mexican clinic.

"Love and no expectations," he said to himself while on the narrow path that led down to the river, to the place Karen's body was found. Across the narrow Big Sioux River, on the Iowa side, he could see a grizzled old codger fishing from the bank, sitting on a portable canvas chair beside a beaten up black and gold Hawkeye

beer cooler. The man waved with his beer hand. JT waved back and headed up the bank that led to the bridge; now he wanted to go up to the middle of the bridge where his father stood looking down at the very place on the South Dakota bank where Karen's body was found. He could imagine his father standing on the bridge and so willing for something good to happen to him. Baby Ruthie was proof to Charlie Tower that Karen wanted him to make his home in North Woodbury, a sign that all his grief and guilt about losing Karen would turn into purpose.

From the middle of the bridge he saw the Iowa side of the river's bank and wondered if he'd even be here today if Karen's body had washed up on the that side of the river. *"Would my dad have even met my mother?"*

He felt he was in-step with Grampa Tower's birthday wish, open to anything, and with no desire for Creative. He moved his eyes back to the South Dakota side of the river and recalled his father telling him after his 2nd meeting with Betsy about the first time he met Ruthie in the bar:

"I wasn't consciously moving my body when I walked into the joint," Charlie recalled. *"When I first laid eyes on your mother...I was feelin'* no pain. *Alcohol was the drug of my choice. Then I saw her walking toward me. Instantly —even though I did think she might own the joint..."* Charlie winked his brown eye like he always did. *"...I wanted to believe that Karen brought me to this woman. I had this burst of thrilling energy come over me. Of course, your mother let me know that night in her little trailer that she felt the same way about me,"* another wink.

306

Still on the bridge: he could see Tower Tavern's parking area getting busy with arriving vehicles as he started his walk around to the backside of the bar, his smile still there from his father's words about his mother.

Soon, to his left, he saw the old Tower trailer and his green heart. Now he was feeling good about spending time with old classmates, many who stayed to live their lives in Superland and supported him by consuming Johnny 3 Sandwiches long after his failure at the free-throw line. They too helped him retire young. *"It's time to be grateful."* And he was, stepping toward the back door of the bar he was open and receptive to whatever comes, thanks to Grampa Tower.

Fooled...Again

Marty Gunderson's Tower Tavern was as busy as any weekend JT had ever seen here, as The Eagles played "Take It Easy" from Charlie's old jukebox that Marty stocked specifically for this reunion. Marty spotted *"Three"* right away from behind the bar. Before JT could stop him, Marty *called out* to one of his employees delivering drinks: "G-nine!" Marty did this every New Year's Eve. JT forgot to tell his friend that it was *unwanted attention*, and that's why he was a no-show to bring in the new year.

Awkward face-to-face nametag encounters were at every turn as reunited classmates talked in one *noisy clatter* of rapt attention and joyous laughter. They were in standing groups of men or women from out-of-town that mixed with local couples and friends that came together. Mary Parrot saw JT from her front-door table where she was handing out nametags and making sure everyone *"printed their name and signed the register."* Mary had seen JT looking over at her and smiled when he started making his way over to her. She was in the mood to fool around with JT about Iris. Mary was a funny/mean person who laughed loudest at *her jokes*.

"There he is!" Mary's loud mouth seemed to be heard above the din just when The Eagles' song ended and there was that gap of *silence* between songs.

JT looked down at the smirking reunion organizer after he signed the register as she printed *John Tower* on his nametag with a black magic marker that he stuck to his shirt after she'd told him to *turn around* and stuck his nametag to one of his butt cheeks, causing her to *laugh so loud* it had to get everyone's attention.

"Well...?" JT finally asked as if Mary was withholding information about Iris.

"Well what?" she could hardly keep from laughing.

"Is she here?"

"Who?" Mary loved this kind of banter.

Just then: along with Mary's negative nod about Iris not showing yet —Marty was staging on all 7 flat screens for the Class of '95 the Johnny 3 video Ruthie and Charlie made of JT's record-shattering first game, dubbed to the R.E.M. song "Losing My Religion," edited painstakingly by Marty for this occasion as the bartender stood on a chair in the middle of the room leading the *chorus of regulars* to insert the lyrics when a shot was made by Johnny 3 from the corner: "Johnny Three from the corner!" Now the entire gathering focused on the brilliant/dying star of their class they all knew as Johnny 3, one of their own who had brought attention to their school. At first: JT wanted to wring Marty's neck for doing this and told Mary above the song, "*This,* is why I didn't show last New Year's Eve." Mary then motioned for JT to follow her over to their corner table that Marty reserved for them by putting a barstool on top of the table, a table-reservation technique Gunderson picked up from Charlie. Then: another *chorus* of *Johnny Three in the corner!* found JT singing along and even watching some of his 3-pointers made in his big game as teammates in the bar cheered shots made until...the recent edited version of Marty's video now shows a barrage of terribly-missed free-throws to the lyrics *"That was just a dream,"* which JT laughed at with his teammates and other classmates until the video mercifully ended for JT.

Then: when Marty stood near JT at the corner table and barked to the room, "One more time!" That's when JT got up and wrapped his arms around Marty, taking away his remote control to keep him from playing the video again.

Then began a steady stream of male classmates over to JT and Mary's corner booth as Eddie Rabbit sang "Drivin' My Life Away," one of Coach Blodough's songs he played on their drive to Colorado, causing JT to look across the room at his framed *Johnny 3* basketball jersey beside his target above the jukebox, where a group of classmates stood looking up at two of Marty's most prized possessions that he'd recently insured for ten thousand dollars on his insurance policy.

Next came one of Charlie's songs on his *no-play list,* "For the Good Times" by Ray Price. JT watched the happy couple slow-dance on the small dance floor in front of the jukebox, causing JT's eyes to move to the green felt of the pool table, one of the makeshift stoner places he and Iris had "used" on cleaning day one Sunday in May when the bar was closed. JT was certain

310

that either that pool table or the ledge under the train trestle was where she got pregnant.

After a couple hours, JT had pretty much mingled with everybody...but Iris. *"Where is she?"* his mind would ask, then he'd catch himself furtively looking around the bar for her. He'd consumed two Johnny 3 Sandwiches and a couple Mexican Cokes, all the while casting off doubts and self-recrimination for the last 6 months of living in oil...*for this. "All that for a no-show,"* his cynical mind kept telling him while he resisted the urge to go to his van and get Creative about her not showing. Just like last New Year's Eve, his mind was telling him to *"get out of here."* Over and over he brought up Grampa Tower's birthday wish...until the battle to resist Creative was lost...when football teammate and local stoner Andy Reese asked JT if he wanted to *go out back and have a bowl.*

"I better not," JT declined with a grimace.

"Whatever happened to Wild Iris?" Andy asked JT.

JT shrugged and said he didn't know.

"Mary said Iris is on the list," Andy said.

Again, JT played it with a shrug, telling Andy he hasn't seen Iris since she moved away with her mother. JT felt sorry for himself now. Here, in his father's old bar, he couldn't help from smiling at his dad's words the bartender often said when someone was down: *"You look about as sorry as a whippoorwill."*

"We never stayed in touch," JT said to easy-going Andy.

"She's one I'd like to see here. Those are the ones that change the most," Andy said before finishing a beer.

Miguel the writer wanted to know what he meant and asked him, "How's that?"

"You know…all wild and crazy in high school… Then they get religious, settle down and have a family. The freakin' total opposite of the way they were… You know what I mean?"

"Yeah…I do," JT nodded that he understood. Then JT told his friend that he has some good reefer.

"Is that…that Creative stuff you smoke?"

"Yeah. Why?"

"Last time I tried that Creative crap…I went home and wrote my ex a letter… Told her *all* the good things about us that I could remember… And I even asked her to be my friend on Facef..k."

"What happened?"

"I never mailed it. The next day I read it and thought, *What's this crap*? Then I tossed it."

***

A bit later, Andy was in JT's van, in the back, so they wouldn't be seen by people coming and going during smoke breaks; they were using Andy's vaporizer with their own stash. JT had just told Andy about finding Coach Blodough's dead body in Blodough's trailer and using his van to deliver the dead body to the funeral home in Elk Point.

"You are shittin' me, Tower?"

"No! I'm *telling you*, Reese, Blodough had *cancer* and I found him in his trailer *dead*."

"Is this comin' from that Creative crap you're smokin'?"

"No! I swear on Blodough's dead body..."

"That's so *freakin' weird*, Tower... I mean, Jesus..."

"Why didn't you just call an ambulance?" Andy was sniffing the interior for any sign of Blodough's dead body.

"I don't know. I just wrapped him in a sheet and slid him across the floor to the door and tossed him into the van. Hell, he didn't weigh a hundred pounds if *that*."

"Coach B was always in good-shape. Hell, he was young too. He must've been in his mid-twenties our senior year."

"Yeah."

After they each took a vaporized hit from their stash, Andy changed the subject:

"You and Wild Iris were pretty hot and heavy at the end of our senior year."

"Yeah."

"What happened between you two? I remember you were *always* together..."

"That's when she moved back to Omaha with her mom... We just didn't stay in touch."

313

"I wonder what she looks like today, JT. I'll bet she's *still hot.*"

"Maybe," JT changed the subject by pointing to his van's front windshield to a black Lexus with tinted glass all-around. It was parked on the space where the Prescott Airstream used to be parked. "Who is that?" he asked Andy.

"Where?"

"That Lexus parked by my old trailer on the other side of the tree."

"I don't know... All I know is I have to take a piss," Andy started to get up.

JT opened the van's side door and Andy left in a hurry. After putting on his blue-tinted shades, JT locked his van and walked over to the Lexus and saw that the license plates were from *Mexico.* Just then: he heard the beginning of Chris Rea's "Fool (If You Think It's Over)" coming from his dad's old jukebox, the same song he and Iris slow-danced to at their pretend prom at her secret place under the train trestle.

"She's here," he said out loud and walked toward the bar's back door in a dry-mouthed Creative stupor.

***

She'd walked across the road and through the casino parking lot to the train trestle. Near the shaded concrete ledge, she smoked a bowl of her Mexican weed to calm her anxiousness about seeing Johnny Blue Eye. There was so much she had to say to him; and now she needed to change her busy thoughts about what was coming.

This was her oil, for like JT, she had no intention of smoking before seeing him. Meanwhile:

***

JT had entered the bar looking for Iris and didn't see Iris or anyone near the jukebox who might resemble her. He scanned the bar for anyone who could be Iris and made his way over to Mary's vacant sign-in table at the front door. There it was: *Iris Prescott,* the last name printed and signed in Mary's reunion register. More scouring the bar for her; and he didn't see Mary or Marty either…until they both walked in the front door together after looking for him outside.

"*Where* have you *been*?" Mary looked exasperated.

"We've been looking all over for you, man. Guess who's here…and looks *as good as ever?"* Marty injected.

"Where is she?" JT asked above the song *he thought* Iris must've played.

"She said to tell you she's going for a walk and she'd be right back," Mary said as JT was out the front door.

He ran across the street through the casino parking lot, and could still hear Chris singing from the jukebox as Mary and Marty watched JT from the bar's open front door.

He ran all the way to the train trestle…and no Iris. Catching his breath, he made his way down the path that led to the river, all the while thinking about how Mary and Marty had fooled him, because how would Iris play that same song and even know it was on the jukebox at

315

all –*if Marty hadn't stocked it for her*. He headed down the path that led to the river, still catching his breath as he walked. When the riverbank came into view: no Iris. *Love and no expectations* came to his busy mind, stopping a collage of things he wanted to ask her. Just then: a woman's voice shouted from above: "Johnny Blue Eye?" He looked up and saw that same skinny girl with the brown curly hair, wearing sunglasses, smiling down at him from the middle of the bridge while leaning on the guardrail and laughing in that familiar, beautifully-loud laugh of stoned nervousness. He hurried up the embankment alongside the bridge and saw her walking toward him, each of them concealing their stoned eyes.

The closer he got, the more he could see how Iris hadn't aged in 25 years. JT removed his sunglasses before reaching her on the pedestrian walkway. He could sense that she was nervous.

"Iris?" he said.

She removed her sunglasses, and at that very moment she saw with absolute clarity that *he didn't know* he had a *daughter* until this very instant upon seeing her Tower left brown eye and the dominant blue right eye. Her mother always told her that he didn't know about her…and his stunned reaction proved that. Seeing the eyes of her father, this Johnny Blue Eye she'd heard so much about…she said:

"I'm Page…your daughter."

"Love and no expectations," he mumbled inaudibly and then she heard, "Page?"

His smile and open arms made her fall into his chest, both laughing in tears of joy as Marty and Mary had obviously staged this part of their reunion on the bridge, for he could hear Chris begin singing for the 3rd time from the bar's open doorway, the *volume* as high as possible. And when they turned west into the late afternoon sun that caused them to put on their shades again, they could see Mary and Marty waving to them from the bar's front door. Walking while holding hands, they talked:

"Whose idea was it to play that song?" JT asked.

"That was my mom's idea. My mom called Mary when my great-grandmother forwarded the reunion letter to my mom in Ensenada. We've been planning this for six months."

"I can't believe it."

"No, it's true!"

"No… I *can't believe* Mary could keep a secret this long."

Mary had played Chris's song 3 times for Johnny 3 on Charlie's old jukebox. The music got louder on their walk back to Tower Tavern. Page knew her parents had slow-danced to that song around the time she was conceived. And then she told JT that when Iris and Libby were on their way to that Mexican clinic to get an abortion, *this song* was playing in the clinic waiting room.

"That was a sign to my mom to keep me," Page smiled.

"I'm glad she did," JT smiled at his daughter before Mary, Marty and Chris welcomed them back to the Class of '95 reunion.

One More Reunion

B ack in Tower Tavern, Johnny 3 introduced his *"daughter"* to every classmate he could (without explaining that this was also *their 25-year reunion*). Every single person who met JT's beautiful daughter could see the Tower genetics right away in her eyes. Anyone who remembered Iris Prescott didn't ask who her mother was. They could see that Wild Iris and JT made a beautiful daughter.

Page knew *all about* Johnny 3 and the Johnny 3 Plan, so she had to get a closer look at *the target* Marty had cleaned and painted and attached a new fluorescent golf ball (the target) to the refurbished oddity that made her father a sports legend around here. Host Marty set Page up with a Johnny 3 Sandwich and played his edited Johnny 3 video of the famous record-breaking game to the in-sync music of R.E.M.'s "Losing My Religion," which fascinated Page, especially when the chorus of regulars led by Marty sang out their lyrics: "Johnny Three in the corner... Johnny Three in the spot...light..." (footage Charlie took of JT shooting his 3s at night on the heart-shaped patio). The missed free-throw footage, then Johnny 3 riding the bench as the song ended was applauded by Page, to Marty and JT's delight.

At the same corner booth, JT and Mary listened to Page as she talked about her early life when she was 10 and still living in Mexico; that's when she became curious about her biological father and his family. She said how her step-dad (*American*) Eduardo "Eddie" Feliz was a handsome local man who adored both Iris and Page, and that her mother married Eddie a month before she was born in San Diego. Soon the newlyweds opened their coffeehouse with the money Ruthie sent Iris for the abortion.

"When *is* your birthday?" JT was curious.

"February eighth," Page smiled.

JT wanted to know more about their life in Ensenada, yet figured if they left the reunion now, "we can be in Elmdale before Grampa Tower goes to bed."

"Oh, my God, yes! Let's go," Page stood up and hugged Mary then Marty goodbye before father and daughter were out the back door after Page took several pics on her phone.

On her walk to her mother's Lexus, Page stopped to look at the green heart-shaped patio, now covered with summer patio furniture and toys. She went over to the heart and took a pic with her phone. JT got behind the wheel of his van and waited for her to follow him in her Lexus, all the while impressed by the fact that she knew about the double birthdays today and the history behind them.

Once on I-29N, as planned, JT called Page on her hands-free speaker phone; that's when she told him that she had a letter for him from her mother. They kept talking about *everything* until reaching his favorite rest area exit, whereupon JT told Page he'd like to stop and read the letter from Iris now.

***

He sat on top of an isolated rest area picnic table reading the letter from Iris as Page was in the restroom. When JT opened the sealed envelope, he saw a cashier's check for ten thousand U.S. dollars made out to *Ruthie Tower*. He unfolded and read Iris's hand-written letter:

"Dear JT, by now you've met your beautiful daughter. In your state of shock, you deserve some answers from me. I couldn't abort the baby and kept the money your mother sent me and opened a coffeehouse with my husband in Ensenada, Mexico. I feared your family would take Page away from me, so I kept her to myself. My selfish fear of losing her, kept her from you, and I'm sorry. My mother and I suffered with great guilt; not only from withholding Page from you –but Charlie and Ruthie too, because they were so good to us. Your mother's money was sent with love and good intentions while we withheld Page from you for selfish reasons.

My husband is an American raised in Ensenada. Both he and Page were born in San Diego. His name is Eduardo "Eddie" Feliz, a good man and husband; and he's been a good step-dad and role model for Page. We all work in the coffeehouse and must thank Ruthie and Charlie for their business savvy. My mother and I know that we opened our doors with Ruthie and Charlie's #1 rule for business: 'Know every customer's name as if

321

they're family –because they are.' Ruthie's cashier's
check with interest is long overdue. When Page was in
junior high my mother and I had told her everything we
know about you and your wonderful family. When my
Granny Prescott in Omaha forwarded the reunion letter
from Mary Parrot we all started preparing for this day
that I know falls on your Tower holiday of 6/18.
Something tells me Mary picked this day for the reunion
for all of us; and Page: right away she believed it was
the perfect time to meet her biological father.

I also want to apologize for our Graduation Day, and
hope you have been able to forgive me for that awful
way I ended our relationship. As far as your forgiveness
of me for keeping Page from you all these years –I'll
have to trust that in time you will. Enjoy your beautiful
daughter, who I named Page…in honor of your writing.
Love, Iris and Libby."

He folded the letter and returned it into the envelope
with the cashier's check; he could see Page leaning
against the front grill of her mother's Lexus. He thought
about what a perfect 6/18 it's been, and how these last
six months of his life have come to be one better-feeling
story. He knew the instant he saw her Tower eyes on the
bridge…there was no sense in looking back. He had
trained his mind with oils to stay in the moment…with
or without Creative…with or without his parents. Gone
was that *false hate* for Blodough, the man who took the
mystery out of the girl he could never rescue. It was so
clear to him that *without Karen…none of us are
here…and…all of us are related.*

***

322

They talked on the phone about their lives most of the way to Elmdale. Crossing the bridge at Big Stone City over to Ortonville at 8 p.m. JT had a plan of surprise in-mind by the time their vehicles parked by the back door of Moe's General Store. Page was impressed with the *rustic charm* of the place her mother had talked about as she hopped up and onto the van's front passenger seat and JT drove them up to Moe House, parking near the cottage door. Before JT could say anything: Charlie and Ruthie opened the back-porch door and headed for the van. When the four of them approached each other, of his gape-jawed parents it was Charlie who spotted the Tower eyes and thought *this is my granddaughter*. But Ruthie thought it was Iris for a bit longer than Charlie had, and her reaction made everybody laugh and embrace into this joyous chatter that soon brought Ronna and Jerry outside to investigate this happy and loving reunion.

The Moe House was soon filled with joyous sounds coming from the parlor, where General Joe and Grampa Tower sat in their favorite chairs. Page made sure she connected with Eldon and Charlie, asking them a hundred questions about their lives. Page knew about *the hailstones* and Karen Mueller, telling her biological father more than once that he should write a book about this. But JT wanted to hear about her life in Mexico. She told her captivated audience that she's always worked in the family-run coffeehouse/bakery. When Charlie asked his granddaughter, "What's the name of your coffeehouse?"; Page looked at her grandmother and said, "Baby Ruthie."

Ruthie was touched. That reminded JT to give his mom her cashier's check and the letter from Iris.

The first hour of 6/19 was gone and JT had just finished writing in his journal about *"the happiest day of my family's life."* He shut off the cottage desk lamp and stood at the cottage front window in the dark, looking out at the darkened windows of the guest room, where his daughter was asleep by now. He was going over in his mind about the letter he'd just written to Iris and would have Page deliver to her mother as he stared absently at Moe House:

"Dear Iris, I was thinking about those nights in my room in high school when I'd hear you crying about your life. Sometimes I would cry with you. And sometimes I wanted to go to you...and hold you...telling you a thousand times how one day your life will be so much better...better than both of us can imagine now. And now it's here, Iris, for both of us. All those fist-pounding nights of wanting a better life are behind us. Proof of this: I witnessed when I saw Grampa Tower meeting his great-granddaughter for the first time this evening before his bedtime. I got to see them together on his 100th birthday with my happy parents right there with us. In this chaotic world, peace and joy have landed on Elmdale...and her name is Page. Who could've planned this perfect night here after that awful game in Watertown? Thanks for giving us Page, and know that now and forever I will always know that I was right to always love you, Miguel Champa."

THE END

Thanks to my library directors
and readers who keep me writing.

www.michaelfrederick82.com